The Secrets We Keep

Angela L Keith

This book is a work of fiction. Names, characters, businesses, organizations, places, events and incidents either are the product of the author's imagination or are used fictitiously. Any resemblance to actual persons, living or dead, events, or locales is entirely coincidental.

The Secrets We Keep

ISBN: 979-8-9925233-2-4 Print

ISBN: 979-8-9925233-3-1 Ebook

For James. I miss you.

Author's Note

Sensitive topics such as drug use, suicide, long-term coma, and bullying are mentioned in this book, and may be triggering for some readers. Read with care and know you're loved.

1

This was my favorite season, when the last of the summer heat thankfully departed and the mornings were brisk. Crisp, burnt orange leaves still clinging to branches that would fall and turn a mucky brown, crunching under my feet on my morning runs. Sweater weather made for the best personal records, but of course I didn't really care all that much about PR's, at least not anymore. I wasn't in competition with anyone else. I knew if I'd really wanted to, I could be top of the pack with the rest of the varsity cross country team, instead of lagging behind. I ran, at my own pace, because lately, running had been the only thing in my life I could control. Running was something that made me feel, but also made me forget, and with the way things were going, these morning runs before my 45- minute commute to school were absolutely necessary.

Nate used to say brisk mornings like this were meant for people like us. I never knew what he meant, and I never cared to ask. It was a time we spent together and that was all that had mattered. He'd lace up his shoes, the ratty Nike's with a hole in the left toe, take a final drag of his cigarette, smear it on the sidewalk and take off ahead of me as if he stood a chance. His lungs burned but he'd said it's what made him feel alive. He kept pace with me, pushed me, encouraged me. It was something that belonged to us, something that I miss.

When I returned from my run this morning my mom was already gone. She'd left her lipstick-stained coffee mug and her favorite chipped breakfast plate stacked in the sink, probably assuming I would wash them before school. Fat chance. A note in her chicken-scratch handwriting stuck to the refrigerator with the heart-shaped magnet I'd made in the 3rd grade.

Margo-Left some coffee in the travel mug. Lunch is in the fridge. Hope pbj is ok. Don't forget, today. 4:30pm-Mom

"It was *one* time," I grumbled, crumpling up the note and tossing it into the trash. The fact that she'd left a note meant today she was at least trying. I sipped some of the coffee and grimaced.

"Blech. No creamer? Gross." I didn't know how she could stand black coffee, so bitter and sharp. Maybe she started drinking it that way because it reminded her of him, I couldn't really say. I made a mental note to add creamer later and headed to the bathroom to get ready for yet another craptastic day of school.

The pipes whined defiantly as I turned on the hot water and waited for it to heat up. This cottage was turn of the century ancient. It was a miracle the pipes still even worked. Mr. Rosenthal, the landlord, who was just as ancient as the house, though an adorable old man with humping shoulders and a near toothless grin, could yammer on for hours about what it was like in this town back in "the olden days" but ask him to fix a hot water heater and he'd look at you as if you'd just asked him to perform brain surgery. Truthfully, this place should be torn down. I'm sure back in the day it *was* once charming, and quaint, worthy of the image that is typically conjured up when one says they live in a cottage, but years and years of making just the bare minimum of repairs had made my humble abode looking more shack-like than cottage. But it was what Mom could afford. So yeah, give thanks, right?

On the counter, my scruffy golden tabby unfurled himself and reached out a paw to thwack me in the arm. "Yes, I see you there, Sir Rusty." I raked a hand through his soft fur. He rolled to his back, wrapped his paws around my hand allowing for me to scratch his tummy, and then rolled off the counter landing with a harrumph.

"That's what you get," I said, pulling back the curtain and climbing into the tub. Through the opaque curtain, I could vaguely make out Sir Rusty batting around at my socks. I remembered when Nate brought him home a few years ago as a kitten tucked into his jacket.

"I found him outside under the porch."

"You know Mom will never let you keep him," I said, taking the little scruff ball from him and setting him in my lap. He purred loud and spastically as he kneaded my leg.

"I think she'll come around." He flipped open the top to his pack of cigarettes, pulled one out and rested it between his lips. As he fumbled around in his pockets for his lighter, I swiped the cigarette from his mouth and tossed it at him.

"Dude don't even think about lighting that in here. Mom may not freak much over the kitten, but she'll sure as shit loose it if she smells this." He shook his head laughing, picked the cigarette off the floor and tucked it into his shirt pocket.

"She knows about the smoking, little sister. She pretends not to know about it, but she knows. So really, does it matter if she smells the smoke?"

"It matters to me. I don't like the smell of it and I don't want my clothes smelling like it. Go smoke in your own room. I need to be able actually use my lungs. You know, for breathing."

"Alright kid," he sprung up laughing. "Have fun with the kitten. His name is Sir Rusty."

It turned out Mom hadn't minded. Eventually. In the end he became more her cat than anyone else's really. He was perched once again in his usual spot on the counter when I pulled open the shower curtains. "Still here I see." I grabbed the hand towel off the hook and used it to wipe the steam from the mirror. After replacing the towel, I gazed at my reflection, let out a deep sigh and shrugged. "What should we do today, Sir Rusty? Natural like always or be bold and go for a dramatic smokey eye?" He let out a squawky meow and jumped down from the counter.

"Yup, my thoughts exactly. Natural it is." I'd never been huge on the whole make up thing. My mom had this amazing ability to blend and combine without looking trashy, but any time I tried to wear more than just a little eye liner on the bottom lid and some mascara, it looked like I was ready to join the circus, or be a hooker, neither of which I was shooting for. So, I stuck with the bare minimum. But every now and then I liked to pretend today was going to be the day I'd go bold.

After brushing my teeth and weaving my long auburn hair into a loose fishtail braid, I slipped on some jeans, my favorite The Decemberists t-shirt, black Converse shoes, and headed out the door for school. It was a 45-minute drive to Marshall Academy from my house, and the morning commute was bumper to bumper traffic hell. My old high school, where I'd gone both freshman and sophomore year, was just a block away.

There were two private Catholic high schools in Valley River, both of which happened to be on the west side of town. St Thomas Aquinas, an all-girls school (no thanks) and Marshall Academy, which had been a pillar of the community since its formation in the 1950's, and was actually where my mother had attended high school. Though a large handful of kids came from various middle schools in the Valley, the handful that mattered came from St. Augustine Middle School, which meant they'd also gone to Mary Catherine Elementary School, which meant they'd formed their clicks long ago, and us outsiders who didn't feed into those schools had to be made of money and smell like it, or have a winning personality. Neither of which applied to me. I was the daughter of a single mom who worked at Price Warehouse, had at best a somewhat likeable personality, oh and I was on an Alumni Scholarship which meant I had to work twice as hard as everyone else to prove I belonged, which I guess was super lame because I'd never wanted to go to Marshall Academy in the first place.

***

"Mr. Fisher is an evil prick," Donny hissed, sliding into the desk next to me. Jillian turned in her seat, eyebrows raised.

"Let me guess, he gave you another C for not showing your work," I said, without looking up. I knew he was about to embark into a full-fledged hand flying drama filled spiel on how much he loathed our calc teacher Mr. Fisher.

"Mmmhhmm. Look, why should I show my work? I mean, I know the answer, who gives a flying fuck how I got there."

"He just wants to make sure you comprehend, or more likely that you didn't cheat," Jillian offered in her sweet charming voice. She was the Mother Goose of our group, and always one to give anyone, including rotten teachers, the benefit of the doubt. "I mean, that's why all the teachers want to see your work."

"Whatever, he can lick my balls. Come on M, back me up here, you know I'm right about him."

"I don't think you're right that he should lick your balls Donny, probably best he stays clear of that general area." I waved a hand in a circular motion in the direction of Donny's neither region.

"Funny. But seriously. You agree he's a prick."

"Well yeah, no arguments there."

Donny shoved his math paper in front of me and pointed to the first problem. "See, like with this one," he tapped the paper as he read. "Alex props up a ladder against a wall. Ladder makes a 23-degree angle from the ground. If the ladder is 10 feet long, what's the expression for finding the distance the foot of the latter is from the wall? It's 10cos23 degrees. Duh, but Mr. Fisher wanted me to like legit write out every single freakin' step including draw the sides. That's why they make us use the fucking expensive calculator."

"Yeah, that's pretty lame." I offered up a sympathetic smile. Donny was wicked smart with just about every subject, especially calculous, but he detested having to validate himself or being put on the spot by authority figures. Or to be told he was wrong. Donny also thought that the world was out to get him for being short, gay, and a red head. Almost everything set him off.

"Look Donny, don't get all '07 Britney about it," Jillian said, applying a thick layer of shimmery red lip gloss. "Mr. Fisher is a jerk no matter what. Like, even if you'd visualized what was being asked, he'd still find something wrong about it. Just the way he is."

The lights in the classroom flickered on an off, Mr. Dan's signature time-to-shut-up-now move. Donny snatched up his math test, crammed it in his bag and turned forward. I chuckled at his adorable lunacy and pulled my psych book out of my bag. Of all my classes, Psychology was my favorite, and as far as teachers went, Mr. Dan was boss. He didn't treat us like we were adolescent dumb-bums who didn't have the first clue about life. I mean, most of us didn't and most of us were lazy AF but Mr. Dan treated us like we were actual people unlike some of the other teachers.

"Ok, so now that we've spent the first part of the semester covering the basics, and we've dabbled a little with learning and memory, I want to spend some time focusing on what happens to the brain after an acute injury, or with neurodegenerative diseases." From behind his desk, Mr. Dan hoisted up a large box, took out a stack of books, and placed them on the first desks of every row.

"'Into the Grey zone. Exploring the border between life and death', by British Neuroscientist, Adrien Owen. His main interest here is trying to figure out what happens to the brain of a patient who is in a coma. Are they alive in there? Can they communicate? Do they feel pain? How much of their brain is functioning?"

The second Mr. Dan said the word *coma*, I felt something in the pit of my stomach knot up. Jillian shifted slightly in her desk to look at me, her eyes narrowing in concern. Go figure, that with all of the freaking topics under the umbrella of psychology, he'd want to talk about comas.

"I want you guys to read this book-," he paused to allow the class to grumble- "then break into pairs and write a 20-page report on your take away, with legit references. And let's make sure to use APA this time ok folks? This will count as 30 percent of your final grade." As the books made their way around the room, and the kids started to gripe to each other, I cradled the book in my hands but didn't open it. I didn't need to. I'd already read the damn book. Three times. The rest of the class paired off, but I got up and pushed my way to Mr. Dan's desk. I bit my thumb nail until he looked up from his computer to see me standing there.

"What's up, Margo?"

"Um, so I was wondering if there was any way I could maybe not read this book or do the assignment?" He stared at me, trying to figure out if I was being real or not.

"You don't like it? I figured you'd get a kick out of this. Thought you loved psychology?" he asked.

"It's not that. I do. It's fascinating, it's just I don't want to do this particular topic."

"Why not?" He jerked up his left eyebrow, something he did when he was agitated with one of us. I'd never before given him any resistance, always graciously accepting any assignment. "What about this particular topic has you acting all squirrely?"

"I'm not acting squirrely, I'm just asking if I could maybe do something else. Any other empirical study or be your guinea pig in some experiment." He furrowed his eye brows. I turned to look back at Jillian, maybe hoping for some kind of back-up but she was thumbing through the book.

"Um, well, it's just that I have a...relative who is kinda in a coma and the topic hits too close to home," I said, just barely above a whisper, and then scanned the class to make sure no one had overheard.

He gnawed on the end of his pencil for a second and then kicked out the chair next to his desk, motioning for me to sit down.

"Is this a particularly close relative?"

"You could say that."

"How close are we talking?"

"I kinda don't like to talk about it," I said. His face scrunched up, as if he were trying to decide if I was being serious or just trying to weasel my way out of an assignment.

"Look, Mr. Dan I'm not trying to get out of the assignment or anything it's just I don't think I'd be in a great mental state to fully commit to it."

"How about you just start with reading the book?" he asked.

"I've already read it. Three times."

"Three? Really, wow." He ran a hand through his unkept sandy blonde hair and let out a deep sigh. He probably thought that reading the book and then writing the paper would somehow help me process, like I hadn't tried any of that already.

He massaged his temples with his index fingers. I hated to be the cause of his annoyance, especially since Mr. Dan was my favorite teacher, but there was just no way I could do this assignment.

"So skip reading it and just focus your paper on your own personal situation. If it becomes too emotional, use that raw emotion in your research. Maybe see if you can draw any comparisons." I nodded, got up and shuffled back to my desk. Jillian waited until I slumped in my seat before she opened her mouth to try and asked what I already knew she was going to ask.

"Don't ask me anything," I whispered to her. She closed her mouth and patted my hand. It's what I loved most about Jillian, why she'd so easily and quickly become my best friend when I transferred. She never pried. Donny on the other hand pried a lot.

"What was that about? Are you in trouble?" Donny asked, flicking his thumb in the direction of Mr. Dan.

"Nothing. Just questions about the assignment," I answered. He tilted his head to the side, narrowing his eyes. He didn't buy it, and I wasn't going to be able to keep it from him for long. Not now that we had this assignment.

"Um, guys, I'm gonna check out of here, head to the library, ok?" I said, packing up my bags. Donny looked at the clock and then back at me.

"We still have 20 minutes."

"Yeah but I mean, Mr. Dan doesn't really care and I'm just gonna go." He didn't argue, even though the way he was pursing his lips told me he wanted to.

My locker door jammed as usual. One would think with the amount of money parents shelled out for their kids to attend Marshall Academy, the school could make sure the locker doors worked. Then again, I was here on scholarship, so really what did it matter if my locker always jammed?

After using a nail file to pry the door open, I chucked the book from psychology into the farthest depths and flipped it off.

"This sucks," I growled, resting my head on the locker next to mine.

"Rough day?"

I jumped, whacking my head on my locker door. Tyler Ashford stood next to me, his thumbs looped through the straps of his backpack, a crooked grin sweeping his face. Apparently I'd been leaning on his locker.

"Sorry. I'll give you your locker back." I slid over to let him get in.

"No no, Adams. If you need a few more minutes alone with it I'll wait." As frustrated as I was with the stupid psychology assignment, I couldn't help but laugh. Tyler was Mr. Popular, but he was also genuinely nice. He always smiled and made small talk-*hello how are classes cool take it easy*-and he never made me wait until he was finished at his locker before moving (unlike the douche-canoe whose locker I was next to last year) but he was a part of the elite inner circle, the most popular of the popular kids.

At Marshall, two levels of popularity existed. First there were the "wealthy but not in your face about it" kids who tended to fluctuate between groups. They were nice to everyone regardless of social standing, typically were involved in some form of student government, and president of just about every club. Jillian was actually part of that crowd. Then there were the "wealthy and we know it, not afraid to show it" kids who drove their parents' BMW's to school and had all basically known one another since birth. They only associated with kids from their circle, and everyone else, especially kids like me- the nerdy book-smart after-school job kids whose parents worked retail, well, we weren't even a blip on their radar.

"You do the calc homework?" Tyler asked.

"Sure did, and no you can't copy."

"Please, you know I have the highest grade in the class."

"Why would I know that?" I slammed my locker door closed, giving the lock a good spin. "Until our next locker encounter," I said and then spun on my heels to walk away only to run right into Tyler's ass hat of a friend Blake Wolf.

"Sorry," I mumbled, meeting his eyes for a second before looking down.

"Whoa watch it there, dork," he said, then laughed his stupid annoying donkey laugh. Why most the girls in the senior class thought he was hot I'd never begin to understand.

2

—·—

The Daily Bagel was quiet for a Monday afternoon. Then again, it was 2:30pm on a school day and I normally came during the peak of the lunch hour rush. I waved to Vinny, the barista as I headed to the back corner of the shop where our usual booth was, surprised to see Jillian sitting there with two drinks in front of her.

"I figured this is where you were heading, so I beat you to it." She slid a cup across the table to me. "They put extra whip and cinnamon, just how you like it." God, I loved Jillian. When I transferred from Valley Central to Marshall, I was so nervous it felt like my stomach would never stop flipping. Kids like me, who grew up in a neighborhood called "felony flats" on the far east side of town, stood out like a sore thumb. Jillian was the student Ambassador and her job was to give new students the lay of the land. She was sweet, open, and didn't care where I was from. She'd told me her favorite band were The Decemberists, who also happen to be mine, and we'd been bestfriends ever since.

I popped the lid off, inhaled, reattached the lid and sipped, savoring the deliciousness that was my caramel mocha. Jillian chuckled, then took a sip from her chai latte. Jillian detested the taste of coffee in any form but she could drink a million chai lattes. In one day.

"So, after you left Donny got into it with Linz about the stupid assignment, but not for anything that you'd think was actually worth arguing, it was about whose name should go first on the paper. Can you believe that?"

"Well, yeah actually I can. They are both pig-headed enough. So, who won?"

"No one! Linz hurled some rather graphic insults at Donny, he threw some right back and then stormed out in a rage. I don't even know why they agreed to partner up."

They were thick as thieves but out of the four of us, Linz and Donny fought the most, constantly, and sometimes went days without speaking to one another. It had been weeks since their last insult hurling, so I wasn't surprised at all to hear any of this.

"What did Mr. Dan do? How did he react?" I asked.

"Oh my gosh, you'd think it was a freakin' episode of *The Real World*. I kid you not, he went behind his desk and pulled out popcorn. If I didn't know any better, I'd say he was rooting for this to happen to use as one of his psychology lessons."

"Oh good, that's perfect. Then they'll start arguing about whose name should go first on *that* study," I said.

"And thus, the cycle repeats itself." We laughed. It felt good, like for one infinitesimal second, I wasn't thinking about how messed up everything was and how this stupid assignment was only going to make it worse. Jillian twirled her now empty cup around on the table. She opened her mouth a few times to say something, but thinking better of it, sucked her lips in, catching the bottom lip between her teeth.

"Say what you want to say Jilly," I sighed.

"Ok like, don't get mad or anything, but when are you going to tell them about Nate?"

I didn't answer. What could I say? How could I even bring it up now after so many years?

"You know you are going to have to tell them."

"Why?" I whispered.

"Because they're your friends and it's the right thing to do. I mean, do they even know you have a brother?" And there it was. They didn't know. I'd never told them. I know that's supposed to be the kind of thing you talk about with your close friends, the basic family life kind of stuff, but I'd never been the type of person who could just be open with another person or group of people. With Jillian it was different because she just sort of had this aura around her, and we'd connected right away, but she also never pried about things, never asked a million questions. The more people I told, the more questions there'd be and I just couldn't deal with all the questions.

"Mr. Dan wants me to focus my project on Nate and his condition," I said.

"You told him but you can't tell Linz and Donny?"

"I told him I have a relative in a coma, but I didn't specify who. He just wants me to read the book and do the report on my comatose relative."

"So, it's going to come out at some point anyway. The longer you put it off the less likely they will be to understand."

"And the second they find out that you knew the whole time they are *really* going to hate me, and probably you for not telling them!" I threw my hands up in frustration, knocking my now empty cup on the floor. Vinny, who'd been walking around cleaning tables, swiped it up as he passed.

"Careful there," he said, tossing the cup in the recycle.

"Sorry, Vinny," I said. "Ugg Jilly what the actual fuck am I going to do?"

"Suck it up buttercup and tell them. I guarantee they won't hate you."

"Linz. Linz will hate me." Linz couldn't stand being left in the dark about anything, and she most certainly didn't like secrets.

"Yeah, you're probably right. I didn't tell Linz my brother had been back from college for a week and she chewed me out for like an hour."

"Well, that's because she's had a crush on your brother since she was in middle school," I said.

"Oh yeah. Forgot about that. Just tell them, ok? I mean, and don't like, rage at me or anything, but it's not really that big a deal. I mean, this secret of yours isn't really secret worthy. So you have a brother in a coma. Yeah, it's something people will wonder about, but it's not like you have a brother who's an axe murderer or anything."

I gnawed on my bottom lip. Maybe my reasons for keeping a secret weren't *exactly* secret-worthy, whatever that meant, but teenagers have all sorts of reasons for keeping something a secret, big or small, and what may seem like not a big deal to one person could actually be a huge deal to someone else. Also, it was way more complicated than even Jillian knew; there were things I hadn't told her.

"You're probably right," I said. "I'll figure it out. Wait, did you already partner up?"

"Kinda? It's just that you ran off and Marcus asked if I'd partner with him and how could I say no to his baby blue eyes?"

I smiled. "It's totally fine. He is pretty irresistible." I glanced at my phone to check the time. "Shoot I gotta go." I gathered up my backpack. "Thanks for coming, Jilly. You're not going to get into too much trouble for skipping, are you?"

"Are you kidding? My mom will love hearing I ditched and that her rebellious tendencies didn't totally skip over me. See you tomorrow."

Rain pelted me as I ran to my Honda. Seemed fitting to end the day with a torrential downpour. Ordinarily I didn't have any quarrels with the rain. I absolutely loved to run in it, but driving in it, yeah not so much. Only one windshield wiper worked and it was very temperamental. Sometimes swishing back and forth slowly and other times spastically as if it were trying to break off my car. Five minutes into the drive the rain stopped and the sun glared. Go figure.

The clock on my dash blinked 3:45pm, but it was always ten minutes fast, plus or minus, no matter how many times I tried setting it to current time. Thankfully traffic on Riverside wasn't terrible, so I'd made it by 4:15 according to the more accurate time on my phone. My mom still wasn't here so I opened Spotify on my phone and shuffled to my favorite Decemberist song. I fished out a granola bar from my backpack, tore open the wrapper, and took an angry bite before digging around for the book from psychology. Then I remembered that I'd tossed it into the abyss of my locker before leaving school. I huffed. Back when the book had first been published, I'd checked it out from the library and read it cover to cover in an hour. I don't know what I'd expected to get from it, answers, yeah, obviously, to the mounds of questions I'd had, but it just left me with even more questions.

I had wanted to talk to my mom about the book, but for weeks after "the accident," she'd all but shut down, spent most her time curled up in a ball under piles of blankets. We didn't talk about Nate, or anything that had happened, even after she'd snapped out of it, for lack of better words. I'd never been very good at talking about the super serious topics with her, mainly because I'd had Nate, so I'd no idea how to talk to her about this book. She'd just been so fragile, and even now, almost two years later, there were moments where she still seemed just as fragile. She worked a million hours as a cashier at Price Warehouse, and when she wasn't doing that, she was dealing with Nate stuff, and on top of that she was still trying to reconcile herself with her faith because she became convinced that all of this happened because she stopped going to church. Sometimes all *that* would become too much, and she'd wind up back under piles of blankets.

Now that we were dealing with the subject of comas for a class assignment, I knew there was no way of avoiding a conversation about it. She was bound to see me with the book at some point and who knew what would happen then.

Deciding to put off thinking about the assignment, I pulled out the book we were reading in AP lit. Half way through the second chapter, Mom finally pulled up. I watched as she got out of her car, locked it, and zombie-walked to the front entrance. The early morning shifts were taking a toll on her health but she'd never admit it, and she'd never miss a Tuesday visit. After she'd gone through the automatic doors, I packed up my bag, locked up my car (though if someone really wanted this hella old Honda civic, they could get in without even trying) and went in.

The hallway smelled a little less like decay this week and more like fresh coat of paint. Canary yellow, like it would help mask the overall feeling of discomfort and despair that quickly enveloped anyone who walked in. South Junction Rehabilitation Center. A friendly place for old people with dementia, in-patient physical therapy and recovery, and for people in comas, though admittedly, my brother Nate was the only coma patient. Ever. In the history of existing as a rehabilitation and recovery center, they'd never had one single coma patient besides my brother. Yay Nate. Great job at being the first.

My mom was sitting in her normal spot-the padded chair at the top left corner of Nate's bed, hunched over him, gently stroking his hair and whispering into his ear. I knew what she was saying. It was the same thing she'd said to him once a week since she'd started going back to church. "I forgive you Nate, God will forgive you too. Just say sorry and He'll let you in." She'd said it five times, like a mantra, gripping the rosary tangled in her fist, rubbing each bead until the paint wore off.

My mom was raised in a strict Catholic family, but as she ventured out on her own, navigating the waters of adulthood, she'd let slide her religious upbringing, and by the time she'd met my dad, who was a self-professed gypsy, never staying in one place for too long, she'd taken a more free-spirited approach to life. Then when the shit hit the fan, when Nate did what he did, when my dad left, when my mom received zero help from her estranged parents in California, she latched back on to Catholicism like a baby to a bottle

As a born-again Catholic, she now was of the belief that Nate was trapped in Purgatory until he could be forgiven for what he'd done. Two years later she was still praying the same prayer, rubbing the same rosary beads, and he was still "stuck" in the same stupid purgatory.

"You know, it's been almost two years Mom. I think you need to up your game with your prayer. Maybe add some holy water or oh get a Priest!" I said, dumping my purse by the door.

"You mock my religion Margo but one day you may come to need it."

"Mmm doubtful, very doubtful." Mom may have fully re-subscribed into all things Catholic, even pulling me out of public school and forcing me to go to private Catholic school, but I didn't buy into it. Now, maybe if I witnessed some grand miracle like, oh hey I know, my brother waking up with zero trace of brain injury, yeah maybe then.

"I'm just saying, either God doesn't care or Nate doesn't." She shot me a look that was both anguish and surprise before turning her attention back to Nate. I should have kept my mouth shut. At least she was trying, and I wasn't making it any easier. "Sorry, Ma. I'm gonna hit up the vending machines. You want anything?"

She shook her head. "Not hungry."

"Ok. Be right back."

To the left of the main entrance was a pathetic excuse for a visitor's lounge. There were four rectangle tables with hard plastic chairs tucked into them, two couches, and three vending machines along the back wall. There was a café in an adjoining room that was meant to serve sandwiches and latte's but I'd yet to see it open, so most people raided from the vending machines. I scrounged around the bottom of my purse for change, bought a couple sodas and a bag of Funyuns. As I walked back down the hall with the bag of oh so yummy chips (can they be called chips?) dangling from my mouth and a can in each hand, I stopped abruptly because I could have sworn, I'd just seen Tyler Ashford, leave the reception desk and head down the other hall.

3

— • —

"It's possible he has a grandparent with dementia, Mar," Jillian said, closing her locker and zipping up her backpack. I'd been waiting for her in the hall first thing this morning to tell her about the possible sighting of a certain popular boy at the rehab center.

"Yeah I know but I'm just saying, it's weird that I've been going every Tuesday for almost two freaking years and I've never seen him there, not once."

"Maybe whomever he was there to see was recently admitted," she offered.

I mulled it over. "Nah I don't think so. I'm pretty tight with one of the nurses and she didn't say anything about new patients."

"It's also possible it wasn't him and those nasty Funyuns you ate played tricks on your brain." She ruffled my head, an act she fully knew I loathed. Brushing the wisps of hair out of my glasses with a low grumble I said, "A-they aren't nasty, they are amazing. B-ok it is a distinct possibility it wasn't him. But what if it was?"

"What do you mean what if it was?" she asked, arching her eyebrows. "Why would it matter?"

"Um what if he sees me there?"

"Are you that concerned?" she asked as we rounded the hall and pulled open the door to calc class.

"Yes. No. I don't know. Guess it's just easier if no one ever saw me there. Less questions to answer. I could just tell him I'm visiting a grandparent with dementia."

"Or, you just tell the truth."

I sighed. She said it like it was so easy, to *tell the truth*. Maybe it was, but unlike the student body of Valley Central where everyone kept to themselves, kids at Marshall were super nosey and yearned for something to talk about. And maybe it was a Tyler lookalike. Not that I'd have to explain why I was there to Tyler Ashford, but it would just be easier if I didn't. At least not until I had a chance to talk to Linz and Donny.

Mr. Fisher barreled in with an armful of papers. "Your tests are graded-," he slammed them down on his desk, "-and I must say not your finest. I mean, I swear I've taught preschoolers who have retained information better than you kids." God, I hated Mr. Fisher. Donny was absolutely right when he'd called Mr. Fisher an evil prick. I swear he was only teaching here because he was coach of the girls' basketball team and they were 7 times State champs.

"I'm hoping your midterms will be better," he continued as he walked the isles passing out the tests. "You're seniors and this is AP Calc. My freshman algebra students have been testing better." When he got to me, he sighed deeply before handing me my test.

"I'm not even sure what you're doing in AP," he smugly remarked, letting the test paper float down to my desk where it slid and continued to float like a feather to the floor. He chuckled to himself as he walked away and I bent down to swipe my test off the floor. Turing it face up there it was. A huge ginormous C. I'd never had a C before. I hadn't even known I was capable of getting a C. I worked really freaking hard in every class, never receiving anything lower than a B+. Sure, calc wasn't my strongest subject, but it was A-freaking-P and I had been smart enough to test into it. I scanned each and every problem, unsure as to what mistakes I'd made to warrant such a heinously low grade. I contemplated speaking to Mr. Fisher after class but knew it would be of no use. He'd had his mind made up about me the minute I transferred here from a school he'd once referred to as "the smelly armpit of Valley River."

I tore a corner off my graph paper, scribbled a note on it and tapped Jillian on her back three times, our signal that I wanted to pass her a note. Covertly, she turned her body so that she could cross her right arm under her left, sliding the note off my desk and hiding it in her math book. As Mr. Fisher plastered a series of equations on the white board, Jillian slid back around and handed me the note with her response-she'd gotten a B. It stung a little. We both knew I was better at calc so the fact she'd received a B and I'd received a C was ridiculous. But what was there to do? Bitch and moan and that was it. *Thank goodness for cross country practice after school today,* I thought as I worked through the damn white board equations.

My threadbare shoelace snapped as I pulled to tighten them. Evidently a little too tight. I rummaged around my running bag, cursing heavily under my breath, having absolutely no luck at all when a sparkly white shoelace flung through the air, hitting me in the face.

"What the...?" I scanned the area for the shoelace assailant. Andy Risko, varsity running captain who was stretching on the grass in front of me waved, a guilty look on his face.

"I'm sorry, didn't mean to peg you in the face," he said. "I saw your shoelace snap, and I had an extra in my bag. Figured you could use it."

"How very noble. Thank you," I said, palming the shoelace. Andy was always super nice to everyone, but he was also friends with Tyler and that jackass Blake, and Blake never did anything out of the kindness of his heart. So, were these shoe laces a gift free of charge or would he be yelling "psych!" any second and snatch them back?

"No worries." He flashed an adorably cheesy smile, jumped up and jogged down the track. Deciding to give him the benefit of the doubt, and because I was in dire need anyway, I took the shiny new shoelace and threaded it through the holes of my old Adidas.

"Now if he'd had a new pair of shoes," I said, pulling the lace tight, smiling when it didn't snap, "that would have been the most noble of gestures." I zipped up my bag, tossed it with all the others and jogged down the track. It felt good to move, to feel the squish of the track beneath my feet and the wind blowing in my face, fighting me as I pushed forward. Sometimes I felt like pulling a Forrest Gump and just running for days. No destination, no plan, no particular speed. Just running until my body gave out. I wasn't naïve enough to think that I could run away from all my problems but it was nice to pretend every now and then, or at least feel that there was something else. Or if I could run far enough and fast enough, I might somehow find that rift in the universe where I inadvertently jump timelines and find myself the "other Margo" whose life isn't messed up. This stupid psychology project was weighing on me, and I knew I needed to tell my mom about it, and I needed to tell the gang about Nate, but I was scared. What if they had all these questions and I didn't have the answers, or if I did have the answers, what if I wasn't ready to talk about it? Would they be pissed because I didn't want to talk about it? Would they be as understanding as Jillian has been?

I used the time running my three miles around the track to imagine each scenario of revealing the truth to the gang, right down to how each one would react and how long each would be pissed. It was a no brainer that Linz would be the most pissed. In this scenario she'd call me a selfish no-good, terrible friend (she probably wouldn't be wrong) and she wouldn't speak to me for two weeks tops. I figured two weeks because it had happened before. Several times, actually. She was easily pissed off. Pretty sure she'd been born with a perma-scowl.

Donny would be hurt the most and though he'd say he understood, he'd be a little less trusting. I'd try and explain that I hadn't done anything to hurt any of them, but they'd all say I'd hurt them by not trusting them enough with this truth. And ultimately, they'd be right, and I'd deal with however they'd want to treat me.

When practice was over, I sent out a group text asking them to meet at The Daily Bagel before school. No sooner had I slid my phone into my bag, Jillian called.

"Hey Jillian what's up?"

"So, you're going to tell them tomorrow?" Her voice was short and wheezy, which meant she was calling while she was dancing. If there was anything she loved more than her three cats and chai tea, it was dancing.

"Yeah I mean, you're right. I need to just do it before we get too far into the project."

"I'm glad you decided to tell them. They won't hate you. Like I said, it's not even that big of a secret."

"What if they do? Hate me?" I asked, fighting tears.

"I won't let them. Gonna go, the dance instructor is giving me the evil eyes."

I tossed my phone back into my bag, unlocked my car and rested my head on the steering wheel. Tomorrow would either suck a whole bunch, or just suck a little, but either way, it needed to happen.

4

—·—

I skipped my morning run to get The Daily Bagel before everyone else. I'd regret it later; my body craved those early morning runs about as much as it did caffeine. Vinny popped out from behind the counter, cocked his head to the side and then looked down at the watch on his wrist.

"Hey Margo, you're here super early."

"Yeah, I have school project stuff to work on with the gang. Best time to meet is in the morning before school."

"Checks out. You want your usual? Cinnamon bagel and a caramel mocha, right?"

"That'd be great thanks."

I hoped he wasn't going to ask about the project while he made my drink. Vinny was the kind of person who genuinely loved to know things about people and took an interest in their lives, so I fully expected him to ask what it was about, and I really didn't want to make something up. Thankfully a handful of college kids walked up behind me eager for their java fix. He handed me my order, winked, and then turned to take their orders. I made my way to the usual back corner booth.

A good fifteen minutes remained until anyone would arrive, so while I finished my bagel, I popped in my earbuds and shuffled through an indie playlist. Half way through an Other Lives song, the gang arrived. Jillian greeted me with her usual warm smile. She looked beautiful as always in a red cable knit sweater that hung off her left shoulder, matching red lipstick, and her thick, curly hair twisted into a messy bun on the top of her head with a few tendrils framing her face. Donny and Linz shoved their way to the booth bickering about something I'm sure wasn't worth bickering over. They slid into the booth with angry harrumphs, one on each side.

"Honestly Donny, I can't believe how moronic you are," Linz hissed, yanking down the zipper to her leather jacket.

"Yeah well at least I'm not an idiot," he hissed right back.

"Wow do I even want to know why you guys are ripping into each other so early?" I asked.

Jillian put down her phone and rolled her eyes. Answering for them she said, "It's so stupid really. They are fighting over who is better at backing up into a parking space."

"Seriously? The tongue lashing is over that?" I asked.

"What? I can't help it if Linz can't freaking drive," Donny said.

"It's not driving you ass-face, it's parking. Backwards!"

"Which requires one to drive! It's like you're basically living up to the stereotype."

She narrowed her eyes. "Oh I know you didn't just go there, because if you did let me just get out my arsenal bag and we'll have a real stereotype war."

"Oh my gosh can you two puhlease stop," Jillian wailed. Donny and Linz crossed their arms over their chests and slouched, eyes set deep into matching glares. Maybe they'd go easy on me since they were too busy being mad at one another. I inhaled until my cheeks fully inflated, and then exhaled.

"Well since the two cats have stopped fighting, I'm just going to jump right in. You probably want to know why I asked you guys to meet before school."

"Yup," Linz said still glaring at Donny. Those two were seriously relentless.

"K well please just promise that you aren't going to hate me."

"What the fuck Margo, what did you do?" Donny asked, straightening himself. I fiddled with the lid to my cup. The words were there, right on the tip of my tongue. All I had to do was spit them out. But instead, I stalled.

"Don't you guys want to order a coffee or anything? You should go get some coffee, here my treat." I pulled my wallet out of my purse. I'd gone this long without telling them, I'm sure I could go another two three four years.

"Margo, stop stalling. Just tell them" Jillian said.

"Just tell us what?" Linz asked.

"I have a brother," I blurted. Two sets of eyes widened.

"Say what now?" Donny asked.

"So like, you just discovered you have a long-lost brother? Like a half-brother from your dad or something?" Linz asked.

"No I mean, like, I have a brother. A full-blooded older brother who I've known all my life."

"I'm so confused," Donny said rubbing his temples. "You have an older brother? I specifically remember asking you when we first met if you had any siblings and you said no."

"I know. I'm sorry."

"Why?" Linz asked, face stone cold.

"Why what?"

"Why not say you have a brother? Are you like ashamed of him or something? Is he in jail? Did he abuse you?"

"No, it's nothing like that. His name is Nate."

"Why are we just now learning about him?"

"Because I didn't know what to say, and then when I did know what to say I didn't want the questions. I have a brother but the thing is, he's been in a coma for a year, well, almost two years now." For a second it felt like a weight had been heaved off my chest. But as their eyes widened and then narrowed, it felt more like the weight had only been shifted to the side.

"He's in a coma?" Linz asked, and I nodded. Next question was bound to be what happened, which came from Donny.

"Just an accident. He was in an accident, he suffered brain damage, he's in a coma and for the past two years he's been at South Junction Rehab."

"The old people dementia place on Barnett?" Linz asked.

"Yeah. It's not just for people with dementia. It's also for people like Nate. Look I didn't want to ever say anything because when I met you guys after I transferred the accident had just happened and I was still processing, and then I never knew how to bring it up."

"What kind of accident?" Donny asked.

"I don't know," I lied. I was going to lie and I had absolutely no idea why. That's a lie. I knew exactly why. I was a coward. These were my friends, my best friends and I was too much of a coward to be open with them.

"Jilly, did you know she had a brother?" Donny asked, flicking his thumb in my direction.

She chewed her bottom lip. "Yeah, I did. But you guys I promise, I told her she should have told you guys a while ago."

"Does you telling us now have anything to do with the psych project?" Linz asked.

I nodded. "Yeah. Mr. Dan thinks my situation could be beneficial to the project and whatever research. I just didn't want you all to have been blindsided by him in class. I wanted to tell you first, and I'm just really sorry I didn't ever bring it up when we met." The table was quiet for several minutes. Linz furrowed her brows, tossed a few looks back and forth between me and Jillian, and then pulled her keys from her coat pocket.

"Welp, guess we should head to class." As she slid out of the booth, I brushed my hand across hers.

"Wait Linz, are you mad at me?" I asked. She pulled her hand away.

"Nah. Not mad. Just bummed we've been friends for two years and you didn't feel you could be real with us but I guess I get it. Or maybe I don't. I don't know. I just really need to get to class."

Donny wrapped his arm around my shoulders, pulling me in for a side hug.

"Sorry about your brother, Mar."

"You're not mad at me? For not telling you about him?"

"No, not really. I mean, Linz is right. It is pretty crappy that you felt you could only tell Jillian, but whatever. I get it. Just remember, we are your friends and we love you, girl. You can tell us anything, and when you're ready to tell us more about what happened, we're here."

"Thanks Donny." I leaned into him. "I really appreciate it."

"Ok well I'd better go. If I don't get into P.E before those lame jock straps do, I'll be miserable all period." He kissed the top of my head, slid out the booth and left. Jillian remained unmoved across from me, eyes still heavy with sadness and confusion.

I sighed. "I know what you want to say Jilly so just say it."

"Why did you lie? And don't say it's because you panicked. You know what happened to your brother, and yeah, it's pretty messed up, but you should have told them."

I chipped away at the paint on my nails. I could feel Jillian's stare boring into me like a drill, waiting for me to explain, but the more I tried to think of something to say that wasn't going to sound like complete utter bull crap, the more I chipped away at my polish. Finally, she sighed.

"I love you to the moon and back Margo, but you have to be honest with us. You can't continue to pick and choose what you reveal about yourself. That's not how bestfriends work. Linz and Donny love you, but if you only ever confide in me and not them, you'll drive a wedge between the group and that's like really going to suck. Please don't make it suck."

With that she slid out from the booth and left. She was right, of course she was. Every fucking thing she said was right. But there were things even she didn't know.

5

— · —

It had been a week since meeting at The Daily Bagel. Jillian was still irritated with me, but she'd never been able to ghost me for very long. Donny was too focused on dodging Blake and his bully-brigade every day, but Linz on the other hand had no problem at all pretending I didn't exist. I'd expected as much because she seemed to be on a rotation with which one of us she was mad. Even though she said she was just bummed, she was acting like I'd personally wronged her. I'm sure I could have just talked to her one on one to smooth things over, but then again, I knew enough about her to know doing that made it worse. She just needed time to get over it, and hopefully she'd forget about it. So while I gave them all time to cool off and forgive me, I focused on work.

Since I didn't have a parent with a disposable income, I couldn't rely on a weekly allowance to get by, so I worked at a small independent bookstore on the east side of town called The Book Shelf. It wasn't much, but the hours were super flexible. I typically worked Friday through Sunday, picking up extra shifts over holidays, and then a full shift in the summer. A nickel over minimum wage give or take, but it was enough money to put gas in my car, pay for whatever personal items I needed, and cover the bills that sometimes lapsed. My mom doesn't know that I do it, but after the third shut off notice from the power company and a late notice from the landlord a few times, it was unavoidable. Sad thing is, I don't even know if she realizes she hasn't paid the bill. When she works long hours and then tries to be attentive to Nate, she sometimes forgets about the bills.

Aside from the whole I-need-money-for-basic-necessities, I really loved everything about working in a bookstore. The crisp smell of new books, the musty smell of the classics; I had always found books to be much more appealing than digital books. The majority of the world may have jumped on the Nook and Kindle bandwagon, but I still held firm to the belief that traditional print was the only way to enjoy reading a book.

My favorite part of any book was the Acknowledgements. I was almost 98 percent sure that most people didn't read the Acknowledgements section unless they had a personal connection with the author, but I felt all the more connected to the story if I knew a little something personal about the author. Even if they said everyone in their lives were pieces of shit and this book was made out of spite or whatever, I loved it and tended to read it before even glancing at the first page.

Most days I worked the register and periodicals, but today I was shelving the new books that had just come in. After unloading my last box of books, I broke down the box, scooping it up along with the other broken-down boxes, and made my way to the stock room. Turning around an isle too swiftly, I collided with a customer, who let out a low guttural "arugh", a pile of books and my boxes crashing to the floor.

"I am so, so sorry!" I exclaimed, crouching down to help gather the fallen books. "I'm such a clutz." I looked up to see I'd collided with none other than Tyler Ashford who was staring down at me with a crooked smile.

"Hey Margo. I didn't know you worked here."

"Yup. Three days a week here I am. Shelving books. Answering questions. Crashing into people."

He chuckled as I handed him his non-fiction book about basketball. How very predictable.

He smirked, as if he'd read my mind. "Don't judge. I like a good basketball memoir."

"No judgments." I threw up a free hand, tucking the folded boxes up under my armpit. "I'm sure you'll find some useful words in there. Real SAT vocab boosters."

He shuffled through his stack of books, procuring a linguistics book by Bill Bryson. "Pretty sure this book covers that. What's the matter, Adams? Didn't think I read smart books?"

I shrugged. "Didn't peg you for much of a reader."

"Oh I read, Adams. I even read the Classics."

"Well color me surprised."

He laughed and I noticed a little too much how his eyes crinkled in the corner.

"So, what are you doing in here? The Book Shelf isn't exactly in your neighborhood," I asked.

"Yeah, I know, but I heard this place has a really neat rare book room."

"You read the Classics *and* you're into rare books."

"Well, a man can be more than one thing, Adams. I can be an athlete and a book nerd."

He pushed back a lock of hair that had swept into his eye. They were icy blue with flecks of gold and of course perfectly symmetrical.

I cleared my throat. "Welp, I should to get back to work. Mr. Ashford as always, it's been a pleasure."

"Later Adams. Hey, try not to take out any more customers."

I rolled my eyes, readjusted my boxes, and continued on to the stock room. There was something really freaking weird going on with the cosmos lately. Tyler Ashford shopping at The Book Shelf? I'd worked here for two years, not counting the year I spent volunteering in the stock room, never once seeing anyone from Marshall walk through the door. The Book Shelf was on the East side of town, home to sketchy strip malls and a bazillion different car dealerships. Absolutely no high end or semi-high-end stores. It was one of the perks to working here versus a big box store, especially one on the West side. It meant that I didn't have to cross paths with any of the richy-riches. I was sure it was just a coincidence, seeing him at the rehab center and now at my place of employment, but still. It was weird. Something about our exchange felt playful and natural, and I don't ever have exchanges with people outside my inner circle that were natural.

***

After handing in my test in psych class on learning and memory, Mr. Dan asked me to swing by after school during office hours. I really couldn't afford to miss cross country practice, since I already leave early on Tuesdays, but he promised to be quick. Plus, he said if I didn't show up it would cost me half my grade. He was messing with me, maybe, probably, but to error on the side of caution I shot a quick text to Coach Cathy to explain why I'd be late and waltzed into office hours.

"Have you made any progress on the book assigned for class?" he asked before I could sit in the chair next to his desk.

"Um, no but I told you I've already read it. Didn't figure I'd need to read it again."

"Where are you at on your assignment? Since you've already read it, you should be miles ahead of everyone else. I'm going to assume you're not though, guessing by the way you're chewing your lower lip."

I didn't respond. What was there to say? I was avoiding the assignment like the plague.

"I had a thought," he continued. "You tell me if you're uncomfortable with it, but I think it would really add to what the class is learning but also maybe help you. Have your parents- "

"Parent," I interjected, "Parent. Just one. My mom. "

"Sorry, parent," he continued. "Has she ever thought about having something similar to this experiment done with your brother?"

I shook my head. "No dice. I read the book when it was first published and I found it interesting, but I don't think my mom would go for it."

"Why don't you think she'd be open to the idea?"

"She believes she can pray him awake."

"You don't think she'd be interested in finding out if he has any cognitive thought in there? See if he understands what's going on around him even if he can't say so, like with locked-in syndrome?"

"She's not about the medical science Mr. Dan. She legit thinks he's in purgatory and if she prays hard enough every day he'll wake up. Besides, even if she wasn't opposed, how would we even go about getting him tested? It's not like there are flyers plastered around advertising for coma test subjects. Also, there's no freaking way we'd be able to afford it."

Mr. Dan scratched his chin. "I know it's a long shot, but what if it was possible? I was thinking of getting in touch with my old college professor who teaches at The School of Neurosciences to see if conducting a similar study would be a possibility."

"I'll ask," I said, rubbing my sweaty palms on the front of my jeans. "I can't guarantee my mom will go for it."

Mr. Dan offered his gentle smile. "Razor. Let me know what she says. If she has any questions, she can call me. In the meantime, get that paper written."

I nodded, rose from the chair and made my way to the door. Before leaving, I turned and said, "Might not want to say 'razor' anymore. Pretty sure people stopped saying that turn of the century." He chucked a hunk of chalk at me, but I dodged it, waved goodbye and left. It was time for me to have a one-on-one with Nate.

6

—◦—

As I pulled into the parking lot of South Junction my phone pinged with a text message notification. Mom couldn't get out of work on time, something about a new manager who wanted her to cover a few breaks before leaving. She'd try to be here before 5:00pm. I felt bad for her. She tried so hard to keep commitments and be punctual, even when I could tell sometimes all she wanted to do was stay in bed all day. She still tried to show up for life, well, for Nate anyway. There were times when it seemed coming to the rehab on Tuesdays was the only thing keeping her together.

I'd told her once that it was okay if she didn't go every single week. Huge mistake. She'd cried for three days, sputtering in between sobs something about how Nate would think she'd forgotten about him if she didn't show up on time at 4:30pm every Tuesday.

"Mom, you have to know that Nate has zero idea whatsoever what time of day, or even what day it is. There's also a pretty good theory that he doesn't even know you're there."

"How can you even say that?" she'd wailed. "You've seen his hand move when I touch him and say his name, you've seen his eyes move when I move. Honestly Margo Annemarie, I don't know why this is so hard for you."

"There's just no proof Mom, that he's actually there."

"I don't need proof," she'd said drying her eyes and tugging at the new silver cross around her neck. "Jesus tells me. And until He tells me something different, I will go every week at 4:30 until Nate wakes up."

I texted Mom back, making sure it was something encouraging rather than my usual sarcastic quips, then shot a quick text to Coach Cathy apologizing profusely for ditching out on cross country practice again. She'd be pissed and for sure make me to a May Day in September sort of practice tomorrow.

When I got to Nate's room, he was being attended to by his nurse, Sari. Her jet-black hair was pulled up in a messy bun and day-old eye liner smudged her lids. Ordinarily she wore her hair half down in ringlets clasped with a butterfly clip, her eye shadow funky bold colors.

"Rough night last night Sari? Don't take this the wrong way but you really look like shit," I said, tossing my purse onto the chair in the corner of the room by Nate's bed.

"No girl, don't even start with me. It's been a rough week. These people up in here are lucky I even bothered to bathe. I've been hit, spat on, projectile vomited on and that's all just been today!" I loved Nurse Sari so much. She was lively and colorful, and full of sass, which was needed in a place that tended to exude doom and gloom.

"Where's your mama today? Isn't she normally here before you?" Sari asked, scribbling some notes into her chart.

"She couldn't get out of work on time. New assistant manager apparently has it out for her or something like that. Just me for a bit. How's he doing?"

"We've just been gabbing about this new reality TV show he got sucked up into and let me tell you he had some serious thoughts about it. And he had some choice colorful words to say about some *Jersey Shore* reboot. I couldn't get a word in edge wise with this one." She tossed me a playful knowing grin. When she'd first been assigned to Nate, she was too nervous to even answer the question- *how's he doing,* especially if it were Mom asking. Over time she'd grown more comfortable with me, in large part because I would make a joke now and then about Nate's long-windedness, and we both accepted that making a running joke about it, finding some form of humor was a far better way to cope, at least for me. She also never asked personal questions about how Nate got to be, well, Nate. For that I was eternally grateful. One less person to lie to.

"Alright girl I'll leave you to it. I've gotta go check the vitals of a new patient down the hall." She gathered up her charts, quietly closing the door behind her. I sat in the chair by the head of the bed, scooting it as close as it would go to Nate. For a moment I just sat there, taking in the sounds. The ticking of the clock on the wall above the door. The gentle hum of the Exit sign next to the clock. The beeping of the monitor that was hooked up to Nate. I picked up Nate's hand, something I hadn't done in at least six months, cradling it in mine, hoping to feel the squeeze Mom always swore she felt. I looked at his face, his mouth slack, a trail of saliva dribbling out. With a free hand I picked up a rag from the bedside table and gently dabbed at his lips.

When I was eight, there'd been this huge lightning storm in January, that was so bonkers it blew the power out for hours. The walls shook so much I was convinced they were going to crumble on top of us. Mom was working and Dad was already long gone so it had just been me and Nate, and I was scared out of my mind. Nate decided to teach me how to play a marshmallow game called Chubby Bunny, which is where you take turns tucking mega marshmallows into your cheek and say the words "chubby bunny", the point being to see how many marshmallows one could stuff in their mouths while clearly pronouncing the words.

I'd managed five before the words just sounded garbled and I choked, spitting and sputtering out a pile of marshmallows. Nate took a napkin and wiped the slobber from my mouth. It felt odd to be wiping the slobber from his.

After I cleaned up his face, I set the rag on the table and stared into his eyes, searching for signs of life. They were open but motionless. *How was Mom so convinced that somewhere in there Nate existed*? I wondered.

"Hey big brother," I whispered. "Mom swears you can hear when she talks to you. I don't think she's right. I mean, I don't know if she is, I guess it's just easier to believe she's wrong." I stared into his eyes, hoping to see some sort of response. Nothing.

"I have this school assignment," I continued. "Mr. Dan, my psych teacher wants me to ask Mom if she would be interested in having some tests run on you to see if there's still some action going on inside your dome. I think we should do it, but I don't think Mom will go for it. She's like born-again or whatever and thinks you just need prayer. I wish you could tell me what to do. What would you want? Know what? It would be so cool if you could like squeeze my hand if you're chill with being a lab rat." Again, I waited. Again nothing. Sighing, I rested my head on our clasped hands. I jumped as the door swung open, and Mom flew in, running into the bathroom.

"Hi honey, I just want to wash my hands. Will you tell your brother I'm washing my hands?" she called out.

"Pretty sure he can hear you and the running water Mom, at least according to your beliefs."

"I could really go without any of your sass tonight ok, honey?" she said, coming out of the bathroom drying her hands on the scratchy brown paper towels. The tight braid she'd left with this morning was now loose and sticking out at all ends, and there were fresh greases stains on her work shirt.

I pointed at her shirt. "Manager make you work in concessions again?"

"Ugg don't even get me started. This was a new work shirt too. This stain will never come out."

I grabbed my purse from the chair by the door as she took my place in the chair by Nate.

"Gonna go to the visiting room for a bit and eat a snack, maybe think about doing some homework. I'll give you guys some time alone. Want me to bring you back anything?"

"No, I'm good. Not hungry. See you in a bit," she said, lips curling up into one of those fake I'm-trying-super-hard-to-be-positive smiles, the ones she's been giving me for the past year. I wish I could tell her she didn't have to pretend to be ok, that she could have a meltdown, be a complete utter wreck. I mean, just looking at her I could tell she was barely coping. She was rail thin (I hadn't actually seen her eat a real meal in weeks), she either slept for hours on end, or hardly at all. When she came home from work, she'd collapse on the couch, looking like she'd been walked all over, which probably wouldn't be far from the truth since most people who shopped Price Warehouse were animals. I don't know if it was a pride thing, but she'd likely fake holding it together until she died.

The visiting room was empty. When Nate first "moved in", I wasn't sure what to expect in terms of visiting rooms. There were commercials galore about retirement centers, and even drug rehabilitation centers where the visitors room, lounge, whatever, was the hub of the whole establishment, where families gathered around tables, holding hands, smiling at one another, probably saying "you'll beat this" or "this seems like a good fit for you, Grandpa." From day one, there have been a total of two people I've seen in here. Me, and Wallace, the vending machine repair man. Most times, from what I've observed, when people come to visit whomever they are here to visit, they remain inside the rooms, with the doors closed, and looking just as somber on the way out as they were on the way in.

Today was no different. Just me and the vending machines. I fed the machines a few dollars, procuring my usual snacks. I pulled up a chair to a wobbly table, rooted around my purse for my phone. I opened Spotify and scrolled around my playlists until I'd found my "sweet indie tunes" and hit play. I cranked my volume up to eleven, losing myself in the melody of a Bon Iver song, munching away. The sudden THUD of a soda dispensing scared the shit out of me, causing me to choke on a Funyuns. After a quick coughing fit, I chugged my Dr. Pepper, which only caused me to burp and sent a shot of carbonation up my nasal cavity, causing the coughing to resume.

"Are you alright over there?" a voice asked from behind me. Swiftly I yanked a bud out from my ear and turned in the direction of the voice. Tyler Ashford (WTF???) reached into the machine, pulled out his Diet Coke, clicked it open, awaiting my response.

"Well, I'm pretty sure I hacked up a lung and burned my nasal cavity but otherwise I'll live." I wiped my mouth with the sleeve of my hoodie. "Question is, what are you doing here and why are you drinking a Diet Coke?"

"What's wrong with a Diet Coke?" he asked, sliding into the chair across from me.

"Nothing, I guess I just didn't peg your type as a Diet Coke drinker."

"My type?"

"Figured you'd be more the Mountain Dew type. Or at the very least a regular Coke."

"I hate Mountain Dew. I feel like it's trying too hard to be 7-UP."

"First of all, those two tastes nothing alike. Secondly, what are you doing here?" I popped a Funyuns into my mouth. His expression changed to a more somber look.

"My grandma was admitted a few weeks ago and I just came by to visit. What are you-"

"Tyler! What the heck, I've been waiting in the car forever. You coming or not?" A younger boy with the same mop of blonde hair and matching blue eyes huffed from the doorway.

"Yeah I'll be right there." He chugged his Diet Coke and tossed the can into the recycle. "See ya later Margo," he said on his way out. I smiled and nodded. The boy waiting for Tyler looked back at me and wrinkled his nose.

"Isn't that the chick Blake calls weird Indie girl?"

Tyler glanced back at me quickly then ushered the boy the rest of the way out without responding. Weird indie girl? Was that really what Tyler's group of douches were calling me? Since when was it a bad thing to be labeled "indie"? That was just the problem with kids at Marshall Academy, I guess. Nerds and indie kids were kicking ass in other schools, and actually outnumbered the Jocks at Valley Central, but apparently, they were still the outcasts at Marshall Academy. I wasn't that surprised, I guess, since half the kids came from rich spoiled families. That might have been my perception and it might have been wrong. My friends weren't that way and they all came from money. They were also nerds into Star Wars and indie music like me so what did that say?

When I got home from the rehab center, I showered, read a scathing text from Coach Cathy about how pissed she was I missed practice, and then called Jillian to tell her about Tyler.

"So I guess it was him you saw there the other day," she said though it came out more like slobbering.

"Jilly bean, take out your retainer. It sounds really gross. Also, it's only 8:30, why are you even wearing it?"

"Well, I didn't expect to be on the phone right now," she grumbled, made a muffled slurping sound, then said, "ok it's out. Proceed."

"Yeah Tyler Ashford was there. And it couldn't have been any more awkward. I choked on a freaking Funyuns"

"OMG!"

"Oh it gets worse. Then I tried to rinse it down with my Dr. Pepper and let out the biggest, grossest dude burp!"

"You didn't!"

"Oh I did. Classy right?"

"What did he say?"

"Just asked if I was ok and then sat down and started talking. I kept my cool but I was totally dying inside."

"What happened next? Did he tell you why he was there?"

"Yeah. Grandma has dementia. Or Alzheimer's. You know, he really didn't specify which. I think he was going to ask me why I was there but then some bratty lookalike came in and they left."

"That must have been Alexander," she offered. "His brother. He's a freshman. They do look exactly alike."

"Well, his brother is a little bitch. He gave me the meanest look and then asked Tyler if I was the "weird indie girl" Blake mentioned. What does that even mean Jillian? I mean, is it a bad thing to have that label?"

"Of course it's not bad. Actually, I think it's awesome. I mean, look at all the amazing indie bands currently out there. They make the best music not just lyrically but also melodically. And there are more people listening to indie music now than whatever is currently popular. What is popular now? Donny would know. Should we call him?"

"Jillian! Focus!" I whined.

"Margo, why does it even bother you? I thought you didn't care about labels?"

"I don't! I mean I don't think I do, I mean, ugg I don't know what I mean. I guess you're right. It doesn't matter what Blake or any of the other quote unquote cool kids think about me."

"That's right. Because while we're having fun at The Decemberists show in a few weeks they'll be, well I don't know what they'll be but we'll be having fun." Jillian never really was good at coming up with insults.

"Once again my dear friend you're right. Ok I'm gonna work on some stuff for school. See you tomorrow." I hung up, plugged my phone into the charger and got to work on some homework. Twenty minutes in I slammed my book closed and shoved it to the far end of my bed. Clearly my brain was not in the right space for homework so instead I turned on the TV and found some mindless reality housewives show. Jillian was right in every way, that it simply shouldn't matter to me that A) Tyler knew I spent time at the rehab center or B) what him and his friends thought about me. In the grand scheme of things, it truly didn't matter. I'd never been bullied by anyone, and I'd never thought about my popularity or lack thereof, not at Valley Central, and not even at Marshall. I'd accepted that my status at school would be what it was simply because of where I came from and I never tried to challenge or question it. Perhaps I never really paid much attention to what I'd been called behind my back because I had mostly been comfortable with myself, and because I had such a good group of friends. That had been enough. But still, why was I bothered?

7

The weekend trip to Portland to see The Decembrists had finally arrived, and thanks to the tension that still existed in the group, I was less than stoked to go. What was that ancient saying? So thick you could cut it with a knife? True to Linz form, she was still holding a grudge against me even though I apologized a thousand times. In a battle she'd be the very first to come to the defense, but lately and by that, I mean since always, I've just found it incredibly exhausting to maintain a friendship with her. I've never expressed those feelings to anyone else in the gang because she'd been friends with Jillian and Donny since elementary school and I didn't want to make either of them feel it were necessary to choose between the two of us. I guess I just wanted this weekend to have as little drama as possible.

"My mom gave us the Subaru for the trip so long as we leave a full tank of gas. So I'm going to need each of you to pony up the dough," Linz ordered. We all riffled through our bags for the gas money, slapping it into her hands. When I gave her my portion she lingered, almost as if debating whether she should count the money, then said, "Donny's riding shotgun."

"That's fine," I said in a hushed tone, sliding into the back with Jillian, who was already busy flipping through a People magazine. Linz shifted into gear, navigating through town towards I-5 with sharp twists and turns, like she was living out a Fast and Furious scene.

We made it to Portland in record time, so after a lengthy check-in process at our hotel, where the clerk asked us more questions than any other guest checking in (probably because we were four teenagers), we killed time huddled on the beds watching reality shows. McCallister's Emerald Hotel, located in the heart of the Pearl District, was by far the swankiest hotel I'd ever stayed in. It was also one of the most expensive. Best Western would have been more than adequate, but Linz of course put her foot down and refused. It was cool though because The Decemberists were playing at the Crystal Ballroom, which meant we didn't have to drive or walk far.

"Good call on staying here, Linz, this place is amazing," Donny said, rolling his suitcase over to one of the queen beds. The wall art was stunning, like being in an actual album cover. The entire room was painted midnight purple, except for the wall with the window, which was a blood-red. There were two curving wall sconces on each wall with amber-colored lights that matched the two lamps on the end tables next to the beds, and the chandelier that hung in the middle of the room was made from sharp fragments of an emerald-colored glass.

"Right? My dad's company always puts him up here when he's got meetings. It's the best," she responded, tossing her duffle onto the couch.

"Alright bitches so how's the sleeping going to happen?" Donny asked.

Linz rolled her eyes. "Well genius, there are two beds and a pull out so I'm guessing we sleep on those." She dove onto the bed closets to the window. "I call dibs on this one."

"And I guess I'm expected to sleep on the pullout?"

"Well Donny, we can always share this bed. You can be the big spoon and I'll be the little spoon," Linz said.

"Hard pass. I'll take the pull out."

We grabbed some pizza from a shop around the corner and returned to our room, sitting in a circle on the floor as we ate. Death Cab for Cutie softly serenaded us from my portable speakers. Wiping sauce off my face I said, "So what's your guys' take on the idea of being labeled an 'indie kid'? Like, is that a bad thing, do you think? Like being called a nerd?"

Jillian cocked her head and looked at me through a side eye. Dodging her glance, I looked around at everyone else. Donny swallowed his bite of pizza, took a sip from his soda.

"So," he wiped his mouth with his napkin, "are you asking like in general or because people around school call you the weird indie kid behind your back?"

So people were calling me that. What the heck? How was I totally oblivious to this? "I um guess I meant in general but if that's what people are calling me..."

"Why is being a nerd a bad thing?" Linz asked. "All the best movies, the biggest Blockbusters, are the product of some genius nerdy mind. Comic book to movie script. Nerds."

"True. Just wondered. Do you guys ever get called weird indie kid or is this just some special name reserved for me?"

"Just you sweetheart," Linz grinned. There was no way I was the only one in the entire student body of over 750 to be called a "weird indie kid" especially since I wasn't the only kid to listen to indie music, I wasn't the only kid to wear converse shoes and prefer independent films to Marvel films. I was however the only kid to transfer in at the end of sophomore year, and from the shitty part of town. But no one had ever mentioned any crazy news stories from "felony flats" that I might be connected with, so the label itself, and the reasons for deeming it "bad" didn't make sense.

"If that's the worst that people call you, you're doing ok," Donny snapped. "Try being the short gay red head. It's like the fucking trifecta. The slew of names I am called on a daily basis by the cool kids is freaking nuts. At least no one says anything to your face."

I felt like a punk for having even mentioned the stupid label. Of course, being called a weird indie kid behind my back wasn't even comparable to what Donny is called, which is also super lame because Donny is one of the coolest people I've ever met.

"You're absolutely right, Donny. I'm sorry. It shouldn't be that big of a deal because being indie girl isn't even an insult, those kids are just too stupid to realize."

"Whatever, it's fine. Let's just not talk about this anymore."

"Agreed," Jillian said. "Let's get cleaned up and head out. I want to get as close to the stage as possible."

The line to get in wrapped around the block and moved at a snail pace. We passed the time by playing Genshin Impact on our phones and once inside, Linz and Jillian ran ahead to secure a spot up front while Donny waited with me at the merch table. In my experience, if you wait until the show is over to hit up the merch, it was slim pickings and I really wanted the shirt with the new design by Carson Ellis.

We were about fifth in line when Donny elbowed me in the side.

"Ow! What was that for?"

"Don't look, but there's some chic over at the concessions who keeps staring at you. I said don't look!"

"Donny, I have to look, otherwise I..."

I forgot how to speak, and think, and maybe, for like half a second breathe. It was her. Her hair was different, blonde now, and long, with pink tips, and her face was a little fuller, but it was her. She was looking at me with both terror and sadness. Donny snapped his head at me, and then towards the woman, and then back to me.

"Margo? Do you know her?"

If ever there was a loaded question. "Uh no, I don't think so. Hey listen, I really have to go to the bathroom, like super bad. Can you just grab me one of the new shirts in a small? I'll meet you at the door."

"Seriously? You can't wait? We're like fourth in line."

"I really have to go. Be right back."

I looked back at the woman who was still staring at me and then took off, disappearing into the crowd until I'd located the bathroom. It wasn't her. It couldn't have been her. It has to be someone who looks like her who just has a staring problem. I jerked the handle on the sink, causing the water to rush out, cupped my hands and submerged my face. After a third splashing, I fumbled a hand around on the wall in search of the paper towel dispenser.

"Here, let me help," a voice rang out and then a wad of paper had been placed into my hand.

"Thanks," I said, wiping my face and then seizing up.

"I wasn't sure it was you, not at first but there's no mistaking the resemblance."

"What are you doing here Khali?" I choked.

"I'm here with a friend to see the opener. I moved back to Seattle." She looked down at her feet and then back at me, watery eyes. "I don't know what to say, Margo."

"I tried calling you," I said. "Three times. I even went to your house."

"I know. I'm sorry. Margo, I was in a really bad place. I was completely fucked up."

"You think you were in a bad place? How about Nate? Do you think he was in a good place?"

She started to cry. "How is Nate? Is he..."

"Alive, barely.

She wiped the tears from her cheeks. I wanted to punch her. She doesn't get to cry over Nate. Not after what she did.

"I know I can't say anything to make things right, and it doesn't matter because you wouldn't believe me anyway, but I just wanted you to know I'm so sorry, about Nate, and I'm clean now."

"Maybe you should tell him."

"I...I can't see him."

"Why not?" I asked.

"I just can't."

It felt like a fireball was rolling in the pit of my stomach, burning to come out. I wanted to yank that fireball out and throw it right in her face.

"You don't deserve to see him anyway. You're the reason he is where he is now, and no amount of sobriety will ever make up for what you've done."

I didn't wait for her to respond. I shoved passed her, tossing my paper towel into the trash on the way out and found Donny waiting by the entrance door with two bags. When he saw me, he let out a sigh.

"Omg what took you so long? Please don't tell me you had to poop."

"I'm sorry. I got lost."

"You got lost? Is that why your face is all red?"

I touched my face. It felt flushed. "Yeah."

"Ok well I've gotten like a billion texts from Linz wondering where we are so let's go. Here's your merch. You're lucky, they only had one size small left."

I shot a quick look over my shoulder, just to make sure Khali hadn't tried to follow me out. Thankfully there was no sign of her, and I didn't have any more run-ins with her during the show, but I was so on edge, searching behind me, and then swatting at the memories that were flooding my mind. Her coming into our lives and of Nate leaving my life, what should have been a kick-ass night was just one big bummer and it sucked because I really just wanted a fun weekend.

***

October was always our favorite month, mine and Nate's. Since we were kids, Nate would take me trick-or-treating, he'd say because our mom always had to work nights, but I knew he loved taking me out just as much as I loved trailing along behind him. He'd put up the biggest fight when I'd ask him to wear matching costumes, but in the end, he'd cave so long as he didn't have to wear tights. As he grew more and more into a pain in the ass moody teen, it became increasingly difficult to convince him to wear a costume with me, but after several pleas and one never-ending pouty face, he'd sigh, take a long drag from his cigarette, put it out on the sole of his shoe and say, *"fine, hand me the damn costume."*

When I'd decided I had become too old for trick-or-treating, we'd spend the night watching those over-the-top gory horror movies on the AMC channel. Mom of course opposed to me watching them because I was only in middle school, so we'd start watching *Hocus Pocus*, and when Mom would fall asleep, I'd microwave the popcorn and Nate would queue up the scary movie. Last year sucked. I'd tried to watch a *Rosemary's Baby* by myself and it felt like I was doing something wrong, breaking some sort of ritual or whatever, which just made me angry at Nate for leaving me, and I'd been trying so hard not to feel angry. I haven't watched a horror movie since.

In the hall closet high on the top shelf and buried under a pile of blankets, was a box labelled "Halloween junk". In it was a hodgepodge of decorations we'd collected throughout the years and hung up around the house every year without fail, even after Nate stopped hanging around. I don't know if it was the run-in with Khali, who I blamed for ruining Nate, or if it were something else, nostalgia maybe, I wasn't sure, but I felt I needed to decorate Nate's rehab room.

After school I drove to the rehab, got the box from my trunk and hauled it inside to Nate's room, placing it on the table, unfolding the flaps as if they were delicate pieces of fabric. I pulled out pumpkin and ghost window clings, so old the goo that made them stick hardly worked.

"I think we should finally toss these and get new ones, Nate," I said, using adhesive tape to stick the defiant clings. Next, I pulled out several plush pumpkins, setting them out randomly on shelves and desks around the room. In the bottom of the box, I found the canvas door-cling of a bat we'd picked up at The Goodwill for fifty cents. In the window on the ledge, I placed a plastic glittery purple Witches' cat. Nate found it in the "free-box" at a second- hand store. I'd pointed out the obvious, that it was purple, not black or orange, which were clearly the typical Halloween colors, and he'd scoffed and said it had character. It was hideous, that's what it was, but we'd put it out every year none the less.

I was standing on the visitor chair stringing up some orange lights in the window when Mom came in, exhaled, and groaned. "Margo, what are you doing?"

I steadied myself but turned to look at her. "Thought I'd decorate a little."

She peered into the box, pulling out a paper witch riding a broom. "I thought we trashed all this stuff."

"Nope. Box was in the back of the closet underneath some blankets."

"Honey, don't you think you should check with staff before you put up Halloween stuff?"

"I don't see what the problem is. Nate doesn't have a problem with it. Here, I'll ask him. Nate? Do you have a problem with me stringing up these pumpkin lights? No? Great. See Mom? Nate doesn't have a problem."

She rested her hands on her hips and cocked her head to the side, lips curling up into a playful grin. "Fine, fine, fine, just be quick and get down from there before you fall and break your neck."

"Mom it's like a foot. I won't break my neck. Ankle, yes. Leg, maybe. Face? Probably. But neck, nope. Not the neck." I jumped down, returning the chair to the head of the bed.

She kissed my forehead. "You're exhausting. Don't you have some chips to go eat?"

Was I so predictable? "Yep, I do. See ya in a bit Mama." At the door I hesitated. Mr. Dan was still waiting for me to talk to her about the psych project, but today was the first day in weeks where she hadn't looked tired. Did I bring it up on a day she was mildly content or when she looked miserable?

In the visitors' room I was surprised to find Tyler seated at my usual table, reading a book for history class and drinking his Diet Coke. I slid my dollar into the vending machine, procured my Funyuns and moved to sit across from him at the table.

"Mind if I sit here?" I asked. It felt odd. Speaking so formal to a classmate.

"Go right ahead," he said and then whipped out a Dr. Pepper from his bag, sliding it across the table.

"You had this in your bag the whole time," I flipped the tab and took a sip, "and yet you still chose to drink Diet Coke?"

"I know what I like," he said, chugging the remaining Diet Coke.

"Then why have this?"

"Figured you'd be here," he grinned.

"Weird."

"Why is it weird?" he asked.

"Well this is only the second time I've seen you here like, ever, so how would you even assume I'd be here today? What if I'd been here yesterday? Or the day before? Have you just had this in your bag for weeks?"

He smiled and said, "You're one of those girls."

"What does that mean?"

"The kind that literally overthinks and breaks down everything, every minute detail until there's nothing left. I saw your Honda in the parking lot when I got here, figured at some point you'd be in here so I got the soda."

"I do that. It's true," I said, popping a Funyuns into my mouth, rinsing it down with some Dr. Pepper. "It's one of my many fun yet annoying qualities. Thank you, for the soda."

"Don't mention it."

"Oh, I'm sure I will. Countless times and say thank you more than a few times. Another annoying thing I do."

He laughed. "You're a funny one. How did I not ever know you're funny?"

"Probably because we've never really said much to each other."

"Oh that can't be true. Our lockers have been next to each other since the end of sophomore year."

"So that must make us best friends!"

"And you're sarcastic! A double whammy!" he laughed and then I couldn't help but to laugh. It felt weird, but yet not so weird to be laughing with Tyler Ashford. He'd never been a straight up jerk to people like his friend Blake was, but I'd never pictured us sitting at the same table laughing, like we'd been friends for ages.

"You used to go to Valley Central, right?"

"If I say yes, are you gonna hold it against me?"

He smiled. "No. Now if you'd said Junction City, maybe. Valley Central has a good basketball team. We played them last year in a tournament. They almost beat us."

"It's the only sport Valley Central excels at. Honestly, I'm not even sure how they had a sports program since half the student body were stoners. I'm not even exaggerating when I say our school resembled the student body in that one Nirvana music video."

He laughed. "Why'd you transfer? Did you not like it there?"

"I liked it just fine. My mom just uh, figures I have a better shot at a good college if I went to a Prep school."

"So, I meant to ask you the last time, who do you come here to see? Got a grandparent in here like mine?" he asked.

"Something like that."

He furrowed his brows. "Something like that? What does that even mean? You have a grandparent in here with dementia or you have a grandparent in here with something else?"

"More like it's complicated and I don't know you well enough to get into it." I hadn't meant for it to come out sounding so clipped, but he didn't seem to take it that way. Instead, he cocked his head to the side and smiled.

"Alright, fair enough. We'll just have to remedy that won't we." He looked down at his watch. "Crap. I gotta go pick up the brother from his basketball tryouts."

"The the disgruntled look-a-like from a few weeks ago?"

Laughing he said, "That'd be him. He's a bit whiny but he's a good kid. See you at school?"

"Yup. See ya."

After he left, I finished my snack and headed back to Nate's room. While Mom sat at the head of the bed holding Nate's hand, I sat in the chair at the small table and proceeded to fully overanalyze the entire conversation with Tyler, because apparently, I *was* that kind of girl.

It was still a shock to me that he'd had the Dr. Pepper ready before I even came into the room. What if I'd already been in and out before he got there, or what if I never went in at all? Then he'd have purchased the drink for nothing. It still begged the question why, and I wasn't buying the reasoning he had given. We saw each other every morning at our lockers, sometimes in between classes and never had he just brought me a drink or anything just because he assumed I was going to be there. What made now, that we both had a reason to be at the same rehab facility, a good time to branch outside of his social circle and be nice to me? I mean, he was *always* nice, but just not thoughtful or considerate.

Maybe I was the one being guilty of assuming I knew the type of person he was. Schools have factions and generally speaking, kids of a factiony feather flocked together. I assumed because he was friends with the school's biggest dirt bag that it must have meant he was one too and wouldn't give a shit about anyone not in his inner circle. But then I thought about Linz, and how she's always kind of a bitch, but none of the rest of us were like that, and Jillian seems to float between factions just fine. Just went to show I guess that people can't be crammed into one social box.

Either way, I decided I wasn't going to turn it into a big deal. If Tyler wanted to make small talk while we were both stuck in uncomfortable situations, I wouldn't brush him off, but it did mean I was going to be very, very cautious.

8

— • —

I was sitting on my backpack on a cold stone bench outside the Chapel before the start of school, flipping through the latest issue of my favorite music magazine, *Under The Radar*, when Mr. Dan came out of the Chapel doors and sat next to me.

"I was hoping to run into you," he said squirming, probably finding the cold hard cement uncomfortable.

"Hopefully not in there." I flicked my thumb back in the direction of the Chapel doors. "My mom may be the super religious type but not me. I don't waste my time. "

"Then don't you think you're in the wrong school?"

"Mr. Dan, be real. You know half the kids here don't go to a catholic church, or probably any church for that matter. They're here because their parents want them to get a good education, go to Ivy League schools so that they might one day live vicariously through them."

"Oh you and your biting wit," he laughed.

"Why were you looking for me?" I asked, folding back the top corner of the page I was on, pulling my backpack out from under me and sliding the magazine into the backpack.

"Two things. The first is your guidance counselor still needs your college application and essay questions, and since I'm your faculty advisor, I implore you to get a move on it."

"Noted. I have it mostly filled out. I'll get it to her next week. What's the other thing?"

"So it's been several weeks since I asked you to talk to your mom about the study."

"I know Mr. Dan, and I'm really sorry. I've been meaning to do that."

He threw up his hands to stop me. "Is what I knew you'd continue to say so I called your mom and talked to her."

No he didn't. Was this dude crazy? "You did what? Why would you do that? I said I'd ask, Mr. Dan."

"I know you did, Margo, but if there's any chance of maybe getting the study approved and even completed by end of year, I need to move on it, and while I understand how sensitive the situation is, I needed to make an executive decision."

"What'd she say?"

"She shot me down. Hard. Said something about him not being a lab rat and shame on me for even asking. Then she called me a whole bunch of choice colorful words before hanging up."

Wow. I'd figured she'd be against it, but I hadn't figured she'd have gone postal on him.

"I told you I didn't think she would go for it."

"That you did. So we'll just carry on with the topic without the study."

As he rose, I said, "I'm sorry she said no." I meant it too. Sure, it was an uncomfortable situation and I didn't want the whole entire psych class to know my business, especially when I haven't been totally truthful with my best friends, but there was a larger part of me that was curious as to what results might have been produced, if Nate was really in there. If the tests revealed he could actually understand what we've been saying to him it would mean we haven't just been talking to a vegetable for the past two years.

***

I decided not to skip cross country practice today, both to avoid any possible tongue lashings from my mother at the center, and to avoid further pissing off Coach Cathy by constantly skipping practice. The season was almost over as it was, and I'd missed too many practices to qualify for State, but that didn't mean I wouldn't have to deal with her angry faces all of Track and Field season in the spring.

I made sure to be the first to finish with warm ups and fell somewhere in the top of the pack with our 2-mile run and cool down.

"Nice work today, Margo," Coach Cathy said as I was changing out of my running shoes and into my sliders. "I applaud you for showing up today. It must have been a real chore."

"Awe come on Coach, I said I was sorry. You can't stay mad at me forever, can you?" Coach Cathy came across as a hard-ass most days but I knew her well enough to know she was also a huge push over who had a soft spot for charity cases such as myself. There had been a few times during sophomore year track season when I had to catch the city bus to school, I think because my mom had to be at work early or something, and the only two times the bus ran from the east side of town to the west was 5:30am and 9pm. Since school started at 8:00, I had no choice but to take the 5:30 bus which put me at the stop outside the school at 6:30, so I'd usually end up sitting on the steps until the campus would open, rain or shine. Coach Cathy lived in the apartment complex adjacent to campus, and after seeing me outside a few times, took me in until school started. She'd become more like an aunt, though I'd never once received special treatment. Sometimes it had seemed my workouts were way worse than anyone else's.

"You're just all full of troubles this year aren't you kid? How's your mom?"

"Oh, you know, the usual, overworked, underpaid, and super tired. She's got a new manager who's a major prick but she takes it like a champ."

"You just make sure you're being good to her, hear me?"

"Yes ma'am. Loud and clear," I saluted.

"Don't ma'am me and don't salute me you look like a damned idiot," she said, pulling me into a hug. I felt the guilt rise up in my throat. I really hated to disappoint Coach Cathy, and I knew that anything having to deal with my brother would hurt and upset my mom thus upset Coach, who'd gotten super close with my mom. I squeezed her back, pulled away and grabbed up my gym bag.

"Gotta run Coach. Good job not making any of the freshman cry today." She shook her head at me and then strutted off, whistle resting in between her lips. I tossed my bag into the back seat, started up the car and looked at the clock. 5:15pm. There was a good probability Mom had already left the rehab.

No such luck. Mom's car was still parked in her usual spot when I whipped into the parking lot. I gathered up my courage and walked in. I wasn't sure what to expect by way of conversation. Would she scold me? She's never done that before. I guess I'd never really ever given her a reason to scold me. I'd never even been grounded. I called any time I was going to be late (with the exception of today), I'd never done anything illegal, I've never even lied to her, so she's never had provocation to actually yell at me. Nate sure, he'd been yelled at countless times growing up. I always sort of figured she'd wasted all her good yelling on him.

I hadn't done anything behind her back or to intentionally make her mad by not yet mentioning the study, but I had a feeling she'd see it differently, having been basically blind-sided by Mr. Dan.

She was sitting in the chair at the top corner of the bed, holding his hand and resting her forehead on his shoulder. Her lips were moving but I didn't hear a sound. She was probably whispering about how disappointed in me she was.

"Hey Mom," I said, slowly placing my purse on the chair by the door. "Sorry I'm late. I really needed to go to practice today and it ran long." When she looked up at me her eyes were bloodshot, burning a hole right through my skull. I was too afraid to speak, so I stood there and waited for her to say something.

"Your psychology teacher called me today, but I'm sure you already knew that," she whispered. "Do you have any idea how it made me feel? To get that call and be asked that question? To be asked if I'd allow for your brother to be part of some study?"

"He wasn't supposed to call you. I was supposed to talk to you."

"Is that supposed to make a difference, him telling me or you?"

"Mom, I don't know why you're making a big deal. Mr. Dan just wanted to know if you'd be interested in something like it, that's all."

She narrowed her watery eyes. "That's all? Making a big deal?" She launched from her chair, catching it before it knocked to the ground. The move was so startling that I backed myself up against the wall, banging my head in the process.

"The big deal is that Nate is not some lab rat! I don't need a bunch of white coats and wires to tell me that Nate is still in there."

"It's not about him being a lab rat Mom, it's about science and dis-covery and because it's been two years with nothing!"

She crossed her arms. "Maybe that's because Jesus is still working on him."

"Did it ever occur to you that all your prayers and rosary beads and candle lighting have been for nothing because Jesus doesn't give a shit-" My words were cut short by the swift slap of her hand across my face. The sting radiated from my temple to my jaw.

"Every day I wake up, pretend to give a shit about taking a breath, about eating food, drinking coffee, going to work. I make my bed, I put on a smile, and for what? No matter what I do I still feel like I've done something wrong. This whole prayer thing, this newly found Jesus thing you think I've fallen into? Did you ever think there was a good reason? I pulled you out of public school and started going to church again because I felt maybe I've done something wrong in the eyes of the Lord, and that's why Paul left us, and that's why Nate acted out, and shot himself, and why he's stuck here like this on that bed. If I'd just raised you guys in the church, raised you like I was, everything would have turned out differently." She dropped her arms to her sides and held her palms open. "I have to believe that Jesus is using this time to work on him, that despite everything I've done, everything that Nate has done, that He still loves us, because if I don't have that faith, if I lose that, what the hell am I doing?"

It was the most real I'd ever seen her be, so raw and open. Even when my dad left, and all the times Nate took off, I'd never seen her vent like this. Shutting down and curling up had always been more her style. We were in uncharted territory. I didn't know what to say to comfort her, because we'd never been the type of mother-daughter who had those heartfelt moments, and while I wanted to understand her point of view, I just couldn't. Or wouldn't, I don't know which. All I know is she was clinging on to some long forgotten religious perspective for answers when there was the possibility of some actual scientific answers. So instead of saying anything, I shoved my hands deep into the pockets of my sweats, shrugged my shoulders and looked down at my feet. After several minutes, she cleared her throat, smoothed her hair back behind her ears and sat back down in the chair.

"I'm going to stay a few more minutes. You should go home. There are leftovers in the refrigerator." She picked up Nate's hand and rested her head on his shoulder. I gathered up my purse and slunk out of the room. I hated this feeling, whatever it was. Disappointment? Guilt? She hadn't yelled, which is more of what I thought she was going to do, but her being so honest made me feel like I'd just done something totally terrible, which actually only made me angry with her. Maybe I was guilty of not taking her feelings into consideration, or being aware enough to ask her if anything was wrong.

I knew she'd grown up with super strict Catholic parents who basically tossed her aside the minute she met my dad and declared she wasn't religious anymore, but I didn't know she was basically blaming the way we turned out, or I guess how her life has gone thus far on not having raised us with religion. I mean, up until the past few years I'd enjoyed everything about our family. Yeah Nate was a dick most the time because, just a guess here, he was having father figure issues, and I hated how he was always coming and going depending on where Khali was needing to score, but back then Mom laughed more, she was playful, and she taught us basic morals, so it's not like we were heathens or anything (except to my estranged grandparents who live somewhere in California).

Still, going back to the possibility of the study, she had her reasons for not wanting it done, what about my reasons *for* wanting it?

As I passed the visitor's lounge, I glimpsed Tyler at my usual table, a bag of Funyuns and a Dr. Pepper sitting in front of him. Though I was curious as to why he had my signature snack ready and waiting, I wasn't in an emotional headspace to chat so I kept heading for the door until he called out to me as I passed by. Reluctantly, I stopped, backtracked and posted up against the frame of the door, one foot in the room and one in the hall.

"Hey, Tyler," I said, offering a weak smile.

"Hey, I took the liberty of procuring snacks." He held up the bag, shaking it back and forth. He looked so utterly adorable sitting there, with his crooked grin, I forgot that I was supposed to head home and instead joined him at the table.

"Thanks," I said, popping open the bag.

"You look kinda glum, everything okay?

"Yeah, I just...my mom and I had an argument, I think, so I'm just a little frazzled."

"You think?"

"Yeah, it's kinda hard to explain. She didn't yell or anything, but I could tell by her tone. I guess it wasn't an argument so much as a disagreement." I didn't tell him about the slap.

"You and your mom disagree often?"

"Not really. Honestly, she's usually too focused on work or being here to pay much attention to me."

"Well I wish that were my situation. My mom is too focused on me."

His mom was Councilwoman Amanda Ashford, and she was a huge pain in the ass. She was also on the Board at school, president of every mom's club, and apparently, she'd gone to high school with my mom and the two didn't get a long at all. Even to this day my mom can never say her name without cringing.

Tyler looked at me like he was expecting more conversation from me but I just didn't have it in me, as much as I wanted to.

"I should go, I have lots of homework. Thanks though, for the snack."

"Yeah for sure, no problem. I hope you work things out with you mom."

"Me too. See you around?"

"Yeah, totally," he replied.

I took the long way home, down Hwy 99 so I'd have more time to think. The more I thought about Mom's emotional state, her inner turmoil with her faith, and how neither of us had ever tried to be close, the angrier I got, which I don't know, maybe it wasn't a fair emotion to have, but the thing is, we never talked about what happened to Nate. She never checked in with me to see if I was okay (I wasn't) and I never asked her how she was.

It would have just been better if she'd yelled at me. She hadn't been void of emotion or anything, I mean, she *did* slap me, but at least if she'd yelled, I think I might have responded better. Sometimes the way we communicate made me feel like I was basically incapable of being real with anyone. I couldn't be honest about any aspect of my life with my friends, and that wasn't because I'd only known them two years. Even at Valley Central, I didn't have anyone I would have called a friend. There were kids I talked to, kids I'd gone to school with since elementary, but not anyone on a BFF level. I'd always had Nate to talk to, and when he started taking off, I'd put all my energy into trying to convince him to stay, I never gave "letting other people in" a chance.

Then when IT happened, and Mom went all catatonic, and Dad couldn't be reached, I didn't have anyone to lean on so to speak. Was this why it was so hard to confide in Linz, Donny, and Jillian? If I'd spent more time letting my mom in, instead of shutting her out, or always trying to take care of myself, maybe then I'd have been better equipped to handle an emotional mom instead of a mute one, and then I wouldn't feel so angry with her for making me feel I'd done something wrong. The look on her face, it was as if she'd thought I was the one to ask Mr. Dan to call her and talk to her about the study. So what though? Even if I had, I wouldn't have known how she actually felt because for as much as I don't confine in her, she doesn't confide in me.

I wish I'd been honest with her when Nate shot himself, even if my feelings about it were contrary to her newly found religious feelings, there at least would have been some understanding on both parts. Instead, what I feel is a mucky combination of anger and disappointment.

And then, to pile on top of that, there was this thing with Tyler, which probably wasn't even a thing. I was more likely reading into it, but why else would he have had my snacks waiting for me not once, but twice? I should be viewing it as a sweet gesture, but instead all I could think about was how weird it was, because I really didn't want it to be a "She's all that" moment. I'd found myself actually looking forward to going to the rehab center once a week because I knew Tyler would be there, even though we'd only really talked the two times. I wanted to talk to him more often because he was fun and easy to talk to. Ugg, I hated that I was even thinking so much about him.

When I got home, I didn't have the energy to do any of my homework, figured I could just get a library pass during first period to finish, so I took a long shower, made some peanut butter-honey toast, then wrapped myself in a dozen blankets in my bed and watched episodes of *Dawson's Creek* on Hulu. At 9:30pm I heard Mom fumble with her keys before finally unlocking the door and dumping her keys into the glass bowl on the table next to the door. After several minutes the floorboards creaked as she walked down the hall, stopping at my door. I half expected her to knock and come in, ask me if I'd done my homework, tell me not to eat in my bed before crawling in to swipe the rest of my food and finish watching *Dawson's Creek* with me. But she kept walking down the hall to her room, flicked off the hall light, gently closing her door. In the morning, there were no sticky notes left on the refrigerator, no coffee in the pot or travel mug, no breakfast.

***

When the bell rang at the end of psych and everyone rushed the doors I lagged behind. Without looking up from his desk, somehow sensing I was still in the room, Mr. Dan cleared his throat and said, "You know Miss Adams, usually when the bell rings and all the kids run out the door, that means class is over."

"How'd you know it was me?"

"It's your scent-a combination of spring fresh flowers and teen angst."

"Funny. Very funny."

He smirked. "You really think?"

"No absolutely not."

"Alright fine. To what do I owe the pleasure?"

"So yeah my mom wasn't very happy with me last night."

"Did she yell at you too?"

"No no, there wasn't any yelling, but it was the um lack of yelling and more the sullen face that gave me the impression. I think she feels she was blind-sided."

"Well kiddo, I did tell you to talk to her."

Of course, he was going to make it my fault. "I know, and I still think you should have waited but whatever. It happened. I just wanted to say I'm sorry she wouldn't say yes."

He shrugged his shoulders. "Meh. It was a long shot anyway."

"I mean, do we *need* to have her permission to do it? Technically Nate's an adult."

"Yes, Margo. We do NEED her permission. Age wise Nate is an adult but in so far as being mentally capable, no. He's not. Your mom is his guardian and conservator and nothing can happen to him without her signing off."

"Can't I just sign the papers for her? I mean, so long as the tests happen on any day that's not a Tuesday she'll never know."

What the hell was I doing? It was like I'd lost all common sense, standing here trying to convince my teacher to do something that was for sure illegal.

"Margo. I may be a rebel in a lot of ways, but I'm not a criminal and what you're talking about is illegal. Look, I don't know the details with your brother's situation, and I'm sure you would love nothing more than possibly getting answers by having this study done, but I just can't reach out to the Neuroscientists unless your mom is on board. There's just no way."

I sighed. What I really wanted to do was cry. "I understand."

Mr. Dan walked from behind his desk and rested a hand on my shoulder, giving it a gentle squeeze in a non-creepy way. "Hang in there."

Hang in there was one of the worst, possibly lamest thing anyone could ever say to anyone. That's all there was to it. I mean, what else is a person supposed to do in an otherwise crappy situation?

9

Last night Mom had been too emotional to fully consider the study, and I'd been too unwilling to try and rationalize with her. She just needed a few days to collect herself, at least that's what I'd told myself, and I needed to figure out a way to talk to her in a meaningful way. I'd show her the book and hopefully be able to get her to see why the study was just as important to me as her prayers were to her. There had to be a way to compromise, because I just couldn't take no for an answer. I needed to know if Nate was still...well...Nate.

When I arrived at the rehab center a little after 4:15pm the following Tuesday, Mom was packing up her purse and heading for the door.

"Hey Mom, you're here early," I said.

She tucked a loose curl behind her ear. "Uh yeah, I got them to switch my schedule around. I'll work in the bakery now and get off earlier most days."

"That's good," I said. She looked at the clock and then down at her shoes. To say it had been awkward between us for the past few days would have been the understatement of the century. She was still upset with me and straight up refused to talk about the study. I'd tried on Saturday after dinner, thinking she'd had enough time to cool down, but she just jabbed her fork into her chicken and excused herself for the rest of the evening. Since then, we'd only managed the basics- hi's, bye's, have a good day. She left for work before I got up in the mornings, and in the evenings, she'd hole herself up in her bedroom, sometimes leaving dinner for me in the microwave. So much for assuming she'd be calm and collected after a few days.

"I'm gonna take off. You cool to visit on your own?" she asked heading for the door.

"Yeah sure Mom. See you at home."

She came in for a loose hug and then left, quietly closing the door behind her. I slumped into the chair by Nate's bed, frustrated, unable to figure out how to make things better with my mom. We were both choosing to shut each other out rather than discuss things, which was making it super uncomfortable, both here and at home. cross country season was over and I was still just working the weekends at the bookstore, so it meant I was home after school every day, which meant we were both home together. Perfect opportunity for bonding, but instead we had been basically pretending the other didn't exist. I studied and she watched TV or read books. It hadn't been a problem before, her not paying attention to me, and me not paying attention to her, but with Nate not around there wasn't a buffer between us.

I accepted that she was going through something, and I really needed to focus on my studies, but I needed her to focus on me and my needs, as selfish as that might sound.

Rather than allowing myself to get too far inside my head I decided it was time for a snack. "So check it Nate, I'm gonna go grab some food. You want anything? No? You sure? Ok be back in a few."

I grabbed my wallet out of my purse and headed for the lounge. I found Tyler posted up at one of the tables drinking his Diet Coke and reading a *Rolling Stone* magazine. He looked up and when he saw me, he smiled, folded down the corner of the page, just like I do, and closed his magazine.

"Hey Margo, what's up?" he asked.

"It's a direction," I said with a coy smile, popping some quarters into the soda machine. I was well aware of how totally lame the response was, but I couldn't help myself. Thankfully he laughed.

"Sweet Dad joke, Adams."

I sat down across from him.

"So really, what's the deal with your weird obsession with Funyuns?" he said, grabbing the bag and tossing it in the air. I snatched it back from him and tore it open.

"It's not a weird obsession," I said, popping a ring into my mouth.

"Really? It's not?"

"Ok I realize that they aren't as conventionally popular as Doritos or Cheetos, but I can't help it. I love them. Have you even ever tried one?"

"Admittedly, I have not."

"Here." I pulled a ring out of the bag, handed it to him. "Try one." He took it from me and mulled it over.

He curled his lip. "It looks like something a cat yacked up."

"Just try it."

He took a bite, chewed a second, then took a giant swig of his drink.

"That's garbage. Pure garbage. You have quite possibly the most terrible taste in junk food."

I laughed, ate another Funyuns. "Everybody has their thing.

"Alright. Well, anything wrong with my choice in chips? There's nothing non-dudely about Cheetos is there?"

I laughed and reached across the table to snag a Cheeto from his bag.

"No of course not. Cheetos are universally accepted as a superior snack."

"But just not your number one choice, right?" he asked.

"Right," I responded. He looked at me and smiled. I felt my cheeks burn. He was so easy to talk to. A little too easy though. Part of me wanted to spend the next several hours sitting at this rinky table talking about stupid things, or not stupid things, anything really, but another part shouted at me, reminding me of who his friends were.

"So, did you work things out with your mom? I saw her come in earlier without you and leave just a few minutes ago. You guys don't visit your relative together?" Tyler asked.

"We didn't really work anything out," I replied. "She's still mad at me but she prefers the avoidance method versus diplomatic discussions. Actually, I guess we both kinda do. The thing is, we don't really see eye to eye on my brother's condition and in the past, I'd just go along with whatever she says, but lately I've been a little more assertive, I guess? Like stating my opinion on the matter and sticking to it."

"Your brother's condition?" he asked. *Crap.* I realized I hadn't actually told him who I come here to see. I also realized I was being way more open and honest with him than I had intended. It had taken me two years to tell my closest of friends, and even then, I omitted part of the truth, yet here I was, having no trouble at all telling basically a stranger, the straight up truth.

"Yeah, my brother is here. He's a coma patient."

"There are people in coma's here? I thought it was just for people with Alzheimer's and Dementia."

"Nate's kinda the only coma patient."

I waited for the next logical question, but he didn't ask. Instead, he nodded and said, "So you and your mom have a different opinion on your brother's condition and she doesn't like it?"

"I mean, I guess I've never really known her position on it, and I'm still trying to figure out my position on it, but let's just say as it stands, we're on opposite ends."

"Do you mind me asking what happened to your brother? Was it a car accident or something?"

The next logical question. I chewed my bottom lip. "No, it wasn't anything like that."

He must have sensed my hesitation because he reached across the table and brushed a hand across mine, sending a heat wave up through my arm.

"You don't have to tell me, you know, if you're not comfortable with it," he said.

"I've just never really talked about it."

"Not even with Jillian?"

"She knows a little, that he's in a coma and why, but not the entire why. I've always had a hard time, like, being vulnerable with people and there are usually whole lines of questioning that come into play when you talk about something heavy like this, and I've just never been good with that kind of stuff."

"Makes sense," he said. "Don't worry, I won't pry or anything."

I smiled. "Thanks. It's just been a really weird couple of years."

"So did this whole thing happen before you transferred? Was it the reason you transferred?"

"Kinda. My mom used to be really religious growing up. She actually went to Marshall Academy when she was a kid. She stopped going to church sometime around meeting my dad and she's sort of been blaming everything that's happened on her losing her faith or whatever. She thought if she changed everything about well, everything, including my education, things might get better."

"Have they?"

I pointed around the room. "What do you think?"

"Fair point. Wait so did you say your mom went to Marshall? Do you think she knew my mom in school?"

I smirked. "Oh yeah, she knew your mom. No offense or anything but she said your mom was a heinous bitch back in high school."

He let out a guttural sort of laugh. "No offense taken. I'm aware of how she was back in the day. My aunt filled me in. Guessing they weren't BFF's, your mom and mine."

I shook my head. "Nope. Not at all."

He reached over and fumbled with the cord to my headphones that was around my neck.

"So, I always see you walking around with these things crammed in your ears. What are you listening to?"

"Music. Duh."

"No shit. I meant *what* are you listening to."

I handed him over one of the buds. "Here, have a listen. You'll love them, I promise." I opened Spotify and clicked on my favorite The Decemberists song. "O Valencia." He didn't yank the bud out of his ear and snarl, so I took that as a promising sign. Half way though the song he nodded, pulled the ear bud out and handed it back to me.

"They sound familiar. Who are they?"

"The Decemberists."

"Oh I've heard of them," he said.

I arch an eyebrow. "You have?"

"Well I don't live under a rock. Yeah I've heard of them. I mean, I don't know many of their songs but I have heard them."

"They're my absolute fave. I've seen them play at least seven or eight times."

"A true fan. I dig it. I don't think I've ever been that into a band to have seen them more than twice."

"Maybe you're listening to the wrong kind of music. What's your favorite?" I asked fully expecting him to say some lame Rap artist.

"You'll think it's weird but I'm legit into classic rock."

"How classic are we talking here?" I asked.

"Like 60's and 70's classic. Blue Oyster Cult, Rolling Stones, CCR. All time fave though is Fleetwood Mac."

I laughed. I didn't want to but I did. It was totally unexpected to hear he liked classic rock. I'd heard him and his friends talk all the time about Drake this Drake that and how and how they'd all just been to see Kendrick Lamar last summer.

"So, let me get this straight. You like to drink Diet Coke and you listen to classic rock. Do your friends know? You're basically a middle-aged man."

"Hence the reason why they sometimes refer to me as Grandpa Ashford on the courts."

I was about to say something in response when his phone began to vibrate on the table. He tapped on it and winced. "Crap. I was supposed to pick up my brother from practice like a half hour ago. I'd better go."

"I should go too. I've got like twelve chapters to read for AP Lit."

"Glad we had a chance to talk. You're fun to talk to, Margo."

If I wasn't blushing before I most certainly was right now. As per usual, I didn't know what to say, how to respond, so like a complete moron, I took a bow. I freaking bowed to Tyler Ashford. Thankfully instead of hurling insults, he laughed hysterically and cleaned off the table.

"I can honestly say I've never been bowed to before."

"First time for everything. See you next week? I mean, obviously I'll see you in school, but like, see you next week here I mean."

"Yeah, I'll be here. Later." We walked out into the hall, he turned right to head for the parking lot, I turned left to get my stuff from Nate's room. I turned around to look behind me and caught Tyler doing the same thing. We both smiled and waved and I realized at that moment I had a freaking crush on Tyler Ashford.

At school the next day I slipped notes into my friends' lockers, old school style asking them to meet at The Daily Bagel for lunch. Sure, I could have sent a group text, but who doesn't like receiving ominous notes in their lockers? Hopefully enough time had passed and they'd all forgiven me for being stupid. I really needed them to forgive me. I was tired of being selective in what I'd say about my life. If I was so easily willing to divulge information about my life to Tyler Ashford, a guy I hardly knew, I needed to be one hundred percent honest with my friends.

When I arrived at The Daily Bagel, I was grateful to see that they'd all showed up. Linz looked disgruntled (not surprised), scrolling on her phone, and Donny and Jillian were bent over a gossip magazine. I slid into the booth next to Linz.

"Hey guys. I'm going to make this quick." I waited for Linz to set down her phone and for Donny and Jillian to look up from their magazine before sucking in a heap of air and emptying my lungs.

"My brother tried to kill himself, it didn't work so ever since he's been in a coma. I know I told you it was an accident and I didn't know how it happened, and I'm sorry I lied, I just was worried you guys would ask questions and I didn't want to answer them, which I also realize is pretty shitty since you guys are my friends and friends tell each other things." I paused to suck in another breath and then continued. "Mr. Dan wants me to get my mom to agree to allow for Nate to be a guinea pig in a psychological study for the class assignment. She refuses, siting religious reasons, I want her to allow it, siting scientific reasons, so we're fighting. There. Now you know the truth, all of it."

Donny let out a low sigh. "Wow Margo, that's super crazy"

"Yeah, tell me about it," I responded, running my hands through my tangled hair. It felt like Thor had lifted a crushing Mjolnir off my chest.

"So, you guys aren't like super pissed at me, are you?" I asked.

"Well, we kinda already knew, kid," Linz said.

"Wait what? You knew?" I snapped my head over at Jillian, who was biting her lip so hard it bled. "What the hell Jillian?"

"Look don't be mad! I couldn't carry it anymore! They kept bringing it up and wondering about the accident and I just couldn't keep making things up. I really don't like lying to people, Margo." Tears streamed down her face and it was like a punch to my gut. I hated to see Jillian cry. Rarely did anything bring her to tears. I felt like the biggest dick of all time

"I get it, it's ok," I said, pulling a tissue out of my purse and handing it to her. Linz slid an arm across my shoulder, which was the weirdest thing ever because Linz didn't like to touch anyone. Ever.

"Dude. I get why you didn't ever say anything. I never told anyone about my birth mom and how she was a cracked-out piece of shit before my parents adopted me. I was always too embarrassed, so I just told everyone what my parents told everyone, that they adopted me from an orphanage in the Philippines, birth parents unknown"

I know this was supposed to be about me coming clean, but something monumental had just happened here. Linz. Opened. Up. It might have only been the smallest nugget of personal information but it was something. Linz never talked about her personal life, and anyone who tried to pry details out of her basically was told in no uncertain terms to fuck off.

"Damn Linz," Donny said.

"It's not that big a deal. My parents are tight so it's all good. Stop looking at me like that, you guys look like morons." And just like that, closed-off Linz was back. I smiled in spite of myself.

"So Margo, you wanna tell us what happened to your brother, you know, what led up to it?" Linz asked.

Donny kicked her under the table. "OMG Linz, could you be more insensitive?" She glared at him, opened her mouth to spit out a retort but I waved my hands to stop her.

"It's ok, that you asked and all, I just, can I not get into it? It's kinda long and complicated and the details are still a little murky." I was grateful that they all nodded. I hated to talk about that day, and the days leading up to it. I'd seen a therapist for a whole month afterwards and even with all her tricks she couldn't get me to talk about that day.

"Thanks again you guys, for not being too pissed at me. From now on you'll get nothing but the truth out of me." It felt like a pie-crust promise, but I said it anyway, hoping it would be true.

"That's all we ask. We love you girl," Donny extended his arm across the table to squeeze my hand. We finished our drinks, cleared the table and headed to the parking for school. Donny wrangled us all in for a group hug which lasted all of two seconds before Linz wiggled free.

"Okay that's enough touching. I'm out. See you morons later." Linz climbed into her Jetta and sped out of the parking lot, Donny following behind in his Forte. Jillian and I lingered for a bit in the parking lot.

"I'm glad you told them," she said.

"Well, I guess I really didn't need to since you covered that base for me."

"I really am sorry."

"I know. I'm not mad. It was selfish on my part to even ask you not to tell them. I should have been straight."

"It's ok."

She lingered, biting again at her lip. It was a wonder the lip was even still attached.

"Do you want to tell me about what happened with Nate?" Jillian knew me better than anyone and I knew I could trust her with my life, but even some things you can't tell your best friend.

"I kinda don't? Please don't take it personally or anything, you're my best friend and I tell you everything but this is just something I don't know if I'll ever be able to tell anyone. Is that ok?"

She smiled, pulled me into a hug. "Yeah, it's ok. I'm here when you're ready."

10

— · —

The book store was crazy busy today. Granted, we were on the cusp of the holiday season. Halloween having breezed by and the loom of Black Friday ever present, basically meant all retail stores would be slammed. Rarely was The Book Shelf THIS level of busy. Most of my coworkers complained about the increase in foot traffic, but I actually liked it. Between running the registers, stocking shelves, and fulfilling online orders, I didn't have even the smallest of seconds to get stuck inside my brain.

Today I'd been scheduled to work the young adult section. Half way through zoning a whole entire shelf just about vampires, I heard a familiar voice from behind me.

"So, is it wrong if I'm Team Jacob? I mean, I'm not going to be kicked in the junk by a bunch of girls for not being Team Edward, right?" Tyler was thumbing through the pages of *Twilight*.

"Just don't say it so loudly and you'll go unscathed," I responded, taking the book from him and re-shelving it.

"Are girls still reading *Twilight* in 2011? Like, has enough time passed to where that's not a popular book to read?"

"Oh no it's still popular, and not just with girls. Men read it too. Grown. Ass. Men,"

"Well now that's just ridiculous. What's your favorite?"

"My favorite what?" I asked, rounding the corner to zone the next isle of books.

"Your favorite genre. What's your favorite genre? You into all these vampire books?"

"Not so much. I tend to stick more with contemporary young adult. Edgy stuff, stuff that makes the banned book lists."

"That's cool. Wanna know my favorite book?"

"Hmmmm, I'm going to guess *Michael Jordan The Life*."

"Oh how you think so little of me," he said putting his hands on his hips. There was something adorable about the way he stood, with his hands resting there on his hips and the corner of his mouth drawn in. Ten bucks says my cheeks were beet red.

"Ok so tell me, what'd your favorite book. "

"*Ready Player One*, though also I really like *The Hitchhiker's Guide* to the *Galaxy*."

"Wow. I didn't peg you for a science fiction nerd."

"That's what you get for stereotyping."

"Well played."

He pulled his phone out from his front pocket, clicked it to look at the time, then shoved it back in.

"Hey do you get a break or a lunch or something any time soon?"

I looked at my watch, frowning. It was 3:15pm, I'd taken a break 20 minutes ago.

"Kinda already had my break."

"Bummer," he said.

"I have to go change out the periodicals. It's usually pretty slow and quiet over there. You can come with if you want, I mean if you need to tell me something, or whatever. I can listen and swap."

He smiled and my heart skipped. I didn't want to be crushing. Why was I crushing? Cramming the fluttering butterflies deep down inside my chest we walked to the front corner of the store and he sat on a bench while I took down past issues.

"Do you like working here?" he asked.

"It beats fast food," I said. "I actually really love it here. Most of my coworkers are either college kids or senior citizens, which is fine because I get along better with older people. I love books and the discount is great. Plus, they offer college incentives so it's a win-win for me."

"Where do you want to go to college?"

"I'd really like to go to UCLA. They have an awesome Psychology department. But I'll probably just stick around here though and go to U of O. I don't want to leave my brother."

"Makes sense. So, you wanna be a therapist or something?" he asked.

"I want to do psychological research. Run tests, studies, figure things out. Get inside the human brain."

"Those are some legit goals." He paused, opened his mouth to say something, but snapped it shut.

"You're wanting to ask if my interest in psychology has anything to do with my brother in a coma and short answer is yes."

"What's the long answer?" he asked. I rubbed my chin between my thumb and index finger.

"Guess that's the long answer too. What about you? Where are you planning to go?"

He frowned and tensed his shoulders. "Well, my parents want me to go to Stanford or an east coast school. Somewhere with great basketball and even greater academics."

"Is that not what you want?"

"Honestly, I don't know what I want to do or where I want to go."

"What about basketball?"

"What about it?"

"Well, I mean, do you want to get a scholarship, play in college, maybe play in the NBA?"

"That's the dream, isn't it? I just don't know if it's *my* dream. I love to play ball, but I just don't love all the pressure. My parents, well mostly my mom, has this idea about where I should go, what I should study, but I just want a say in where I go, ya know?"

I didn't know. I'd love to have even half the opportunities Tyler had. His parents had connections, people who knew people who knew people at good Universities. I was pretty sure Tyler could totally bomb his SAT's and still get into whatever IVY league college he wanted, though I knew well enough Tyler was smart and he'd score higher than anyone on his SAT's. He had a double-whammy advantage. Smart, and his parents were rich, oh and he'd most likely get a basketball scholarship.

But there was something in the way he carried himself, shoulders fluctuating between tense and slouch that said the game and his involvement in it was becoming more of a weight than he wanted to carry.

"Hey, you've heard of this music event in Portland called December to Remember yeah?" he asked.

I dumped a load of magazines into a box and turned to face him, dropping my hands to my side. Anyone who had any decent taste in music knew what December to Remember was.

"I'm aware of it," I said, playing it cool.

"The Decemberists were supposed to play but had to pull out last minute. This band called Lord Huron is playing? Have you listened to them?"

"Yeah of course, I love Lord Huron. Little surprised you like them since you're like this classic rock guy."

"Hey I'll just have you know even though I'm heavy into classic rock, I also love the whole umbrella of rock, and that includes your indie rock. I even know who Umbrella Waistcoat is."

This was probably the most startling of things he could have ever said because Umbrella Waistcoat was a super lo-fi local indie band that really only had an internet presence, usually playing smaller venues in Valley River.

"I can tell I've totally shocked you with that," he laughed. "Anyway, Lord Huron is playing the day after Thanksgiving. You think you'd wanna go with me? To December to Remember?"

Tyler was actually asking me to do something with him, like a date, I think, but I was scheduled to work Black Friday, and even if I wasn't, there's no way I'd be able to afford a trip up to Portland.

"The day after Thanksgiving? Shoot. I have to work. It's Black Friday. Super busy day here. Actually, the whole season is busy, I can't really take any time off."

"Oh, Ok I get it." He slid his hands into his pockets and frowned. It felt like all the pleasant air in the space between us had been sucked out and replaced with an icy chill. "Well, I should go. Let you get back to work. See you in school."

Before I could say anything, he spun on his heels and weaved through the book isles to the exit door, leaving me with a weird feeling like he was mad at me for something but I didn't know what. I hadn't lied, or made up an excuse not to go to a concert with him. I really did have to work. I needed to work. Hopefully tomorrow I'd be able to meet up with him at the lockers and ask him.

I didn't see him at the lockers at all the following day, and we didn't have any classes together. Two days later, I'd been running late getting to school because my crappy Honda decided to stall on the freeway not once, but twice. Tyler was at his locker swapping out books when I got there.

"My ancient piece of shit car forgot how to function. What's your excuse for being late?" I asked, sliding my backpack off my shoulder and opening up my locker. I expected him to glare or ignore me, but thankfully he didn't.

"Dentist appointment," he smiled wide, shoveling a little more coal onto the low burning fire in my heart.

"Ah yes, you must take care of that award-winning smile of yours. You can't get buy on your basketball skills alone."

"You're hilarious, Adams. Hey listen-" He stopped mid-sentence just as his friends Griffin and Andy came out of the media room and hollered his name. Tyler looked from me to his friends, a slightly panicked look invading his face. He slammed his locker shut and greeted his friends with fist bumps.

"Dude you missed morning practice, Blake's gonna give you shit later," Griffin said. When he saw me standing next to Tyler he nodded.

"Hi Margo," Andy said.

"Hey Andy," I replied quietly. I looked up at Tyler but he refused to look back at me. He fiddled with the lock on his locker, rocked back and forth from heel to toe. The warmth in his face was gone, replaced by something else, discomfort maybe; his lips pinched together and his eyes spastically shot from side to side.

"Sorry guys, had stuff to take care of this AM. I can handle Blake. You skipping second or something?"

For one quick second he looked down at me as if he'd just remembered I was still standing there, right next to him, sharing the same freaking air.

"Naw just getting stuff from the office for the sub," Andy said.

"I'll come with," Tyler said slinging his backpack on and walking away. I watched him as he left, hoping he'd turn around and wink or flash a crooked smile, but he didn't. Funny how fast people shifted when the status of their popularity was about to be jeopardized. Either Tyler was just as much a douche as his friends, pretending to like me out of convenience, or he was too afraid of his friends knowing he was a nice guy. It didn't make any sense because Andy had zero problem acknowledging me. I really didn't want to believe he was a jerk because then that would mean I'd allowed myself to feel something other than distain for a member of the douche troop.

***

For eleven months out of the year, the halls of the rehab facility looked exactly the same. Same canary yellow walls, same framed photographs of serene fields, same smell of stale air accompanied by a heavy feeling of despair. When December finally rolls around, it's like new life is breathed into the halls, into every room and even the residents seem a bit more alive. Strands of bright Christmas lights are hung in uneven waves down the length of the halls, cotton balls stretched out to their max are glued around the door frames, and in the center next to the nurses' station, a 6ft Douglas Fir is erected, wrapped in miles and miles of garland, lights, and red and silver glass bulbs. For one whole month the resident's smiles were a little bigger, their guests actually seemed happy to visit, and the staff would make their rounds humming holiday radio tunes.

Nate had never been keen on Christmas. He said it was a dumb holiday where people put on masks and pretended to be nice to each other. I don't know if it had anything to do with Dad having left in December, but his crappy disposition usually pissed Mom off because she'd always enjoyed the sentimentality of the holiday, and it was actually the only time she ever tried to be all religious, wanting us to go to Christmas Eve Mass and all that.

He was such a punk about the holidays, but every year I managed to catch him in what he thought was a private moment, laying under the Christmas tree with all the lights out except for those illuminated around the tree, humming "O Christmas Tree."

Last year we were still too emotional to think about Christmas and decorating, but this year, in the odd chance that it would make a difference, maybe in the hopes that if by some random fucking miracle all of Mom's prayers were working, I wanted Nate to have his Christmas tree. I found a used 4ft artificial tree at a second-hand store, bought a new strand of super bright twinkling lights, and planned to make it look like the holiday spirit basically vomited in his room.

I was super late getting to the rehab center since the lines were long at the store so I had to full on sprint from my car to the doors while hauling the tree and a box of decorations. Right as the automatic doors opened, I barreled into Tyler as he was coming out of the Center. It had been a week since he blew me off in the hall, and while he'd slipped a few notes into my locker, I'd tossed them without reading and avoided him at school. What did you say to someone who was ashamed to be seen speaking to you? Even if he was afraid of what his friends would think and that's what the notes would have explained, I was still too hurt to just brush it off, choosing instead to ghost him.

When we collided, I dropped the box, garland and plastic balls rolling out. Were we going to make a habit out of literally running into one another like this?

"Hey Margo, I've been trying to get ahold of you for like a week," he said, scooping up the balls and dumping them into the box.

"Yeah, sorry. I got your notes. I've been busy."

"Look, about last week at the lockers-"

"It's fine," I said, cutting him off. I had been standing right there, I was well aware of what was happening. I didn't need him to insult my intelligence.

"You don't owe me an explanation, Tyler. I know where I stand and where you stand. We don't need to pretend that line doesn't exist just because we see each other here once a week."

Even when he pouted his face was still stupid attractive. "I'm sorry about that. It was a dick move. Plain and simple. I didn't mean to make you feel, rejected or whatever. I'm really sorry."

I couldn't tell if he was saying that to safe face or if he *were* genuinely sorry. I so desperately wanted to tell him to fuck off and never speak to me again, but that damn stupid-hot grin of his sucked me right back in, and then he said something next that made it worse.

"So last night I listed to every single Decemberists album. In a row. And I loved them." He handed me the last strand of garland that had fallen from the box. He gently took the tree from my arm and we walked down the hall to the visitor's room, even though I was supposed to be heading for Nate's room.

"Really? Even 'The Hazards of Love'? That must have taken you all night."

"Oh it totally did."

"But why?"

"Because you like them."

He fed a few dollars to the vending machine and brought back a Diet Coke and a Dr. Pepper, sliding the latter across the table to me. I checked my watch, aware of the time and that I was now really fucking late. He clicked open his tab and continued.

"And because I ended up going to December to Remember and watched like three bands play and the last one, who was it, oh yeah Band of Horses, I really liked them. So I listened to all their albums on the way home from Portland, and then all of The Decemberists."

"Wow. I'm super impressed and maybe just a little jealous," I laughed, sipping from my Dr. Pepper. "I really am sorry I couldn't go with you. I wasn't making up excuses not to go. I really did need to work."

"It's ok, really. I get it. Truthfully, I kinda got in a lot of trouble for going. I missed two basketball practices and my mom totally chewed me out. Also I took my brother with me which got me in even more trouble because he missed practice too."

"Yeah but admit it, it was worth it."

"It totally was. Would have been even more worth it if you'd been there," he said, running his hand through his blonde locks.

I knew I was blushing so I pulled my knit scarf up higher around my face. I was a total noob when it came to flirting and recognizing when a boy was flirting with me. I guess it could be chalked up to the fact that I'd never actually had a boyfriend before. When you're working, going to school across town, running, and visiting a comatose brother, it didn't invite a lot of time for dating. Plus, what would I even say when asked about myself? *Hi my name is Margo. I'm like ten bucks away from being on welfare, my brother tried to kill himself, and my dad left us?* Not really the ideal girl. So it'd always just been easier to keep to myself, and that included any boy crushes.

Tyler Ashford was not making that easy. The way the left corner of his mouth pulled up slightly when he spoke, how he smiled with both his mouth and his eyes, the way his hair slid into his face. I could see why so many girls were attracted to him. He could have his pick of any girls at school so why he'd even waste his time flirting with me, if that's what he was doing, I don't know, I could be reading way too much into his comments. I mean, if he were into me would he be too ashamed to be seen speaking to me at school? Let's be real here, it's Marshall Academy and the kids there are dicks who thrive on social status and money. Of course, he'd be too ashamed to be seen speaking to a girl from the East side. Even so, I just knew I felt good around him and I wanted to be here with him.

"Maybe we can go another time. To see them play," he said. I nodded, pulling the scarf down away from my mouth.

"For sure," I croaked. "They usually play Britt Fest down in Jacksonville every summer. It's a great outdoor venue."

"How many times did you say you've seen them? Six times?"

I hiked up the sleeve of my left arm jacket and turned the inside of my wrist to face him, revealing a tattoo of an open heart and underneath it eight dash marks. He took my wrist in his hand and traced the heart and dashes with his thumb. It felt as if my whole body were slowly going numb starting at my toes and trickling up my spine coming to a stop at the base of my skull.

"Eight times, and you tattooed it to your wrist. That really is dedication."

I gently pulled my wrist away, sliding the sleeve back down, hoping my racing heart would calm.

"I'm sure it might seem a little silly to get a tattoo of a band or something representing it, but music is so important to me, and not just for the obvious reasons. It's a form of therapy. Sometimes when shit just gets too real, I use music to cope, and The Decemberists have always been my go-to."

He smiled, drank a little from his Diet Coke. The way he sat there looking at me, like I was the only one in the room (admittedly, like always, we were actually the only ones in the room), like I was always the only one in any room unnerved me, but in a good way. Who cared if come tomorrow he pretended I didn't exist when we passed in the halls? I wanted to be in this moment with him, in any moment like this where it was just the two of us being real, even if it meant at school I didn't exist.

"What are you thinking about over there?" he asked, leaning closer to me over the table.

Blushing I said, "Trying to figure out what's going on here. What's your angle?"

"Why does there have to be an angle? We're just two people connecting."

"Yeah but why? I'm not one of you. I grew up in felony flats. I'm not rich, I'm not popular, and I drive a shitty Honda."

He reached across the table, taking both my hands in his. I gasped at the unexpectedness of his actions. "You're real Margo. It may not seem like it, but I'm scared shitless to do anything or say anything that my friends or family won't approve of, but you aren't afraid to be you. I know I dissed you at the lockers last week but you have no fucking idea how insecure I am."

He stopped talking and started to pull his hands away but I tightened my grip on them. Everything I was fighting not to feel about Tyler started to crash into my chest cavity like violent waves. His blue eyes bore into mine like they were trying to see into my soul and before I could actually register what I was doing I leaned across the table and kissed him.

I'd kissed exactly one guy my whole entire life and that was at the eighth-grade graduation dance. I'd known Robbie Miller since the fourth grade when he moved to Oregon half way through the year and we'd been assigned desk partners in Mrs. Maine's class. He had floppy brown hair, huge green eyes, and would slide Skittles onto my desk when the teacher wasn't looking. At recess we would swing together. When middle school rolled around, he'd been accepted into the popular crowd while I was still floundering, trying to find my click. We didn't talk much but on the last slow song of the dance he asked me to dance with him.

"Won't your friends make fun of your or something?" I asked, looking to the back corner of the gym where his gaggle of friends collected. He looked back at them, shrugged his shoulders.

"Eh who cares. I'm moving to Washington next year anyway so it's not like I'll see them," he said, placing his hands on my hips. I rested my hands on his shoulders. You could stick a freaking steam boat between us, there was that much space.

"You're moving?" I asked.

"Yah, my dad's company is transferring him again, up to Seattle."

"That sucks."

"It's alright," he shrugged.

We danced the rest of the song in silence, allowing for ourselves to slide a little closer with each shuffle. When the song ended, fully aware of the awkwardness that was a middle school dance, I unwrapped my arms from his neck and clasped my hands together about to thank him for the dance and say good luck when he leaned in, pressing his lips to mine. His were salty-sweet like Cracker Jacks. When he pulled away, I was vaguely aware that I was smiling but upon hearing the snickers from the a-holes in the corner I spat out a goodbye and ran out of the gym like a moron.

Tyler's lips were soft, gentle, and as he parted my lips with his tongue just a little, I felt a similar panic rising from within and like the moron from before, I pulled myself away and bolted out of the chair.

"I gotta go," I said, grabbing the box of ornaments with one hand and the tree with the other.

"Wait where are you going?" he asked.

"My mom, I was supposed to meet her in Nate's room ages ago. She's gonna be pissed, I think. I'll see you, um tomorrow? Ok bye." I sprinted down the hall aware of his lingering gaze and of how totally stupid I was.

I came to a screeching halt outside the door, bursting in to find Mom still there, tangled in pink garland, swearing under her breath and spinning around trying to get out of it.

"There's just so much of this stuff! I got carried away and now it's trying to eat me." I set the tree and box down on the ground and ran over to my mom, grabbing up the loose end of pink garland and helping her to twirl out of it.

"I'd ask you what the hell you're doing with this crap but I think I already know. It's safe to say you've actually gone insane."

She stopped and stared at me stone cold. "That's not funny, Margo. Mental health issues are a real thing."

"Yeah, Mom I know. It was just a joke."

I thought she was going to argue, maybe slink over to the bed and curl up next to Nate, but she didn't. Instead, she actually cracked a smile and tickled my nose with the end of the garland.

"Tell better jokes." She hopped down from the chair and pointed towards the tree. "You got a tree?"

"Yeah I mean, it's nothing special but I saw it at that second hand store next to the bookstore, thought it might be nice."

Then she did something I wasn't at all expecting. She laughed, and not just a little giggle, but a full-on tear-inducing laugh.

"Have I missed the joke?"

She walked to the closet, yanked open the doors and pulled out an artificial 3ft fiberoptic tree. You had got to be kidding me.

"You got a tree, sort of."

"Guess smart minds think alike, or something. I picked this up last week. I don't know, I mean, I know we didn't do anything last year, but it didn't feel right. Honey, you know how much Nate loved Christmas."

He didn't, but I didn't have the heart to tell her that, not when she seemed happy. Christmastime had always been more her thing. When we were kids, she took the normal holiday celebrations and cranked it up to eleven. The merry songs, the cinnamon-pinecone scents that filled the house, the piles and piles of ugly-sweater sugar cookies, Mom made a big hoopla out of it. When Dad left, she worked even harder to make sure Christmas had still been special, but she must have missed all the signs from Nate, his eye rolling, his grumbles, that he just wasn't into it, with the exception of the tree.

"Why the pink garland, Mom?"

"Believe it or not, but that's all I could find left in the store."

I pulled out the red and silver packs of garland from my box. "Welp, you're in luck because I also found this stuff at the store. It's bald in places, but still totally functional."

I set up the tree and Mom and I spent the next hour stringing the lights and decorating with the stuff from my box.

"So honey why were you so late today? Thought you didn't have to work on Tuesdays."

"Yeah sorry, the lines were long at the store and then my soda got jammed in the vending machine, so I had to hunt someone down to get it for me." I wasn't ready to tell her about Tyler.

"You know that stuff will rot your teeth."

"I'll brush really hard."

With the garland and lights now strung, I set about rummaging through the box of ornaments-a collection of misshapen plastic red and silver balls, and little Santa figures with bits and pieces broken off. They were totally tacky, but I thought Nate would have liked them. Or maybe not. Maybe I didn't ever know a damn thing about Nate, and maybe neither did Mom. If we had, he probably wouldn't have ended up here.

Mom left to procure hot chocolate. When she returned, she pulled out two small candy canes from her bag and plopped them into the cups, handing me one. We turned off the room lights and sat at the little table in the corner drinking the hot chocolate and watching the little twinkling lights around the tree.

"This would be a beautiful sight to wake up to." She reached across the table and took hold of my forearm. "We did a great job honey. This will be the year." I took my candy cane out of my cup, tapped it on the corner before sticking it in my mouth. I wanted to believe her, but I had a feeling she would without a doubt say it again next year, and the next year, and probably the year after that.

"So Margo, how's that assignment going, the one in your psychology class?" she asked.

"Oh um Mr. Dan decided to have me work on something else, so now I'm doing it on REM and sleep cycles." It was scary how easy it was becoming to tell lies.

"That's good. I didn't like the topic anyway."

"Obviously."

"Well not just for the obvious reason, I just think the subject matter is a little too mature and complicated for a high school psychology class, that's all."

I bit my lip to stop me from arguing with her, or at the very least from mentioning the study. Or even just talking about our difference of opinion on the matter. I should tell her why it meant so much for me to have a brain study done, and say it has nothing to do with fighting her religious beliefs or whatever. But I decided to once again keep it inside because I didn't want to ruin her good mood. Tomorrow she'd be a completely different person. No smiles, no jokes, just mopey, tired eyes and crying when she thought she was alone.

"I should probably get home, start on some psychology homework." I downed the rest of the hot chocolate, trashed the cup and gathered my coat. "See you at home?"

"Yeah I'll be right behind you. I'm gonna clean up here. Bye honey." She blew me a kiss as I left.

11

— • —

I hadn't seen much of Tyler in the week that followed our kiss. I had expected him to slip notes into my locker, since that seemed to be his style, but there was nothing. I looked for him in the halls after school and between classes, but with basketball season in full swing, he was always in the gym. What would I even say to him? *Hi sorry for mauling your face with my lips*? Who knows what he must have thought after I'd kissed him and then bolted like a complete spaz. There were seriously several major steps I'd skipped, like establishing a mutual attraction for starters. I liked him. A freaking lot. Even though I didn't want to like him, I did. But did he like me? I wanted to believe he did. I mean, why else would he be going out of his way to talk to me at the center and buy my favorite snacks? He could just be this totally nice guy, but also, he could just as easily ignore me on Tuesdays and stay in his grandma's room, or just, like, eat in silence in the visitor lounge. No, something told me he liked me, or again, maybe it's what I wanted to believe. Either way I never thought I'd be so bold. I desperately wanted to tell Jillian, confide in her, see if she thought I was bat shit crazy but that would mean I'd also have to tell Linz and Donny since I said no more secrets, but I sure as shit wasn't read to tell them that I had a crush on one of the most popular boys in school. Jillian was the only one who wouldn't totally flip since she sees good in everyone and fits into all the clicks, but Linz and Donny would straight up cut me.

Since the following week was Christmas break and Mom knew she'd be swamped at work, we celebrated Christmas with Nate early. At 4:30pm, I met Mom at the center where we watched *White Christmas* (my least favorite holiday movie), and then exchanged a few gifts. We left a few for Nate under the tree just in case our little Christmas Tree miracle worked.

"I'll meet you at home. I'm gonna clean up, and then say Merry Christmas to Sari," I said.

She nodded, kissed my forehead. "Alright, honey. Don't stay too late."

"I won't. Bye, Mom."

She walked over to Nate, bent down and grazed her lips across his forehead. After whispering in his ear, she left, grabbing my hand and giving it a gentle squeeze. I held her hand, feeling now was as good a time as any to bring up the study again. Mr. Dan hadn't brought it up, and I wasn't even sure if there would be time before the end of the year, but I wanted to try.

"Hey Mom, I know you said you didn't want the brain study done, but I just wondered if you've maybe given it any more thought? Maybe changed your mind?"

She closed her eyes and exhaled, sliding her hand out of mine. "Honey, can we just please get through the holidays and then we'll talk?"

I nodded, even though I knew that basically meant she hadn't thought about it, we wouldn't talk about it, and she was still leaning towards a big fat no. But there was no use arguing about it now, especially not at Christmas.

"Sure, Mom. Drive safe. I'll be home soon."

After she left, I swiped up the waste bin and walked around the room to collect torn bits of wrapping paper and our paper plates. I'd just bent down to unplug the tree when there was a soft rap on the door. I set the bin down and walked to the door, gently pulling it open to see Tyler standing there, hands in the pockets of his coat. My entire body flushed at the sight of him.

"Hey," he whispered. "I was at the Nurses' station and saw your mom leave. Thought you might still be in here since you didn't leave with her and your car's still out front."

"Yeah I just wanted a few extra minutes with my brother. We're busy at work next week so I'm not sure we'll make it up before Christmas."

"Can I come in?" he asked. I nodded, opening the door and stepping aside. He slid in and walked over to the small end table. I closed the door and sat down in the chair at the table opposite of him realizing that aside from the nurses, no one else had ever been in here.

"How's he doing?" Tyler asked, nodding in Nate's direction. I hated answering that question. It was always the same- *how's he doing, he's doing good relatively speaking, has there been any change, nope he's still a vegetable.* At some point people stopped asking.

"Ok I guess. He doesn't do much. He's actually kinda lazy, just lays there." Tyler's eyes widened for a second before registering my statement as a joke. I couldn't stand people who walked on egg shells around me or who lacked a sense of humor. This whole situation was tough and depressing enough. I relied on humor, as dark as it was, to cope.

"You should tell him basketball is a great workout."

I smiled. "I know I'm making light of the whole situation, but I feel if I don't, I'll go crazy."

"I get it. We all have a coping mechanism. So, are you ready for Christmas break?"

"I guess," I said. "I work like every day basically open to close but it's fine. The money will be nice. How about you?"

"Yes. Absolute yes. I have been so freaking busy with school work, basketball practice, games, Mom's charity shit. I could use a break."

I couldn't help notice the way he leaned against the wall. My mom used to watch this show when she was a teenager where the protagonist pined after this hot stoner guy who was always leaning on his locker. She was super obsessed with the way he leaned. I thought it was something weird to think was hot, the way someone looked when they leaned against things, but in that moment as Tyler was leaning against the wall, balancing on the left side of his body with his hands in his pockets, I totally got it.

"So, um, about last Tuesday in the visitor room," he said shifting his weight. Well there it was. Looks like he was going to bring it up after all and I didn't know what the fuck I was going to say. Plead temporary insanity maybe.

"Yeah I don't know why I did that," I said running my hands through my hair, hiding my face. "Anyway, can you just forget that happened?" He pushed off the wall, walked around the table and kneeled down in front of me. He gently smoothed my hair away from my face, tucking the strands behind my ears. His left hand trailed down my jawbone and came to a rest for a quick second at my chin.

"What if I don't want to forget it?" he whispered. "What if I wanted to ask you out, like on a date? Would you say yes?" Would I say yes? I'd scream yes, but there was a part of me, a small panicked voice in the far corner of my head telling me to say no, that it wasn't a good idea, that I needed to save myself from being hurt. Still, the way his blue starburst eyes rested on mine, deep and warm, I chose to ignore my stupid head and follow my heart.

"I'd say yes."

He took hold of both my hands bringing them to his lips. As he was about to say something his phone vibrated in his pocket. Dropping my hands, he dug out his phone, and frowned as he read a text.

"It's my mother. She wants me to pick up my brother from practice because she's working late, again. So how about I text you about the date?"

"Sounds like a plan," I said. He leaned in, lightly kissed my cheek before rising and heading for the door. As he opened the door, I realized he didn't have my phone number.

"Wait Tyler you don't have my phone number." I got up from the chair, took his phone out of his hand and entered in my contact information. I handed him back his phone letting my fingers linger a little on his.

"See you later," I said. He smiled and then closed the door behind him. I leaned my back up against the door, closed my eyes and let out the biggest sigh. Had I just agreed to go on a real date with Tyler Ashford?

***

Nate had had a lot of girlfriends. He went through girls like tissue paper, never dating the same girl longer than two weeks. He said he liked to keep his options open at all times, but I think it had more to do with commitment issues. The only thing he'd really ever been able to commit to was the brand of cigarette he smoked. Marlboro Reds. Then he'd met Khali and everything for him changed, but that was beside the point. I'm sure had our father stuck around to give him sound dating advise, he might have treated girls better, spent more time getting to know them, form a bond, steer clear of the bat-shit crazy ones who spelled their names in a ridiculous way.

Anyway, the one and only other time I'd gone out on a first date I had just turned fourteen and Mom made Nate chaperone. He'd just returned from Seattle with a broken heart and Mom thought he could use the distraction. The guy, Chase Brandis I think was his name, was the son of some lady Mom worked with. He was homeschooled, loved all things sci-fi, played the cello, and had also never been on a date before. Naturally that must have made us soul-mates. She'd set up the date and Nate drove us to Camp Putt. I hated mini golf but I didn't want to sit through a movie with a boy I barely knew and I was told jogging was not a suitable activity for a date. It was horrendous. Small talk made me nervous so I babbled incoherently most the time and he said maybe all of ten words. I wasn't sure if it was because he'd been nervous, or just maybe lacked a lengthy vocabulary, but I recall his palms being so sweaty he could barely grip his putter, and it had nothing to do with the heat. It was only like 78 degrees that day. Nate seemed to have found the whole thing amusing. He sat at an umbrella covered table in the café trying so hard to keep from busting up, which was a nice change from the sullen-faced zombie boy he'd been since returning from Seattle. Before the date he'd told me to be myself and not talk too much, which I feel was just setting me up for failure because he knew I babbled when I got nervous.

By the end of the evening, I was so happy to drop Chase off and go home. When Mom asked how it went, hands clasped at her chest, a gleeful expression on her face, I rolled my eyes and told her never to set me up with any of her friends' kids again. She'd agreed and I'd never had a first date since. I wished Nate were awake so he could tell me how to act, what to say, how not to babble so much. Tyler and I were able to talk normally in the visitor's room and any time he saw me at work and school, but in a private setting like a date, I'm sure I'd find some stupid way to make it awkward.

When I woke up in the morning I fumbled around my nightstand for my glasses, slid them on and checked my phone. There was a text from Tyler sent some time after I'd gone to sleep.

> Tyler: Hey M. Hope this doesn't wake you. Couldn't wait. The Remedy is playing McDonald Theater on the 21st. I know you're working a lot over the break. But I'd really like to take you. What do you think? Do you like The Remedy?

Okay, I may have been an indie girl through and through, but I loved me some 80's synth. My bosses at the bookstore were adamant that music produced in the 80's was far superior to that of any decade, therefore bands such as The Remedy and The Smiths were on heavy rotation daily. I opened my calendar app to check my work schedule. Thankfully I had the morning shift, so I texted back,

> Margo: I love The Remedy. Sounds like fun. Can't wait.

As if he'd been sitting by the phone eagerly awaiting my response, he responded right away.

> Tyler: Score. Doors open at 7. Pick you up at 6. Where do you live?

Ack. The dreaded "where do you live" question. Tyler lived in a huge Colonial in the ritziest part of West Valley River, where the doctors and Judges and other made-from-money families lived, and while I was pretty sure he knew I lived in "felony flats" I wasn't at all ready to let him see my house. Granted, it wasn't the most run down of all the houses on the street, but still. We were lucky if we got to park in front of our house most days. I texted back that he could pick me up from the bookstore, which made sense anyway since I had to work.

Now that the date was set, I didn't see how I could possibly get through the next two days thinking clearly. Thankfully I was scheduled to work a shit-ton of hours, and the gang was having a Christmas get-together tomorrow night at Jillian's house. That would keep me from obsessing about the date and thinking about all the ways I was bound to muck it up.

****

Jillian lived in the Laurel Hill Valley neighborhood in a five-bedroom Mediterranean style house. It was more room than her family could possibly need since Jillian had only one sibling, and neither parent worked from home. Her father was one of the top premier architects in the Pacific Northwest, so the house was, for him, more of a statement piece. Jillian's bedroom wasn't technically the master bedroom, but it was just as big. French doors with rose gold handles opened up into a large space that looked like a page torn out of some Greek goddess mythology book. The walls were painted pale blue with grey-white clouds, a four- poster wooden bed took up space in the middle of the room adorned in soft silvery curtains and tiny twinkling white lights. Her en-suite bathroom, larger than my entire bedroom, had both a jacuzzi tub and a rain fall shower.

None of it seemed to matter to Jillian though, which is one of the things I loved most about her. She was girly and flighty and sometimes fickle, but she had a tremendous heart and was probably the only person I knew who actually cared about everyone, no matter their social standing at school, or how much money they did or didn't have. As corny as it sounded, she let her heart decide who she was friends with, not anything or anyone else.

Christmas in the Cogburn household was a big deal. We're talking the whole shebang-white twinkling lights in every square corner of the house, two massive Christmas trees (one in the foyer, yes she has a foyer, and one in the family room), mossy colored garland twisted around the banisters, wreaths, poinsettias on the tables, and their entire street was referred to as "Holiday Lane" since all the houses banned together to decorate their yards, each year choosing a different theme. This year was Nutcracker. There were also multiple company holiday parties, one for Mr. Cogburn's architect firm and the other for Mrs. Cogburn's restaurant, oh and since Mrs. Cogburn is Jewish, they also have a huge Menorah in the window.

Jillian, Linz, and Donny had been having Christmas get-together's there since middle school, and when they included me last Christmas, I was super reluctant because I was still trying to figure out how to even have holiday cheer with Nate being in the hospital, but the second I walked in I felt like I'd been a part of their tradition for years, and I couldn't help but feel all the feels. Her house was purely magical during the holidays. We wore matching Christmas pj's, stuffed our faces with piles of pasta Mrs. Cogburn brought back from her restaurant, and watched a Christmas movie. This year it was *National Lampoon's Christmas Vacation,* which just so happened to be my all-time favorite holiday movie.

Half way through the movie, Linz lunged for the remote and pressed pause. After pouring a ton of Mike & Ike's down her throat she said, "I just need to say it, and I know you, Margo, are gonna be pissed or whatever, because this is your fave, but I just do not get this movie at all, like, how is it even enjoyable? It's not even funny."

I wiped my buttery popcorn fingers on my fleece Grinch pants, gulped down some Dr. Pepper.

"How you gonna be dissing on *National Lampoon* like that?" I asked.

"For real. None of it's funny. The cousin in a snow hat and bathrobe? Dumping a what was it? RV sewage into the drain? That's not funny."

"Uh yeah it is."

"Also, have you even seen the other movies in the franchise? The kid Rusty is A) a different actor every time and B) sometimes he's older and sometimes he's younger."

"I think they do that on purpose," Donny said.

"It's part of the running joke with the franchise, Linz," I said, just dumbfounded that I was even having to justify the awesomeness of this movie.

"I actually don't like any of the lame 80's movies we always watch on movie nights."

"Then why do you watch them with us? Why do you never give any input?"

"I don't know, didn't want to ruffle feathers I guess."

I scoffed. "What do you call this?"

She shrugged her shoulders. "I dunno, a light nudge?"

Jillian slid off the couch and stood in front of the TV.

"Ok how about this. Maybe everyone can put in their choice and we can pull from a hat or something."

"What are we, twelve?" Linz said.

Donny chucked a marshmallow at her. "At least she's trying, biotch. How about we just alternate."

"What if one of you idiots chooses another stupid 80's movie?"

"You just suck it up until it's your turn and then you can pick a stupid Noir movie we all know you're going to pick."

Linz groaned. "Fine! Whatever. Okay, we'll alternate."

"Halleluiah it's settled," I said, lunging for the remote. "Can we please just finish the movie? We're just getting to the best part."

After the movie we opened our secret Santa gifts. My gift was from Donny. It was a framed tour poster from The Decembrists that was designed by Carson Ellis and signed personally by all the band members.

"Oh my goodness, Donny this is amazing!" I exclaimed.

"Good I'm glad you like it," he beamed. "I wrote to them half a dozen times asking for the signatures. I said you were their biggest fan and told them about your tattoo."

"Shut up! Wow Donny, thanks. This is literally the best gift ever." I leaned over and squeezed him.

"I'm sure Tyler Ashford will get you something amazing," he said in a hushed tone. I snapped my head up and stared at him.

"Oh don't give me that deer in the headlights look honey, you're not very good at it. I know Tyler asked you out and I know you said yes."

"How? How'd you know?"

"Well for starters I've seen the way you look at him in the halls. Second, I heard him talking to Andy about it the other day in the locker rooms."

Great. This was just what I needed. If Andy knew, Blake would know in no time which meant he'd for sure put me on blast. Sensing my panic, Donny rested a hand on my knee.

"Chill girl, you're ok. Andy is a standup guy. You shouldn't have anything to freak about."

"How do you know that?"

"Please. He's an alter server at my church and a backup eucharistic minister. Also, he's on leadership team. He may run in the same group as Blake and his crew but he's not an ass."

Well that was semi comforting, but I guess also not very surprising considering how nice Andy had been during cross country season. I thought he was trying to work some angle but turns out he really was just being nice.

"Wait, Donny you go to church?"

We'd never talked about our religious beliefs or lack thereof, but I guess I'd figured he wasn't so much a church goer since he complained about the once-a-month Mass Schedule, and used air quotes whenever he mentioned organized religion.

"Honey I may be gay but I'm not a complete heathen. Yes, I go to church," he said, making the sign of the cross with his right hand. "Every. Damn. Sunday."

"Um, I haven't told the others yet, I'm still trying to process. I was going to wait until after the date to tell Jillian and Linz. Can we keep it between the two of us?" I asked. He grumbled, jutting his pinky out towards me and looped it with mine.

"Girl, you know I hate secrets," he said rolling his eyes, "but I won't say anything. For now. I can't believe you haven't even told Jillian."

It was a little unnerving that Tyler had told Andy he'd asked me out. What if Donny was wrong about Andy, what if he was disgusted and tried to talk Tyler out of it? Or worse, what if Andy told Blake? What kind of verbal assault would I be walking into at school in January? But then I remembered the shoe lace and how kind he always was at practice. I had to believe that Donny was right, because I really wanted to go on this date and I didn't want something so lame as worrying about what his friends thought to spoil it, even though I was fully aware that was the exact thing I was doing right now with my own friends. It's just that I wanted this thing, whatever was going on between us, not to be sabotaged before it even started.

***

Tyler was on time picking me up from the bookstore. Part of me thought he was going to flake and I'd spend the evening consulting the time on my watch, triple checking for texts that would have explained his absence. That's what was supposed to happen right? It's how these sorts of things played out in the movies. Popular guy asks out the not so popular, nerdy but cute girl, she accepts like the complete naïve idiot she is, gets all gussied up (people don't use that word any more I think) and then gets stood up and blasted on social media later. So, I sunk into a plush chair by the window and got lost in the latest edition of *Under the Radar*, catching up on some much-needed indie music news when a light tapping on the window startled me, the magazine sliding to the floor. I whipped around to see Tyler leaning (damn his leaning) against the window in loose fitting ripped-knee jeans, grey chucks and a KISS t-shirt. It occurred to me that I'd never seen him in what would pass as normal clothes. At Marshalls he always wore polos and starched jeans, or athletic clothes. Tonight, he was dressed so chill I hardly recognized him. And then there was that damn smile. The left side pulled up slightly more than the right, teeth bleach-white and perfectly straight. He was definitely someone ripped right out of an Abercrombie catalogue. I smiled back, mouthed that I'd be right out. I swiped up the magazine and put it back on the shelf, grabbed my bag and met him outside.

"Well look at you Sir, don't you look like a normal person," I said sizing him up.

"What's that supposed to mean?"

"I mean you're not wearing your signature jock polo and jeans."

He nodded and laughed. "Yeah believe it or not but my over bearing mother demands I wear the polo shirts. She says appearances are everything and I must keep them up. I actually hate polo shirts."

"So, no KISS t-shirt?" I said pointing to his shirt.

"Oh fuck no. She doesn't even know I have this. I left the house in a polo," he smirked. We crossed the parking lot to his car, a shiny black BMW. He opened the passenger door and let me in.

"And they say chivalry is dead." I slid across the heated leather seats. I'd never been inside a car with heated seats unless you counted cracking open hand warmers and sitting on them as heated seats. The hint of pine and sandalwood invaded my nostrils. It was exactly how I imagined his car would smell.

He closed the door, walked around to the drivers' side and eased in.

"Full disclosure," he turned to face me, holding his hands up. "I'm super stoked to see The Remedy. I watched a concert DVD with my dad a few years back and ever since I've been hooked."

"Wait, Dr. Ashford likes The Remedy?" Tyler's dad was Chief of Staff at the hospital and an amazing neurosurgeon. He's what my mom calls real life McDreamy, which I guess is a reference to some character in a popular medical show, and I never would have pegged him as a fan of rock music, not with his wife being so prim and proper. He also wears loafers and cardigans to all of the school's silent auctions. I fashioned him more a Mozart kind of guy.

"He's huge into music. He even listens to heavy metal during surgeries."

"No way."

"Yeah way. He says it keeps him both fully pumped and totally relaxed at the same time."

"What about your mom? Is she a metal head too and this whole time I've just been thinking she is a straight up square?"

He laughed. "Oh yeah no, she's a total square. She's more of an adult contemporary kinda person. Lionel Ritchie, Rod Stewart. Barry Manilow probably. I think at some point in her youth she used to like rock music, because there are pictures of my parents from back in the day at concerts and stuff, but now I think she feels a person of her political standing has to have more refined taste when it comes to music."

"How does she feel about your dad and his musical preferences?"

"Well, I think she'd prefer his tastes would have chanced along with hers, but nope. He's all rock all the time."

I smiled and traced the open-heart tattoo on the inside of my left wrist with my thumb. I never would have guessed this about Tyler and his family, and I know it's just one aspect, but for me, music was a huge deal. It didn't define who a person was, but it certainly helped shaped them. But I'd made assumptions based on what? Outward appearance that his family couldn't possibly be cool enough to listen to good music? I didn't like that I'd allowed myself to give into stereotyping because in truth, there was so much about Tyler, and well I guess his dad too for that matter, that made me feel connected on some level to Nate, maybe because just like Tyler and his dad share this love and appreciation for good music, I share it, well used to share it with Nate, and it was no small coincidence that we just so happened to be going to see one of Nate's all-time favorite bands.

We parked a few blocks away from the actual venue so that we wouldn't have a difficult time leaving when it was over. I'd been to enough shows at the McDonald Theater, and countless other venues to know fighting the crowd was always hell.

After a bag search and a quick trip to the merch table (admittedly I did do a quick scan of the area just in case a certain someone might have been at the show) where Tyler bought us a couple band t-shirts, and then we pushed our way to the front of the stage. There was something unspeakable about being as close to the stage as possible, especially if it were a dope band. The way you could feel the rhythm pump through you as the floor shook, the vibration in the ears that without a doubt would cause partial deafness later but at the time seemed totally worth it, the idea that for two whole hours you were somewhere else without a care in the world, just losing yourself in the lyrics and melody.

"This is so great! We're so close to the stage!" Tyler shrieked. His eyes were full of excitement and so wide I felt for sure they'd pop out of his sockets. I took a mental snap shot of Tyler in this particular moment where his grin covered up his entire face and where it seemed he didn't give a fuck about what his mother thought, where his friends were, or how well he'd done in basketball. It was the same sort of face Nate had when he was feeling on top, usually at a concert or after one, where for just a few moments I really did believe he didn't give a fuck.

"Yeah it's awesome," I replied as he slipped his hand into mine and the house lights went down.

After the show our adrenaline was sky high so Tyler decided it was imperative we eat ice cream. Fun fact. I loved ice cream the most on cold blustery days. No good reason other than I liked that I didn't have to devour it before it melted and gave me a wicked case of brain freeze. We drove a few blocks to Ice King on 19th and Agate. While most of the ice cream shops in town switched over to their out of season hours in early September, Ice King was always open until midnight, mainly because it was the only ice cream shop surrounded on all four corners by concert venues and figured people would want ice cream after two hours of singing along.

At a table in the back sat a couple who looked to be in their early 20's sharing licks from a chocolate and vanilla swirl cone, which kinda grossed me out given the whole pandemic thing.

A group of high school girls gathered in a table towards the entrance eating their ice cream and gabbing about whatever, barely stopping to catch a breath. As soon as one girl finished another began. If Donny and Jillian were here, they wouldn't be able to resist sitting in a table somewhere in the back but still within eyesight of the gaggle of girls pretending to narrate their conversation.

I ordered one scoop of vanilla and one scoop of dark cherry with gummy bears while Tyler ordered some triple chocolate and Oreo concoction. We slid into a small booth and I shook off my coat, folding it over my purse and merch bag. Tyler crushed up the Oreo's in his bowl, swirled them into his ice cream scoops, and after taking a huge bite, grabbed at his head with both hands. I tried to stifle a laugh but failed.

"Brain freeze brain freeze!" he exclaimed.

"And that is why you don't shove a whole freaking spoonful of ice cream right into your gullet," I said taking a normal sized bite, curling my lips over my teeth to avoid the icy sting.

"Ok so maybe eating ice cream in the winter was a bad idea,"

"No way I love it. It melts slower."

"So, what did you think of the show? Did you like it?" he asked.

I took another bite and said, "It was amazing. Truly amazing. I don't even think I have the proper words to describe it. Nate would have loved it. The Remedy was his favorite band." I don't know why I said it. "Was" like he was dead and gone. If I was actually being honest with myself, I'd say part of me already thought he was, but the mere fact that I'd actually said it like he *was* startled me.

"Do you mind if I asked what happened to him? What really happened?" Tyler asked, swirling his spoon around his ice cream. I could have avoided the question, made something up that was some version of the truth. It would have been easy. I'd been doing it to almost anyone who asked about him. Tyler stared at me with his deep glacier eyes. "You don't have to tell me, if you don't want."

I wasn't aware that I was picking at my cuticle until Tyler reached over and grabbed my hand. "Nate had this girlfriend, Khali. He met her I think at the bus station. He had this need, more like a necessity to get on a bus now and then and let it take him somewhere. Didn't matter where, just somewhere that wasn't home. I think it was hard for him, trying to figure out how to be a man or whatever. My dad left when Nate was 10 and it was so abrupt it kinda messed him up. My mom was an emotional wreck after. I mean, she did her best but she wasn't equipped at all for trying to parent a teenage boy. So, they ended up butting heads a lot, and Nate would just leave for a few days, but he always came back."

I paused to swirl my ice cream around in my bowl, then took a bite. "One day he met a girl, Khali, who was waiting for a bus to Seattle. Some punk rock girl with purple hair and a nose ring from San Diego. Anyway, he followed her to Seattle and they started dating or whatever. I know they lived together but it was off and on. He'd come home every couple of months, but they got pretty serious and I didn't hear much from him. One day about a year or two later he came home looking like shit. Hair long and scraggly, cheeks gaunt, skin clinging to his bones. There were marks all over his arms but he swore they weren't from drugs, which yeah right, that was a lie. Anyway, he said she'd broken up with him and took off with some guy who I think was her supplier. He tried to get over it, be normal, but he got pretty depressed. Stopped showing up for work at the mini-mart by our house, stopped eating, spent all his time on the internet."

I took a long drink from my water glass. "Then he just kinda snapped. He walked down to the bus station and tried to get a ticket, but he couldn't get one because his card had expired and he didn't have any cash. So then he started harassing the guy at the booth, pulled out a gun and started waving it around, freaking everyone out and then he shot himself in the head. Instead of dying, he became a vegetable."

I'd stirred my ice cream so much it now looked like soup. My body trembled, and I could feel hot tears stream down my cheeks. This had been the first time I'd said out loud what had happened. My therapist had tried for a year to get it out of me. I didn't want to be known as the girl whose brother went nuts at the bus station and tried to kill himself, which I'm so sure I would have since the whole story had been circulating the news channels for days. Why was it so easy for me to be telling Tyler the truth when I couldn't even tell Jillian? He must be thinking the worst of my family right now, but his face was unreadable. I didn't like it. My palms were starting to sweat. I was half a second from running out of there, but then he got up and slid into the booth next to me, taking my hands in his.

"I'm sorry about your brother, and about what you've had to go through these past few years. I'm sure it hasn't been easy," he said.

I let out a sigh of relief. "You're not, like, disgusted or whatever?"

"Disgusted? Why would I be disgusted?"

"I don't know. Maybe disgusted is the wrong word. Freaked out?"

He shook his head. "Not even a little."

"Well I would be if I were you."

"Why?"

"Because my family is just one giant shit show"

He kissed the top of my knuckles. "Show me a family that isn't."

He was looking into my eyes with such depth I felt like I was about to basically let him see inside my soul, tell him every stupid thing I was thinking, everything I'd ever done.

"Anyway, now you know. Please just don't tell anyone. It's just that I don't like all the questions and you know how fast the rumor mill turns at that school."

"I won't tell anyone Margo, I promise." As he laced his fingers through mine, my nerve endings ignited, shooting electric jolts through my entire body. The feeling was both terrifying and exciting, and swiftly interrupted by the sound of someone pounding on the window. Upon seeing it was a group from school, including Blake, I quickly pulled my hands away from Tyler, shoving them under the table onto my lap. Great. This was just what we needed. Tyler looked from me, then to the group standing outside, and then slid out of the booth.

"I'd better go talk to them or Blake will never stop. I'll be right back." I smiled and nodded, rubbing my hands up and down my legs. He walked out to join his friends. Blake playfully punched him in the shoulder. The girl with them holding Blake's hand I recognized as Erica Raade who was a senior at Churchill but used to go to Marshall Academy up until last year when she was expelled for smoking pot in the freshman bathroom. She stared at me through the window, trying to connect a name with my face. Her eyes widened and then she turned to Blake and whispered something into his ear. Blake looked through the window, locking eyes with me. I quickly pulled out my phone, pretending to be texting. He must have said something to Tyler because Tyler turned his head to look at me and then turned back to his friends. I felt completely uncomfortable. I didn't need to be out there to know what they were saying. I knew it was about me. The way Blake jutted his thumb out at me, face pinched as he spoke to Tyler, it just made clear that anything amazing happening between us was just an illusion. I didn't belong with Tyler. I wasn't part of his social circle and there was no way they'd ever accept me. I was imagining a scenario that would not, could not ever possibly play out.

I shoved my phone into my purse and slid out of the booth just as Tyler came back in.

"Where are you going?" he asked.

"I have to go." I shoved past him, darting towards the door. A burst of winter wind slapped me in the face and I wrapped my scarf tightly around my neck. Behind me the door was pushed open and Tyler stumbled out after me.

"Margo wait! Where are you going? What's wrong?" he yelled. I willed my legs to move faster but he caught up to me, grabbing my arm gently and whipped me around to face him.

"Is it your brother? Did something happen?" he asked.

"Tyler, come on. We both know this isn't going to work," I said throwing my hands up.

"Why do you say that?"

"You know why. Because you're you and I'm me. You're Tyler, captain of the basketball team. Marshall's golden boy. Your parents are freaking loaded, and I'm just Margo, the weird indie girl from the flats whose mother is a cashier and who barely has 50$ to her name." The tears that had welled up in my eyes poured down my cheeks.

"That's not fair Margo," he moved closer to me but I stepped back.

"It's not about what's fair or unfair it's about what's true, and the truth is we are just too different." I turned to go but he moved in front of me and gently cradled my face in his hands, eyes boring into mine with fierce desperation.

"Margo, I don't care who my parents are, or who my friends are, and I don't care about what neighborhood you're from. I just want to be with you." He lowered his face to mine until our lips met, gently at first but then he parted my lips with his tongue and kissed me with so much passion and hunger I'd forgotten about all the risk. All the doubt and hesitation in my mind disappeared, as if someone had flipped a switch. I knew now with certainty that I wanted to be with him and I didn't care what people would say. Sure, it could all go up in a freaking blaze (que Taylor Swift song) but at that moment I didn't care.

12

—◦—

I wish I could stop time. Or at least slow it down. I wasn't ready for Christmas Break to end. I was working crazy holiday hours at the bookstore, but when I had any time off, I spent it with Tyler. It didn't matter if it were only for a few minutes or a few hours, we made sure to see each other every day. On nights that I worked late he'd come by with tacos from Gordita Tacos after his club basketball practices and we'd cozy up in the reading nook on my breaks.

If a decent movie was playing at 10:30pm at Cineflix, I'd shoot a quick text to Mom that I was seeing a movie with Jillian, then rush through the closing procedures at work to meet him there. We'd share a bucket of popcorn and compromised on sharing a Cherry Coke.

Sometimes we just sat in his car, heated seats on full blast, because I was totally going to take advantage of the feature, and listen to music, talk about our favorite movies, or TV shows, our favorite books, or just make out. There was a lot of making-out.

We never discussed the ending of Christmas break and what would happen when we went back to school. Would we walk the halls together holding hands? Would we tell our friends we were dating? Were we even dating?

We'd never actually referred to one another as boyfriend/girlfriend, but I'd like to believe it was implied with the level of making-out that was happening.

The night before the start of winter term, I laid in my bed, unable to sleep, staring out at the moon through the slit in my *Doctor Who* curtains. Right about now would be a super fab time for the Tardis to randomly appear in my bedroom with Tyler inside exclaiming, "It's bigger on the inside!" and whisk us away. I thought of how tomorrow would play out, all the scenarios, hoping for positive outcomes, but my stupid brain only thought of the negative ones which in turn produced a train of thought that spiraled into a wicked anxiety attack. What if when I got to school and saw him at his locker, he smiled at me, and as I reached for his hand, he laughed a gut-splitting laugh then brushed past me with his group of friends? Or what if I get to school and he's told everyone that we hooked up and that I'd spent the rest of the break stalking him? I hated this. I hated how my brain spiraled.

I flipped to my side, fumbled around the nightstand for my phone to check the time. 11:30pm. Hoping that Tyler was still up, I shot a quick text.

MARGO: Can't sleep. Nervous about tomorrow.

I waited a few minutes. Nothing. Ten more minutes, still nothing. I closed my eyes willing for sleep to come so that I didn't have to cry myself to sleep when my phone pinged.

TYLER: Don't be.

I sighed, rolled over and pulled my blankets up over my head. I needed to trust him but I just didn't know how.

***

Nate used to say that when you're unsteady and you need something to set you straight, blast a song until you can feel it radiating through your bones. My song of choice was always "Midnight City" by M83. Even with the lame saxophone solo at the end (there's not one redeeming quality about the musical instrument, and frankly I felt the people who chose to play it were major ass hats), the song was the melodious kick in the pants that got me going.

I sat in my car the next morning, ear buds jammed into my ears, song blaring, hoping that today when I walked into the halls it wouldn't be to a shit-ton of glares and whispers. As the song ended, I grabbed my bag from the back seat, locked up my car and made my way into the school. If ever I felt like a deer caught in the headlights, it was today. Every step felt like I was sludging my way through a swamp, every eye that met mine held a judging nasty remark behind it. I'd always let my assumptions get the best of me. Today they were straight up *running away* with me. Better yet, they were trampling me into the mud. In my mind I was Simba in *The Lion King* and all these damn eyeballs on me were the freaking stampeding antelope.

I turned down the hall towards my locker and slowed my gait. He wasn't there yet. Letting out a sigh, I stopped at my locker to unload my lunch and swap books. As I closed the locker door and turned to make my way to first period, I saw him walking towards me in a new crisp red polo, jeans, and grey converse shoes surrounded by his usual entourage. I thought about turning around and losing myself in the crowd, or ducking into one of the classrooms, but his eyes found mine and when he stopped in front of me, he pulled me into his arms. My face was pressed into to his chest, but I could still feel the eyes of his friends boring into my back.

"Stop looking so terrified," he whispered into my ear. "I told you not to worry."

"Uh dude, what's this?" Blake snarled. I pulled myself away preparing to bail when Tyler grabbed hold of my hand, gently lacing his fingers with mine. When neither of us said anything, Blake spoke up again.

"You guys are a...thing? I saw you guys at the ice cream shop but...when did this happen?" He wasn't good at masking his disapproval. Tyler shrugged his shoulders. "Dunno man, it just did." Winking at me, he pulled me along and we walked down the hall, students moving away as if we were walking down the parted Red Sea.

"Everyone is staring," I said.

"Let them. Like I said, I don't care."

When we got to my first period class, he kissed me (in front of everyone!) and I dove into my seat fully aware of the gawking faces in the hall.

In language arts I knew by the pissed look on their faces that my friends heard about me and Tyler. Jillian refused to look at me while Linz glared a hole right through my head.

"Heads up they're pissed," Donny leaned over to whisper.

"What gave it way," I retorted.

"Don't get snippy with me girl, this your fault." Donny went full Rue Paul when he felt the need to defend himself.

"Uggg fine you're right," I grumbled, then turned around in my chair to face them. "Okay I know you guys heard something about me and Tyler, so let's have it."

Neither of them said a thing.

"Jilly?" She didn't even look up at me.

"Linz?" Epic eye roll.

"Oh come on Linz, I know you have something to say."

"Yeah ok I do have something to say, Margo. What in the actual fuck? You're dating Tyler Ashford? Since when? I didn't even know you liked him. Jillian, did you know she liked him? Was this another one of your selfish secrets?

"No, it's not like that," I said. "He visits family at the same rehab center my brother is at and we got to know each other. It's not like we've been secretly dating."

"Why did you never say any of this?" she demanded.

"I don't know because I really didn't think he liked me and I certainly didn't expect to like him. It just happened. But I swear I didn't keep it from you guys on purpose. I was just scared that I was being duped or something." She was about to respond but Mr. Danvers walked in. She snapped her mouth shut and then crossed her arms over her chest, slumping into her desk. She'd probably hold this against me until graduation.

I knew I wasn't going to be able to focus on a word Mr. Danvers said, so instead I passed a note behind me to Jillian explaining that I didn't tell her about Tyler because I didn't want her to get stuck keeping another secret. She clicked her pen a few times, furrowing her brow, scribbled a few lines and then slid the note back onto my desk. Thankfully she wasn't mad at me, but she felt, and no surprise here, I shouldn't have kept my newly formed relationship with Tyler a secret, oh and that I was being super selfish. Again. Also, she didn't like the development (she even underlined that part three times) but she was going to be supportive since I was her best friend.

The rest of the morning all anyone could talk about was us. The Tyler and Margo development. Tygo, because Margler just didn't flow. Every corner I turned kids stared and whispered. In the bathroom girls would quiet down the second I walked in and as soon as I left, they'd laugh and start up again. Occasionally someone would slide up next to me and ask, "Is it true? Are you and Tyler Ashford like, a thing?" Since we'd never actually labelled it, I'd shrug my shoulders, respond, "Yeah I guess so?" and then the whispered comments would continue.

Lunch was awkward. We sat at our usual table in the back-left corner of the cafeteria, no one saying a word. I *so* would have preferred Linz's ranting and raving about some injustice in the world, school, or friendship instead of this stupid lame awkward silence. A few times Jillian would look up and open her mouth to say something, the peace-maker side of herself itching to get out, but a sharp glance from Linz made her snap her mouth shut.

I wish Tyler and I had the same lunch period. We could go hide in the library or lecture hall and he could hold me in his arms. That's where I wanted to be, wrapped up in his arms, breathing him in. Even if we didn't say anything at all, even if all we did was sit there wrapped up in each other, the silence would be so much more fucking enjoyable to this one.

When the final bell rang at the end of the day I bolted. I just wanted to go home, curl up with my cat and watch a cheesy 80's movie. Between the sea of stares from kids in the hall to the unbearable silence between my group of friends, I felt like every ounce of my being had been drained from my body. After a quick trip to my locker for school books, I put my head down and rushed to the parking lot. I dug around my purse for my keys as I walked and was surprised to find Tyler leaning against the door of my car.

"Hey, what are you doing here?" I asked.

"I have independent study last period and it's closer to the parking lot than the lockers so I figured I'd just meet you over here." He slid to the side so I could unlock my car.

"Do you have to work today?" he asked

"No, no work today. I don't work until Friday actually.

"You wanna hang out?"

I sighed. I did want to hang out but I also just wanted to be alone. "I was thinking about just going home. I'm so drained. Besides, don't you have club basketball practice?"

"Skipping it."

"Seriously? Won't your Coach be pissed or something?"

"Nah," he shrugged. "He'll get over it. You want to hike up Skinner's butte?"

"It's like 40 degrees out."

He stepped closer to me, zipping my coat up to my chin before kissing my forehead.

"I'll keep you warm."

How could I say no to that? "Fine."

My favorite place for a run had always been Skinner's Butte. The various trails, the rock wall, the breathtaking scenery, a perfect escape. I met Tyler in the lower parking lot and we hiked to the top. Tyler pulled a ratty blanket out of his backpack and we snuggled next to one another on a bench. With his arms wrapped around me, I rested my head against him and felt at ease. Being here like this felt so natural. Why couldn't everything else?

"I love it up here," Tyler said, wrapping the blanket tighter around us. "I came up here a lot when my mom was campaigning."

"Why's that?"

"Too many people in and out of the house and it was the same time as all the basketball tournaments. I needed a quiet place to come and collect my thoughts. This was it. This exact bench. I even carved my initials in the corner over here." He scooted over to show me the TAA scratched into the wood. I traced each initial with my fingers. He dug his keys out from his pocket and began to carve an M under the T. "What's your middle name? Let's be totally cliché and carve both our names."

"It's Marianna."

"Margo Marianna Adams. Beautiful."

"Thank you," I blushed. "My mom says it's a family name. I think it's her grandmother's name and my grandmother's middle name."

"What's your grandmother like?"

"No clue. I only really remember meeting her once, when I was five after my dad left. She lives in some retirement home in California and she and my mom don't talk."

"Really? That sucks. How come?"

"Guess my grandmother didn't like my mom's life choices. Mom grew up in a super religious house and when she was studying abroad in Italy, she met my dad who was like this total new age kinda guy. How did my mom say my grandma described him? Oh yeah, a scoundrel. Anyway, she got knocked up and basically disowned by her parents."

"They disowned her because she got pregnant?" Tyler asked.

"Pretty much. That and my mom had decided she didn't want to be Catholic anymore. I think the only reason they even came to see us after my dad left was to say I told you so."

"Can I ask about your dad?"

"You can but there's not much to tell. He left when I was five, something about how he didn't like being tied down and he missed traveling and we were all just dead weight"

"Have you talked to him, since he left?"

"Nope.

The wind picked up, quick and crisp, blowing my hair into my face. Tyler chuckled, pulling his arms out of the blanket to sweep the hair over my shoulder.

"How's your brother? Any signs of improvement?" he asked.

"No not really. I don't expect he will any time soon, to be honest. I just wish my mom would agree to let him be tested."

"Tested? For what?"

"In my Psychology class, Mr. Dan assigned this book to read that talks about a man in a coma and some tests that were run on him to see if he can understand anything. Mr. Dan wanted to see if my mom would be ok with the same tests being done on my brother and she won't even consider it."

"How come?"

"She thinks God has Nate in a coma for a reason and if she prays enough and apologizes for her backsliding that he'll wake up. She doesn't want science getting in the way of that."

"What would the knowledge that he can actually understand you guys have anything to do with God healing him or whatever? I mean, it's not like the tests will actually wake him up or anything."

"That's what I said but she just won't hear it and it's super frustrating because I just need to know if he's still in there."

"Think she'll change her mind?" he asked.

I shrugged, burrowing myself deeper into him. "Who knows. Ugg it sucks."

"So, you wanna talk about today? About how things went at school?"

"Blech. It sucked. The way the entire student body stared at me today."

"Oh, come on now, I'm sure it wasn't the entire student body. Isn't the High Five team away at some tournament?"

"You don't think everyone was staring and talking about us?"

"I'm sure they were, but that was to be expected, ya know? The student body always has to have something new and interesting to gossip about, and we were the something new and interesting. It's just kinda how it is."

"Yeah but you're sort of used to all that stuff, Mr. Popularity. I'm a nobody who suddenly became a somebody and I don't know what to do about the stares."

"Just don't let it get to you. I mean, in the end the only thing that matters is how you feel about me and how I feel about you. Everything else is just background noise."

It was easy for him to just pretend that everything else was background noise. He's always been in the limelight and when people stare at him, they weren't ever saying anything bad or whispering behind his back. There'd been plenty of whispers and gawking eyes when I'd transferred, *who was the new girl, did she really transfer from Valley Central, was she into drugs, how come she doesn't drive a BMW,* and once people had figured out there was nothing left to talk about because I wasn't a trust-fund baby, I'd been able to fly below the radar. This was precisely why I'd made sure no one knew about my brother, because then I'm sure I'd have always been the topic of conversation. I had been right to be worried about school today, and while my feelings for Tyler were as strong as feelings could be, I wasn't sure his would always be strong enough, especially not with Blake.

As if the cosmos knew I'd been thinking about him, Tyler's phone rang, and it just so happened to be Blake.

"I'll call him back," Tyler said. As he slid the phone into his pocket it pinged five times with text messages. Tyler yanked it back out and scrolled the texts. Blake called again. Tyler sighed and then answered.

"Dude, what's the deal? You'd better be dying or something. Yeah I know practice was today. So what? Coach will get over it. Yeah I'm with her, she has a name bro." As he continued to argue with Blake, I laid down across the bench, pulling the blanket up over my head, wishing I could melt into the cracked wood. After the call ended, Tyler crammed the phone back into his jacket pocket and pulled the blanket down from my face. He was smiling but behind the smile was frustration and anger.

"Everything ok?" I asked.

"Yeah. Just Blake being a dick."

"He really doesn't like me very much."

"He doesn't like anyone very much except for himself. Coach is pissed and wants to talk to me asap."

"Oh, ok." I stood up, folded the blanket and handed it to him. He shoved it into his backpack, and we climbed down the hill. As we walked to the cars, I stole several glances at Tyler, trying to get a good reading from him. He was clearly bothered, obviously by what Blake had said, but he was good at hiding it. Was this going to be too much for him? I wanted to ask, but I was afraid to hear him say it. This was the happiest that I had allowed myself to be and I didn't want to lose that.

"I'll see you tomorrow?" I asked. He smiled, leaned over and kissed me. I got into my car waited for him to leave before getting into mine where I promptly broke down and cried.

13

—·—

Mom was tucked under a fleece throw blanket on the couch, gently snoring, the remote-control seconds from sliding out of her loose grip. Her chestnut brown hair was piled high on the top of her head in a messy bun, a few rogue strands sweeping across her face. Even with the unkempt hair and the shadows that had taken up residency under her eyes, she was still beautiful. She had the kind of face women envied, the kind of face that was smoking hot with makeup and naturally stunning without. I know I sure as hell envied it. Instead of inheriting her perfectly symmetrical hazel eyes, sharp, pointed nose, and lush pouty lips, I inherited my father's auburn waves, eyes that were just a little too close together, and a short stubby nose. I was confident enough in myself to accept that these features were cute at best, but nowhere near beautiful, like my mom.

Sir Rusty, who'd been curled up on her feet lifted his fuzzy head, meowed. "Hey to you, Sir Rusty." I scratched him under his chin before collecting the dirty plates from the coffee table. I rinsed them off and placed them into the dishwasher. After making a pb&j I headed to my room, placing the plate on my desk, shaking the mouse to wake up the computer. As I took a bite, my phone rang. It was a group FaceTime. Oh good. I'd hoped to end the day with an ambush.

"Hey guys," I said, mouth still full of sandwich.

"You have peanut butter on your face," Linz said.

I swiped the sleeve of my arm across my mouth. "So, what's up?"

"Hey M," Jillian began. "We wanted to talk to you about the whole you and Tyler thing."

"For the record," Donny said, gesticulating, "I'm totally cool with you guys."

Jillian nodded. "I'm cool with it too."

"You are? Because you wouldn't even look at me all day today."

"I know, and I'm sorry. I was kinda trying to process. I really am fine with it."

"Hello! Am I the only one thinking straight?" Linz yelled, squirming in her chair.

"Linz..." Jillian began but Linz cut her off.

"No don't "Linz" me. I'm serious guys. Margo, you've been so full of secrets and now you're dating Tyler and you didn't have the balls to tell your best friends." She threw up some air quotes at "best friends" and it stung. "He's not a good guy Margo. Him and his whole richy- rich gang are all jerks, or have you forgotten that part?"

"He's not like the rest of them Linz," I yelled, fighting back tears. "You don't even know a thing about him. All you know is he has money. That doesn't make him a bad person."

"It's not about him being rich. If you haven't forgotten Jillian is loaded. It's about him being friends with a group of assholes who beat up on Donny regularly. Last year when Blake pantsed him at the assembly did you see Tyler come to his defense? No, he was too busy laughing with the rest of the assholes."

"Thanks for dredging up that nightmare memory Linz," Donny mumbled.

I took a few calming breaths to keep from losing my shit. "Okay, I know that his friends are jerks, but you have to trust me when I say he's not like them at all. I know I should have told you we were dating. The thing is, he's sweet and thoughtful, and I really, really like him and I'd like for you guys to give him the benefit of the doubt. Please." By now the tears I'd fought to keep in were falling down my cheeks in hot salty sheets.

"Margo, you know I have your back, and I trust you. If you want to date Tyler, you should. Just do us a favor, please stop keeping secrets from us," Jillian said.

"I promise," I said, wiping the snot from my nose with my other sleeve. I was a gross mess.

"Fine, whatever." Linz grumbled. "Just know, I still think you're making a huge mistake and he's going to break your heart into a million pieces, and when that happens, I'll be here to say I told you so."

"God Linz, could you be any more of a raging bitch?" Donny said.

"Uh yeah probably!" Linz replied. Donny puffed up, prepared to say something else but Linz hung up before he got the chance. There was a soft knock on my door and then my mom opened it a bit.

"Margo, honey are you ok? I heard yelling. Are you crying?"

"I'm ok Mom, just on the phone. Done now." I hung up and snatched a tissue from my desk.

"You sure everything is ok? Why are you crying?" she asked.

"Nothing is wrong Mom," I said blowing my nose. "Just lame high school stuff. I'm gonna do my homework."

"Alright sweetheart. Clean yourself up first, you look terrible."

I went to the bathroom to cleaned myself up, my face now blowfish puffy and crusty from peanut butter. I twisted my hair into a braid, went back into my room and collapsed onto my bed.

***

I was elbow deep in my lit book when I felt a thick hand grasp my shoulder and squeeze.

"What the...!" I yelled out, the book spilling onto the floor. Ms. Cork, the librarian whipped around the corner, eyes bulging at me. "Miss Adams please refrain from yelling in the library!"

I scrunched my face as I bent down to retrieve my book. "I'm so sorry, Ms. Cork!"

She scowled at me before returning to her work. I spun around to find Mr. Dan leaning against the desk behind me, hand over his mouth, suppressing a laugh.

"Dude, not cool Mr. Dan. Not cool."

"You were about to throw out a curse word, weren't you?" he asked playfully

"Of course I was," I said. "I'm a teenager. We all curse, especially when you sneak up behind us." He sat down in the chair opposite of me, sliding a document across the table.

I scanned it. "What's this?"

"It's a letter from one of my grad school professors. I'd told him about the grey zone study back before your mom said no. He really wants to see it happen so he's written this letter for you mom. He wants her to reconsider."

I sighed. "Come on, Mr. Dan. I couldn't convince her and I'm her own flesh and blood. There's no way this letter from some rando will do the trick. She's like legit stuck in her ways."

"Would you just try for me, kid? This is a great deal. He said his facility can take care of all the arrangements. The transportation, the cost, all of it."

"Why don't you call her and tell her about the letter, or like call her in for office hours or something."

His face went stone white. "Yeah, no."

I laughed. "Mr. Dan, are you afraid of my mother?"

"You weren't on the receiving end of that phone call."

I shook my head, folded the letter and slid it into my backpack. Whether or not I was going to give her the note later, well that would remain to be seen. Maybe I was just as much afraid of her as he was, based on our last conversation about the topic, but I'd at the very least humor him.

"Can't promise you she'll say yes. She might even tear it up right then and there."

"Welp, at least you'll have tried." He rubbed his hands together and then pushed off from the chair. "I'll leave you to your lit book. *Like Water for Chocolate.* Yeesh." He winked before leaving.

I arrived at the rehab center to find Tyler pushing an elderly woman down the hall in a wheelchair. Her long silver hair was swept to the side, and as they strolled, Tyler hunched over her shoulder, softly smiling while he listened to whatever she was whispering into his ear. He stopped in front of me, stepping to the side of the wheelchair, straightening his posture.

"Grams, this is my girlfriend Margo," he projected, taking hold of my hand. It was the first time he'd ever introduced me as his girlfriend. I extended my free hand to his grandmother.

"Hello Ma'am it's a pleasure to meet you." She took my hand in hers, and I gasped as her freezing bony fingers clamped around mine. She smiled, the skin around her eyes crinkling slightly in the corner. They were the same icy blue as Tyler's but clouded. Abruptly she dropped my hand, eyes narrowing.

"Who are you? Why are you touching me? You're not my Amanda. Amanda! Amanda!"

I looked to Tyler, panicked. He squatted down in front of her. "Grandma, this isn't Mom. This is my girlfriend, Margo."

She swat at him and then gripped the corners of her shawl. "Who are you? I don't know you."

"It's me, Grandma. It's Tyler."

She just stared up at him muttering the word NO over and over.

Sari moved around from the nurse's station, grabbing onto the wheelchair. "It's alright sugars, I'll take her. Mrs. Mahoney let's get you back into bed, okay?" Sari turned her and wheeled her around the corner. Tyler ran a hand through his hair, sighing as he walked into the visitor's room. I followed him in, wrapping my arms around him.

"Her lucid moments are getting to be less frequent. They said pretty soon she won't have any at all."

"I'm sorry Ty," I said, burying my face into his chest. He kissed the top of my head before sliding out of my arms and sitting in a chair. I got us drinks from the vending machine and sat across from him.

"Know what sucks the most? My mom never visits anymore. Claims she's too busy running the town, but I know she just doesn't want to deal with her own mother anymore. And do you think Alexander visits? Nope. Just me, and she only remembers who I am half the time."

I reached across the table and grabbed his hand. I wanted to tell him that I understood, but I wasn't sure it would come out making any sense, or if it was even relatable on the same level. Neither my father or my grandparents have been to see Nate. There was a slim chance my father knew, because my mother hasn't spoken to him in years. I know she's told her parents but why would they care to come visit a grandchild they'd met only once?

"Know what else sucks?" he asked. "None of my friends ever ask how I'm doing with it. To them grandparents are just these wrinkly people who send money on birthdays but for me, my whole life my grandparents have been solid. When my gramps died do you think any of them called? Nope. Well, Andy did but that was it."

"Fare-weather friends. You can always tell who your real friends are, the kind meant to be in your life for the long haul by how often they show up."

None of Nate's so-called friends ever reached out when he had his accident. Actually, none of my "friends" from Valley Central ever did either. Kinda made me wonder if I was proving to be a fare-weather friend with my circle of friends.

We'd only been dating a few weeks, not nearly enough time to have witnessed every side to a person, but I was beginning to see that there was a vulnerability to Tyler, one that I gathered not even his closest of friends ever saw. I sucked hard core at being honest and vulnerable with my group of friends, but at least they showed they were there for me.

Behind us, a throat cleared. I looked over my shoulder to see my mom leaning against the door frame grinning back at me. Her frizzy hair was piled in a messy bun, ink stains splattered on her white wrinkly shirt. Even disheveled, she still looked stunning. Noticeably different today were her eyes. No dark circles.

"Sari said I might find you in here. Who's your friend?" she asked.

"Mom, this is Tyler." I pulled my hands away from his, smoothing them in my lap. Tyler bolted up, knocking his chair to the ground, walked over to my mom and extended a hand.

"Hello Mrs. Adams. I'm Tyler Ashford. Pleased to meet you."

She shook his hand arching her eyebrows. "Ah yes, you're Amanda Ashford's eldest."

"Yes Ma'am. Guilty as charged." He shoved his hands deep into his pockets.

"I didn't know Margo had a boyfriend. Margo, honey, why didn't you tell me you have a boyfriend?".

"I thought I mentioned it. Anyway, it's new and we're sort of keeping it on the DL."

"Ok, I won't pry. You guys are very cute together."

"Mom!"

"No need to get all teenagery on me," she laughed waiving her hands. "I'll wait for you in Nate's room. Tyler, it was a pleasure to meet you."

"Yes, likewise. Have a good evening." Apparently, he was Mr. Popularity and Mr. Manners.

"Sorry about that. Guess it was bound to happen."

"It's ok. She seems real chill."

"Far from it. Mostly overworked, underpaid, and in denial about her depression." He arched an eyebrow but I brushed him off. "Anyway, I should go be with her."

I gathered up my coat and bag while Tyler picked up the knocked over chair and recycled our cans. He walked me to the door, kissing my forehead before leaving. I took a few deep breaths before entering. Who knows what Mom will say when I walk in. Mom looked up from combing Nate's hair and smiled. As she opened her mouth to speak, I threw up a hand to stop her.

"I know you want to ask questions so let me just sum up for you. Yes, I'm dating Tyler Ashford, we started dating some time over Christmas, no it's not serious, or maybe it is I don't know. Yes, we've kissed, no we haven't had sex."

"Hi honey, how are you? How was your day?"

"Mom, come on. You know you were going to get up in my grill about it."

"I think it's great that you have a boyfriend. I didn't even know you were interested in anyone."

"You don't care that it's Amanda Ashford's son?"

"Don't be ridiculous. It doesn't bother me at all. He seems like a very sweet boy and as long as he's kind to you that's all that matters." It was awesome how chill Mom was being about Tyler. I guess since everyone at school had an opinion about the relationship, his popularity, my lack thereof, and since his mom hadn't been very nice to mine back in the day, I figured she'd disapprove as well, which was totally stupid. Nate's girlfriends had always been straight-up bitches but she'd always treated them as if they were freaking princesses. It was a no brainer that the problem here was me and my stupid assumptions.

***

Teenagers love to have something to talk about. No, not love. Love isn't a strong enough word. *Yearn.* Yearning for gossip, they are artists when it comes to taking a small kernel of knowledge and making a big hoopla about it. I admit that I have been guilty in participating in the gossip game. When Blake and Amanda had their first epic blow up at a rivalry football game and all the stories started circulating, I soaked up every one of those rumors. It always seems like harmless little fun until the day the rumor mill churns about you.

In the weeks since Tyler and I had been dating, I'd heard so many untruths whispered about myself I'd lost count. And these weren't the fomas of Kurt Vonnegut's "Bokononism". No, there was nothing about the things said that when strung together would make me braver, stronger, or live happier. They just plain sucked and basically were the product of bored rotten rich kids. Do you think there was anything lame said about Tyler? Nope. Just me.

The most common untruth was that Tyler had lost a bet. Like some '90's teenage movie, he'd lost a bet (when asked the nature of the bet, no one could say) and had to ask me out. Joke was on them because I was confident in myself to know that I looked cute, albeit nerdish, with or without my glasses. Then there was my personal favorite, that his mother was paying him because my mother begged. They got a little dark and twisted too. One untruth was that we'd had drunken sex and then I'd faked a pregnancy to get him to stay with me. When asked about if I were still pregnant, word in the quad was that I'd aborted it but hadn't told him yet. I would seriously love to meet the author of these outlandish rumors. They deserved some sort of a plaque or medal for creativity. Or a punch in the face for stupidity, preferably the latter.

Tyler was great about brushing them off, a learned skill from his mother's campaigns. At first, the rumors bothered me, all these unkind untruths whispered in the halls, but I found it's easy to grow thick skin when your other half is a rock. For as much as he'd declared he was self-conscience, he was excellent at standing his ground with his friends and not letting the whispers get to him. Not that I needed the reminding, I knew how the school worked, but he'd be quick to pull me into him and tell me that eventually they'd move on to something new to talk about. It also helped to have a group of friends that didn't mind a good cat fight. Linz was still very livid with me but she was the first one to step up to anyone she heard trash-talking. The school nurse promised that Samantha Eubanks' nose was only bruised, not broken.

While most people seemed content with whispers and snide remarks, Blake was the only one who adamantly refused to accept our relationship. When Tyler and I would walk hand in hand to meet up with his friends in the courtyard (it was more like Tyler dragging me along behind him. I was so uncomfortable around his friends), Blake would jump up, mumble something under his breath and then bolt. It was like he couldn't stand to be seen with us. His disapproval never escalated into anything violent, until one day it did.

My lit class ended early so I went to the lockers to meet up with Tyler. He was hanging out there on the benches in the middle of the hall with Andy, Blake, and Griffin. As I slipped my hand into Tyler's, Blake growled.

"Seriously, don't you have like a class to be in?"

"It got out early," I said, keeping my chin up. I refused to let him beat me down.

"Great. Don't you have a next one?" He cracked his knuckles, a habit he does when he's annoyed. I'd witnessed him do this countless times whenever he argued with Griffin or when Donny spoke up in class.

"Chill out, Blake," Tyler hissed, pulling me closer to him. Blake slid down into the bench, crossed his arms over his chest.

"Nah, man. I don't think I will. I'm over this...whatever this is," he said, pointing between me and Tyler. "She doesn't belong with you, dude."

"That's not really up to you though, is it Blake? I mean, Tyler can date whomever he wants," Griffin said from behind the bench. Blake jumped up, turned to face him. They stood nose to nose.

"What the fuck did you say, bro?"

Griffin kicked at the bench with his foot. "I mean, why does it matter so much to you? Because it shouldn't. She's a nice girl, and Tyler should be able to date her without you freaking out."

Blake's stone-cold eyes bugged out and his lips pursed like he was unable to process the fact that his own flesh and blood, his identical twin, had called him out in front of everyone. There was a little vein in the left side of his face, right at the temple that was pulsing rapidly, a sure sign that he was about to fuh-reak. Slowly, he walked around the bench. Before any of us had time to register what was happening, Blake cocked his arm back then lunged forward, his fist cracking Griffin in the nose, crimson blood spilling out as Griffin tumbled backwards to the floor. Tyler let go of me and jumped over the bench, grabbing onto Blake to hold him back as Andy crouched down to help Griffin to his feet.

"What the hell, Blake!" Griffin yelled, covering his bloody nose with his hands.

"I think you broke his nose," Andy yelled. Blake pushed back against Tyler, but Tyler pivoted and tossed Blake up against the lockers, pinning him there.

"Get off me!" he yelled, trying to muscle out of Tyler's hold.

"Calm down. What is wrong with you!" Tyler tried to keep Blake pinned but he was eventually able to break free just as the chemistry door opened, Mr. Hogfoss popping out.

"What's going on out here?" He looked at Blake who was straightening his shirt, chest heaving, then to Tyler who had moved in front of me protectively. "Mr. Ashford, Mr. Wolf...Griffin why is your nose bleeding? Have you boys been fighting?" He ducked back into the classroom and then reemerged with a paper towel, applying it to Griffin's nose.

"Just a misunderstanding, Mr. Hogfoss," Griffin said under the paper towel. Mr. Hogfoss let go of Griffin's face and walked towards Blake, carefully eyeballing him. "That right, boys? Just a misunderstanding? Because you know fighting isn't tolerated."

"Yes, sir. Just a misunderstanding," Tyler said.

"Alright then. Griffin, get yourself cleaned up and then checked out by the nurse. The rest of you get back to class." Mr. Hogfoss closed his door and the bystanders dispersed. Blake snatched up his backpack and cradling his fist started for the door, bumping right into Donny as he entered the hall.

"Out of the way," he growled, shoving past him. I winced as I heard Donny's head crack against the lockers.

"I'd better go help Griffin. And then go find the Coach. Somehow, I know he's gonna hear about this." He kissed my forehead and then grabbed Griffin's backpack, following him and Andy down the hall. I ran to Donny, linking my arm in his.

"Hey are you ok?"

Donny rubbed the back of his head. "Um Margo, what the hell is going on? Did I just see Griffin leave with a bloody nose?"

"Yeah. Blake punched him in the face."

"Blake did what? He hit his own brother? Do I even want to know why?"

"Because Griffin doesn't share Blake's opinion that Tyler and I shouldn't be happening."

"Awe honey." He wrapped his arms around me and we walked down the hall. This school really sucked.

***

It was one of those rare February days where Oregon decides it wants to snow, flurries at first, light and damp, then as the wind picks up, snowflakes dumping in giant sheets. I sat at a window table in The Daily Bagel waiting for Jillian. We hadn't spoken much in the past few weeks; when I wasn't working or at the rehab center my free time was spent with Tyler. I'd never wanted to become one of "those girls" who totally blew off their friends once they got a boyfriend, but all I wanted to do when I had any free time was be with Tyler.

I watched as Jillian parked her Subaru, wrap her scarf tightly around her neck and slosh through the wet snow. She opened the door, stomping the snow off her boots before entering. After offering up a weak smile, she ordered a drink and slid down into the chair opposite of me. She unwound her scarf, slowly as if she were unwinding our friendship. Had I messed things up beyond repair?

"What about this snow, huh?" I offered, pathetically attempting to ease the tension with lame small talk. She wasn't buying it.

"What are you doing, Margo? You know you suck at small talk. And about the weather? Seriously?"

"I don't know!" I threw my hands up. "I'm just trying."

"Well stop. You sound stupid." She glanced down at her drink but I could see the smile forming in the corner of her mouth.

"I'm sorry," I blurted. "I don't know what I'm doing. With like, anything. I don't know how to have a boyfriend and friends too, I don't know how to just be up front and honest about my feelings with you guys, and I feel like I'm messing this up." I gestured between the two of us.

"You're not messing anything up."

"Really? Then why does it feel like we're not friends anymore?"

"If it feels that way it's because you're pushing away, Mar. Look I get that you have a boyfriend, and it's new and exciting and you want to spend all your time with him. Remember when I started dating Kyle Nowak last year?"

I took a long drink of my coffee as I tried to recall.

"Oh, that's right. I totally forgot that you dated him for a few months."

"Yeah, and remember how I hung out with him all the time and we barely hung out?"

I nodded. "I think I gave you crap about ditching your friends for some dude."

"You did, you were kinda bitchy about it," she laughed. "But we were cool, you know, once I figured out how to balance."

"Yeah, but then you broke up anyway," I said.

"Only because he kept pressuring me to have sex. I wasn't ready and…"

"You dumped his ass," I interrupted pushing my fist across the table. She smiled, meeting my fist with hers.

"I'm just saying I get it, you wanting to spend time with Tyler. I know you'll figure out the balance."

I rested my head on the table and groaned. "Ugg why does this have to be so complicated? I just like him so much but it's so hard to be his girlfriend you know? I can handle Linz and her objections, but it's Blake who is so not making this easy. You heard what he did at school right?"

"Pretty sure the entire student body heard. I can't believe he punched his own twin brother. That dude is certifiable."

"I just don't get why he cares so much. Like, why does it matter if Tyler dates outside of their stupid social circle?"

"It's all about appearances with that group," Jillian said.

I took off my beanie and shook out my hair. "Yeah but it's not with Tyler," I whispered.

Jillian pulled a tissue out from her purse and handed it to me just as tears spilled down my cheeks.

"Why is it so easy for you to float in an out of their social circle? I just don't get it."

"It's history, babe. I've gone to school with half those kids since pre-k and I can't help that our parents all run in the same circle more or less. But you know what Mar? Who cares, no seriously. Who. Cares. You like him and he likes you. Just enjoy it. And in the meantime, stop pushing us out."

I laughed, snot pouring from my nose. "Gross. Just gross." Jillian gagged, and then we both exploded into a fit of laughter, the kind you feel deep in your soul.

***

Donny took great pride in his appearance. From his perfectly styled hair to his unscuffed shoes, his ensemble was always on point. So, when he showed up to psych wearing a tattered black hoodie over his button-down t-shirt, his hair flat and disheveled, and mud caked to his shoes, alarms were sounded. Oh, and not to mention the huge blue-black shiner on his left eye. This was not how he looked this morning when I saw him before school started.

"What the hell happened to you?" I leaned forward to whisper after he slid into his desk. He narrowed his eyes at me, flinching. "Shhh, nothing, stop looking at me."

He pulled his notebook and pencil out from his backpack and then turned to face Mr. Dan. His fingers gripped the pencil so hard I could hear the splintering. Dirt had built up under his nails, like he'd been digging. Donny hates the dirt. He was slightly mysophobic. I slid a note to Jillian to ask if she knew anything about his appearance, but she shook her head no, then passed the note to Linz. She shrugged her shoulders.

Mr. Dan sat at his desk taking roll, his eyes scanning the room as people responded, and then stopped when he got to Donny. "Everything ok there, Donny?" Donny looked up at him, then around at everyone in the class who were all by now staring.

"Uh yeah fine. Just fell, earlier. I'm ok though."

Mr. Dan didn't look convinced, but he didn't pry. All through the lecture I stole glances at Danny, which he ignored, his face covered by the hood he'd pulled over his head. When class was over, I knew he'd bolt for the door so I jumped up from my desk and stood in front of him.

"Seriously, Margo," he sighed, "can we please not do this?"

"Do what? Stand up? Gather our backpacks? Oh wait, I know, talk about our periods?"

Linz rolled her eyes at me. "Margo you're annoying. Can't you just give him space?"

I opened my mouth to respond but Donny gently touched my forearm, shaking his head.

"No, it's ok. It's stupid of me to assume I could keep it quiet, I mean look at me, I look like shit."

Linz muttered under her breath, slid on her backpack, motioned for us to leave the classroom. We followed her through the hall and outside onto one of the benches. Donny winced as he sat down. I sat next to him taking his hand in mine.

"It was Blake, wasn't it?" I asked. He kept his gaze fixed on his shoes, nodding.

"So, what happened? Why did that little shit stain attack you this time?" Linz asked, crossing her arms tight across her chest.

"So classically cliché. I was using the bathroom by the gym because I'd just come from TAing for Mr. Shosh. Blake was in there with Andy and I walked past them to use the far urinal. Blake gave me this snarky look and next thing I know I'm being shoved up against the wall and he like yells something about how I looked at his dick. So then I said there was nothing much to look at, and then he started to kick me and punch me. Andy kept trying to hold him back but you've seen his skinny untoned arms. I grabbed one of those stupid urinal cakes, rubbed it into his face and ran out of there."

"What about the mud? On your shoes and your fingernails?" Jillian asked. Donny looked at his nails then rubbed them on the front of his pants.

"Yeah so I cut across the football field and slid in the freaking mud. I didn't have time to clean properly so I grabbed this hideous hoodie out of the lost and found and came here. I'm so sick of this!" He broke down, hiding his face in the sleeves of the hoodie. Donny learned long ago to form a hard shell, bullies would be bullies no matter what. For the most part he'd been able to defend himself and still keep his swag but everyone has a breaking point. I wrapped my arms around him. Jillian dug in her bag, pulling out a pack of Wet Ones and wiped at the dirt and scrapes on his face. Linz wrestled a wipe out of the pack and worked at the dirt under his nails before moving onto his shoes. The bell for the next class had long since rang but none of us cared. We'd skip class and face the consequences. As we tended to Donny, none of us saying a single word I realized just how much I never should have shut any of them out of my life, how I should have just confided in them, all of them, every day as much as I did Jillian because no matter how often we fought or had disagreements, when there was trouble, we came together.

I couldn't focus in the rest of my classes; my brain a hot pile of frustration and hatred for Blake. How could anyone be so callous? I just didn't get it. I thought Tyler would have some sort of insight, them having been some variation of friend since childhood, but he was just as baffled.

"He's been that way for as long as I've known him. It's like he always has something to prove and he doesn't know how to channel his emotions."

"Ok, well how do you explain Griffin? He's like, the exact opposite."

"He's part of Blake's problem, I think. See with them it had always been a competition. Who came out of first, who took their first steps first, who spoke first. Griffin was born one minutes ahead of Blake, and he's kinda always been the favorite. I think Blake resents him, feels there shouldn't be favorites since they're twins but anyone can tell his parents clearly treat Griffin better."

"That doesn't excuse his behavior," I objected.

"Hey I'm not defending him. And I've told you before that we're not close, our mothers are best friends so we kinda just got thrown together when we were in diapers. I'm just trying to shed light."

We jumped as the hall doors burst open, Blake and Donny tumbling out followed by Andy, Griffin, and Alexander. "I can't believe you narked on me!" Blake grabbed a fistful of Donny's hair and threw him into a patch of grass. Without thinking I jumped up and took off towards them. Tyler grabbed for my arm to stop me but I swerved out of his way. I didn't know what I was planning to do, taking on this beefy meat-head whose left bicep was larger than my entire face, who could flex and knock me back. But it didn't stop me from charging full speed, ramming into his chest with the full force of my shoulder. He gasped and grabbed me as we both tumbled to the ground. My shoulder felt like I'd been hit by a semi and blood tasting like hot iron gushed into my mouth, either from the fall or from Blake's fist plowing into my face. Within seconds Tyler descended upon him scooping his arms under Blake and pinning him to the ground.

"You fucking punched my girlfriend, bro!"

"Don't bro me. That bitch pummeled me!"

"I don't give a shit if she pantsed you in front of everyone and your tiny dick came out. You don't hit a girl, especially not Margo." He released Blake who spit blood onto the ground.

"Screw her and her friends. They're nobodies, and as long as you're with her you're a nobody too." Blake wiped the blood from his mouth with the back of his hand before turning and stomping down the field towards the parking lot. Alexander shifted his weight from one foot to the other.

"You're making a huge mistake, Ty," Alexander said.

"You don't know what you're talking about Alex."

"I know you're throwing away a perfectly good friendship. Where's the loyalty?"

Not waiting for a response, Alexander spun on his heels and ran after Blake. Tyler ran a hand through his hair, wincing from the pain in his wrist. He knelt down beside me, using the sleeve of his shirt to wipe my lip.

"Are you okay?" he asked. I rubbed my shoulder, the throbbing pain reminding me just how stupid I was. "All things considered..." I mumbled, then turned to Donny who sat where he'd landed with his knees pulled into his chest. I smoothed the hair out of his eyes.

"You okay Donny boy?"

"Peachy," he mumbled. I wrapped my arm around him and held him there until the doors to the hall burst open and Jillian and Linz barreled through, collapsing beside us. Jillian cradled Danny's face in her hands gently turning it from side to side.

"Well, good news is, you're still beautiful."

He smiled, wincing a little. "Girl, that idiot could hit me a thousand times and I'd still be beautiful."

"Hey man," Tyler rested a hand on Donny's shoulder, "I'm real sorry about Blake. He's an ass."

Linz scoffed. "Yeah we know your friend is an ass, pretty boy," she said, emphasizing the word 'your' and pointing at Tyler.

"Chill out, Linz," I said. She snapped her head at me and glared.

"What? They're friends, aren't they? I mean, we're not going to sit here and pretend that Margo's new boyfriend has zero blame in this."

"It's not his fault Linz. He didn't tell Blake to beat up Donny. Besides they aren't even friends, not really."

"So they don't eat lunch together, go to movies together, shoot hoops with one another?"

"Look, there's a lot you don't understand about...about Blake and..." Tyler tried to explain but Linz jabbed her pointer finger into his chest.

"Don't you dare try to make excuses for that ridiculous excuse for a human being!"

"Linz, he's not making excuses for him, God! Can't you just chill out?" I said. She opened her mouth to spit something out but Donny threw a pine cone at her.

"Really? Did you just peg me with a freaking pine cone?"

"Enough Linz, ok? Just...enough. It's not Tyler's fault. Just chill."

Linz rubbed her temples with her fingers. "You're all idiots," she said before turning and walking away from us back into the hall.

Tyler squeezed the back of his neck. "Man, is your friend always this intense?" Whether from hysteria, adrenaline or what, Donny keeled over into a fit of laughter. I looked to Jillian, see if she had any idea what the heck just happened, but she shrugged her shoulders clearly just as confused.

"You have absolutely no idea how accurate that statement is," he said between laughs, and because we knew just how sadly true that statement was, Jillian and I fell to the ground laughing and hugging Donny, Tyler standing over us watching, a look equal parts amused and confused sweeping his face.

Once we'd composed ourselves, Donny left with Jillian, and Tyler walked me to my car. After putting my backpack in the back seat, he gently turned me to face him, touching the cut just above my lip.

"You sure you don't want to put ice on this before you leave?" he asked.

"I'm sure. Tyler, really. It hardly hurts anymore and I don't think it will swell." Lies. It hurt like hell.

"Yeah ok well what about your shoulder?"

"It's fine!" I rotated it around the socket biting my tongue to keep from screaming. I could tell Tyler didn't believe me but he wasn't going to push. Instead, he pulled me into him, wrapping his arms around me, resting his chin on the top of my head.

"I feel really bad. You know, about what Blake did, what he does to Donny."

"You wouldn't have been able to stop him."

"Maybe, maybe not. If I tried harder to like, be his friend maybe he wouldn't be such a dick."

"He'd be a dick regardless. His own twin can't even get him to stop being a bully, what makes you think you'd be able to change him?"

"Your friends will never like me, because of him, because of where I come from."

I didn't say anything. What could I have said? He was right, of course he was. No matter how hard I tried to convince them there would always be something happening to make them disagree. Though mostly it was Linz who vocalized her issues, the reservations were still present with Jillian and maybe even Donny too. They were just better at keeping them at bay.

Tyler kissed the top of my head and uncurled his arms from around me. "I'd better go. I'm pretty sure Alexander has already told my parents about today."

"You think you'll get in trouble for what Blake did?"

"I don't know. Like I said, our moms are best friends. They'll be pissed when they find out I didn't back him up."

"But he was beating someone up! You think they would have wanted you to actually help beat someone up?"

"I don't know, Margo!" He threw his hands up. "I just know that when Alexander tells my mom that I chose some nobody over my friend she'll be pissed."

I placed my hands on my hips. "So now Donny is a nobody?"

"That's not what I'm saying Margo. I don't mean I think he's a nobody, I'm saying my mom will think that. You just don't understand." But I did understand. That's what sucked about this whole thing. It wouldn't matter that Donny was the nicest, most compassionate person in the entire world. The fact that he wasn't rich and that he wasn't straight would forever make him a nobody, just like I was a nobody for being poor and the sister of an attempted suicide. I didn't want to end our day on a sour note so instead I kissed him, told him to text me later.

On the drive home I blasted Santigold and thought about all the ways my relationship with Tyler would eventually go wrong. At some point, his friends would ditch him, because that's just how his group of friends were- super fickle and quick to bounce.

And my friends, though they'd pretend for as long as they could to be okay with Tyler, they too would ghost me, but be classier about it, probably make it look like it was me ghosting them rather than the other way around.

My mom claimed she was chill with us, but who knows for how long, and I don't even want to think about how Alexander has painted me out to look to Mrs. Ashford.

Then there was the topic neither of us had actually discussed. What happens after we graduate? Even though I'd applied to UCLA as well as U of O, I wasn't going to school out of state. I couldn't leave Nate. Tyler applied to a handful of schools but mostly east coast schools. What would we do if he did go back east? Have a long-distance relationship? Those were a joke. I couldn't think of one long distance relationship that worked out, ever. Nate tried it with his girlfriend and look where that got him? What if Tyler went to a school in California? Would we call it close enough and see each other on weekends? For how long would that last? No matter how I looked at it, my thoughts spiraled into the same conclusion every damn time. My relationship with Tyler was doomed to fail.

***

My assumptions about Mrs. Ashford proved to be correct. A few weeks after the whole Donny incident, I was working an early morning solo shift at the bookstore. Late February was notoriously slow at work so I usually opened the store by myself and manned the register and the floor. No biggie. I was organizing the magazines behind the counter when I heard a soft high-pitched cough from above me. Rising up and turn-ing around my skin froze as Mrs. Ashford placed several books on the counter in front of her. Her blond curls fell loosely down her shoulders, ice blue eyes the same as Tyler sizing me up, assessing my worth. When she smiled, the left corner of her mouth curled upward, also the same as Tyler. He was a carbon copy of his mother and it freaked me out.

I straightened my shirt, meekly smiled and began to scan her books. "Good morning. Did you find what you were looking for?"

She sucked in and paused before saying, "More or less. Your store is very small and your non-fiction selection is sparse, but I managed to find something worth reading."

"That's good to hear," I nodded, sliding her books into a canvas tote. I knew her little trip to this side of town was no coincidence. No one of her stature ever came all the way over here to book shop unless they knew exactly what they wanted and the big box didn't have it. No, she was here specifically for me.

"If I'm not mistaken, you're Christa Adams' daughter?"

I hesitated, unsure if I would be walking into a trap by answering. "That I am."

"And you know who I am, dear?"

"Sure do. You're Mrs. Ashford. You're on City Council, board of directors at my school, and you and my mom went to school together,"

"Yes, that's right. Haven't seen her around much these days." She brushed loose strands of hair away from her face,

her nails perfectly manicured, the gaudiest diamond wedding ring ever resting loosely on her boney finger.

"Yeah well, she works a lot," I said curtly.

"And you know my son, Tyler Ashford."

I opened my mouth to respond but she cut me off. "Oh but of course you do. It seems that the two of you are dating, which I must say is news to me."

"Oh? He didn't tell you? Well, you know how us teenagers can be. Forgetful and stuff." I was trying my best not to come unhinged. She had some sort of an angle she was working and I really didn't want to feed into it.

"Yes. Forgetful and stuff." Her eyes narrowed. She was gearing up to say something more but before she could I crammed the receipt into her tote and slid the tote across the counter.

"Well, thanks for coming in. I hope you enjoy your books. Pleasure to finally meet you."

She slid the bag off the counter, slowly draping it over her shoulder, continuing to stare into me with her icicle eyes. She'd been dismissed and she knew it, and clearly didn't like it. Pulling her lip up into a sneer, she waived her manicured hand at me.

"Yes, dear. Pleasure. Do tell your mother I said hello."

I pushed down the bile that was creeping up my throat. The gal of that woman was beyond ridiculous. As if she cared enough about my mother to actually say hello. Her words dripped with so much spite I was surprised she didn't choke. I didn't know how Tyler could stand living one minute under her roof, but it wasn't like he had a choice, I mean, we can't exactly pick our parents. Judgment and prejudice ran through her veins thicker than her blood. Even before I'd transferred, I was well aware of who she was, her freaking face had been plastered to every city bus, and when she was campaigning, her commercials popped up on every local news station just about every hour. I thought she was a tightly wound kiss-ass from the start. The only way she'd ever approve of me dating her precious son was if we were the richest people in Valley River.

14

— • —

March blew in full of vengeance and mayhem. The ground thawed in sections bringing false promises of spring to the daffodils, who sprout only to be sorely disappointed weeks later when a random snow storm blows in. It was mostly rainy days though, thick black clouds blanketing the sky. We all wore our hoods pulled tightly over our heads, shuffling single file, hugging the walls in an attempt to keep dry under the overhang of the buildings. The school was split into four wings and each building was far enough away that you're completely soaked by the time you got from one to the other, and true Oregonians never bothered with an umbrella. Clearly this school had been built by some dumb company not familiar with the moody weather pattern of Oregon.

The gang had to work on a government project at lunch, so I met Tyler in the library to eat. By the time I'd ran from my locker to the library on the far east corner of campus, I looked like I'd just gone swimming fully clothed. Mrs. Sheffield, the assistant librarian glared as I opened the door and shook off my coat, leaving giant puddles in the middle of the floor. I looked at her sheepishly and shrugged my shoulders.

"Sorry, Mrs. Sheffield," I whispered, hanging my coat on the rack by the door. She rolled her eyes at me and turned back to cataloging. I found Tyler hunched over a book at one of the research tables, dragging a blue highlighter across the words on the page in a hungry sort of manner, gobbling up whole paragraphs at once. Sliding into the seat next to him, I pulled his book out from under him and examined the pages.

"You know you're really only meant to highlight what you feel are the most important parts, not every single word on the page."

He pursed his lips, snatching the book back and turning the page. "I have a paper due in AP Lit in a few weeks I feel like I have zero clue what I'm doing. Mrs. Card split us into groups and we each have to write a paper critically analyzing this stupid short story from a different perspective, and I was assigned the feminist perspective. How the hell am I supposed to write from a feminist perspective when I'm a dude?"

"You don't have to have a vagina to be a feminist, genius," I said, taking his book again and flipping it closed to look at the cover. It was a short story by Joyce Carol Oates that I'd read many times, "Where are you going, where have you been".

"This is a great story."

He rolled his eyes. "Sure it is."

"No really, it's actually one of my favorites. It was inspired by a really good Bob Dylan song."

"For real? My dad plays Dylan all the time. What's the song?"

"Here, just listen to it." I took out my phone, scrolled through my music until I found my Bob Dylan songs, clicked on "It's all over now, Baby Blue" and handed him an earbud. When the song finished, he removed the earbud, handed it back to me.

"I've heard my dad play this song. I don't see how in any way it has anything to do with the story though."

"I didn't say that they were directly related, I just said she drew inspiration from the song. Look, it really isn't that difficult to think like a feminist. Read *The Feminine Mystique.* That should help."

"The feminine what?" He looked as if I'd just told him to pierce his nipples. I burst out laughing, forgetting where I was until the harsh "shhhhhhhhh" spat out by Mrs. Sheffield. I slapped a hand over my mouth and nodded.

"You're killing me, Smalls," I whispered. "Ok I will help you with your paper."

He leaned over and gently kissed my lips. "You're the best."

"Things I already know for 2000, Alex." I pulled a string cheese from my lunchbox, carefully tearing the wrapper so as to avoid another epic shushing by Mrs. Sheffield.

"So, since you're the best, you won't mind coming to my house one night this week for dinner."

I tore so hard on the wrapper the stick of cheese flew out of my hands landing on the table in front of us with a thud. Tyler reached over, grabbed the cheese and handed it to me.

"Here's your cheese, Hulk. What was that about?"

"Nothing, you just caught me off guard," I said, wrapping the cheese back in its wrapper and cramming it into my lunch box. I'd lost my appetite. "Did you just ask me to dinner, at your house, like with your family?"

"Well it'll be at my house but I was thinking with the family down the street. The Maisel's make a killer brisket. Yes Margo, I mean with my family."

"I don't think that's a good idea."

"Why? Do you have to work, because we can have it when you have a night off."

"It's not just my work schedule. Tyler, your mom doesn't like me. She only wants me to come to dinner so she can further show me just how much she doesn't like me."

"That's not even true." The slight catch in his voice told me he was zero percent convinced of his own statement.

"I told you about how she acted when she came into the bookstore, like I was just some poor white trash trailer park reject."

"I'm sure you just misread it. Or maybe you didn't. I don't know. My mom is a bitch most times. Either way, I think it would be good if you came to dinner so my parents spend time with you, get a chance to know you."

It wouldn't make a difference if they got to know me. I'd never be wealthy enough to even be in the same room as their son. His eyes though, they were pleading and I could tell it would mean a lot to him. So of course, I'd go. I knew how to suck it up and be the bigger person. I'd been doing it all of my life. Someone should give me a freaking Tony Award for how well I could act.

"Fine, I'll come to dinner. I don't work Thursday night."

He grabbed my hands, beaming. After kissing my palms, he said, "It's going to be great. You'll see. And if any of them says anything rude or disrespectful at all, we'll bounce. I promise." What was it Mary Poppins said? Something about never making a pie crust promise?

***

Today's psych class had been a nightmare. Nothing monumentally horrendous had happened, there weren't any class fights, Mr. Dan hadn't assigned a complicated project, well, any more so than the current one, but he had been in a mood, and thanks to ye ole rumor mill, I learned it had something to do with a major fight and subsequent break-up between him and his long-term girlfriend. How the bulk of the student body even heard about it, since from what I know Mr. Dan tends to be a pretty private person, is beyond me.

The waste basket sat overturned on the floor by the door, pieces of chalk were piled up as if they'd purposefully been dumped out, and Mr. Dan sat folded over in his chair, elbows resting on his knees, fingers smoothing down his eyebrows. As I walked by to my seat I stopped and tapped on his desk.

"Everything alright, boss?"

Without looking up he shot an arm out, pointing a short stubby finger to words written on the chalkboard-

SIT DOWN, SHUT UP, READ ABOUT LEARNING AND MEMORY. I continued to my desk, sliding in and pulling my psych book out of my bag.

"A moody Mr. Dan is *so* not a fun Mr. Dan," Donny said, flipping the pages of his book. The bruises across his face had lightened, now a greenish-yellow, the cuts on his lip mostly healed.

"You heard what happened right? That his GF had been cheating on him for like, over a year and then he totally caught her in the action?" Linz said.

"He didn't catch her in the action exactly," Donny chimed in. "He just saw them out in public together holding hands or whatever."

"When did it happen?" I asked.

"Saturday night. Word is he was at the movie theater with some of his guy friends and he caught them in line at concessions. They had this huge blow out right there. Bunch of kids from school saw it and I think someone even filmed it."

Of course, some kid filmed a hugely personal matter and posted it for all to see. "Damn. That sucks" I said.

Mr. Dan cleared his throat, glaring in our direction. I mouthed the word *sorry* and flipped my book open. I guess just because you're a teacher doesn't mean you're immune to school gossip. Whatever happens in your personal life, if witnessed by anyone, especially any one of the gossip brigade, it wasn't personal anymore. What sucks is when you're a teacher, it just seems you never get away from it. You do something bad or worth talking about in high school, it gets talked about. You do something bad, or I guess just have anything with a little action happen in your life as a grown up, it gets talked about. People just suck.

When class ended, I told Jillian I'd catch up with them later, then waited around until the room cleared. Mr. Dan had said only what was necessary all period, answering questions regarding homework assignments, clarifying items on the study sheet, all with deep sighs and eye rolls in between. Now, he sat with his cheek rested on his desk, lips squishing together like a fish, his arms hanging down in front of him. I sat with my hands folded in my lap, staring at him, waiting for him to say anything, or even just blink.

"This school just sucks the life right out, doesn't it?" he slurred through fish lips.

I nodded. "Every last bit."

Slowly he sat up, the cheek he'd been resting on a bright red, shaking his arms to life.

"You've heard, I'm sure, about my public dumping?"

I nodded. "That I have. Uh, if you want to talk about it or anything..."

He scoffed. "Nah. I'm good. Kinda blurs the lines between teacher and student. Besides, if I give it enough time, one of you dumb kids will do something stupid and I'll be yesterday's news."

I hated to see my favorite teacher so worn down. Which is why I feel my next statement was totally justified.

"So yeah, I talked to my mom and she's going to agree to the study."

He arched his eyebrows and curled his lip up to a half smile. "Oh yeah? What changed her mind?"

"Uh well there was the letter, from the doctor, and I think she saw how important it was to me." I hoped Mr. Dan couldn't see the beads of sweat I felt pooling up on my upper lip.

"Good. Yeah, this is good. I think we can still make it happen. I will call the testing facility and then give your mom a call in a few weeks to go over the details once I hear back."

My stomach clenched and I had to squeeze my hands together to control the anxiety I could feel creeping into my neck. It was just a quick spur of the moment action, telling him my mom had said she'd do it. I didn't actually think he'd have to talk to her. "Oh, you have to speak to my mother? Wh...why is that?"

"Because, Margo it just makes sense for me to talk to her beforehand, you know, since it's my project." He flicked his wrist over, glanced at the time, then stood up. "I need to get something to eat before my next class. I just realize I haven't actually eaten in a few days. Anyway, please just tell your mom I'll be in touch. And don't forget about your paper." I nodded, slid out of my desk and left with the understanding that that I was royally fucked.

I yanked my phone from my pocket, texted Tyler some series of emoji's I hoped he'd understand and told him to meet me on the benches outside the Chapel. I sprinted there and sat on a bench, gnawing at my thumb nail until my finger bled. I couldn't keep my legs from jiggling. I spotted Tyler rounding the corner by the cafeteria walking with some friends. He smiled when he saw me, laughed at something a friend said and then headed over to me. When he saw my mangled thumb, he sat down next to me, taking my hands in his.

"They make these things called nail clippers so that you don't have to chew your nail off."

"It's a nervous habit."

"So what's up? Your text was a little weird. I have no idea what any of those emoji's have in common." He turned his phone towards me to show me the text, but I pushed it away.

"Yeah I have no idea I just mashed a bunch of keys together to get your attention. Ty, I'm totally and completely screwed. I told Mr. Dan I gave my mom the note from his doctor friend and that she'd changed her mind and agreed to have the tests done, only none of that's true."

"Okay, well then why did you tell him that?"

"I don't know! I guess I felt bad for him because of what happened with him and his girlfriend and because having the whole school gossip about you sucks and he looked like he just needed a win."

"So you lied to him? Margo, how do you think he'll feel when he finds out your mom never actually agreed?"

I buried my head in my hands. There was no good way out of this. Either I beg and plead with Mom to change her mind until I'm blue in the face, or I tell Mr. Dan I'd lied before he has a chance to call my mom. Both of those options sucked.

Tyler pulled me upright, wrapped his strong arms around me and held tight.

"It's okay. Everything is going to be okay. I think."

"You think?"

"I mean, it's probably going to be easier for you to tell Mr. Dan that you lied, since you're sure your mom won't change her mind, and he'll probably be super disappointed in you but just tell him you felt bad for him and you weren't thinking when you said it and you're sorry. You're his favorite student. He won't stay mad at you forever. Or..."

I looked up at him. "Or what?"

"You try talking to your mom one more time."

"Ugg somehow that sounds even worse."

***

I hated skirts. And dresses. Basically, anything with frills and lace. When I was little my mother dressed me in a skirt or a dress every day, the sparkly kind with layers upon layers of glittery tulle, butterflies and stars on plaid and polka dot. In first grade, when I'd come home from school covered in dirt, holes picked into the tulle, tears up and down my tights, Mom finally tossed her hands up yelling, "alright girl, you win. No more dresses," and I traded the dresses and Mary Janes for jeans and Converse.

Mass schedule at school was a royal pain because girls were required to wear skirts or dresses, which I always felt was lame. What was so wrong with a nice pair of dress slacks? Nothing, that's what. I'd spend the whole day shifting uncomfortably in my desk, tugging at the hem. Some girls just weren't cut out for girlie clothes.

I'd had to reschedule dinner at Tyler's twice due to work conflicts, which I too happily welcomed, but I couldn't put it off any longer. There was only so much of Tyler's pouty-lipped puppy dog face that I could stand. When Mom asked what I was going to wear, I ran my hands over my t-shirt, smoothing down the edges.

"This. It's not a formal dinner or anything."

"Margo, you can't wear jeans and a 'Hugs not Drugs' t-shirt to a family dinner with Mrs. Ashford."

"Why not? It's the perfect way to say I support her anti-drug campaign."

Mom rolled her eyes, spun me around and guided me to her bedroom, repositioning myself in front of her closet.

"You're going to wear a dress. I happen to have a lot of dresses that never see the light of day. Let's find one in here, shall we?"

I groaned. "Mom, you can't be serious. A dress? Why can't I just wear a good pair of khakis?"

"Because! She already things we're trash. Let's not dress like we are."

"Mom, khaki pants from The Gap are not white trash."

"Well, it is if you're her," she said, her tone equal parts bitter and sad, pulling out a long-sleeved knee length crushed velvet dress and holding it up to me. As she rummaged through her jewelry box, softly mumbling under her breath, I tried to summon up the courage to tell her about the letter from the test facility, and about what I'd said to Mr. Dan, but I couldn't do it. She'd been happier these past few weeks, spending fewer days crying when she thought I wasn't paying attention. Her smiles were less forced. I didn't want to be the reason for a setback. Plus, it had been a while since she'd taken an interest in anything in my personal life, and her wanting to help me look nice was kinda, well, nice.

"Ah! Here they are." She turned to me with a pair of dangly silver tear drop earrings, held them up to my lobes. "Good, they won't be too long." She folded them into the palm of my hand and draped the dress over my arm, turning me and ushering me out of her room.

"Ok, go put these on. I'll heat up the curling iron. We'll do loose curls."

I closed the door behind me, leaned against the door and closed my eyes. I felt like the worst daughter ever. Why couldn't I have just kept my differing opinions about Nate to myself and let my mom have this? Why was my need to know greater than her need for faith?

Deciding to push these feelings down and deal with them later, I kicked off my jeans, yanked my shirt off and slipped into the dress. The top hugged my ribs while the bottom hung loose and flowy to my knee caps. The sleeves came to the middle of my wrist but had giant holes at the shoulders. Mom knocked three times on the door, opened and gasped.

"Oh, honey you're a vision."

I rolled my eyes, shrugging my shoulders up and down. "What's with the sleeves? Did you actually cut these?"

She laughed, readjusting the sleeves. "They are called peekaboo sleeves."

"Well they're ridiculous."

"You're ridiculous." She picked up the earrings from my desk, handing me one at a time. I threaded them into the holes in my ear, shook my head back and forth feeling their weight. I only ever wore studs, so it felt weird to have something so heavy dangling from my ears, though it wasn't anything compared to the weight of guilt that was accumulating on my shoulders.

After Mom curled my hair and weaved it into a waterfall braid, I brushed mascara through my eyelashes and sat at the kitchen table to wait for Tyler. I told him I'd drive to his house but he insisted on picking me up, some nonsense about it being the gentlemanly thing to do. Besides, there was only so long I could put off not showing him where I lived.

The sound of the doorbell startled me out of my seat. Smoothing down the front of my dress, I walked the few feet from the table to the front door. Tyler stood on the porch holding a bouquet of red roses, his jaw slack. His eyes widened and I instantly felt self-conscious.

"What? Why are you staring at me like that?" I asked, wrapping my arms tightly around myself. He lowered the roses and took my hand.

"You look amazing. I mean, you always look amazing but I've never seen you in a dress before. I mean, of course I have, on Mass days but...you're stunning."

"That she is," my mom said from the kitchen sink, a dish towel draped over her shoulder.

"Tyler, it's good to see you again." She pulled off her yellow rubber gloves and walked to stand beside me at the door. Tyler let go of my hand and extended his to my mom.

"Good to see you too Mrs. Adams. May I come in?"

"Sure, make yourself at home," she said stepping aside. Tyler stepped between us and walked into the living room, taking in his surroundings. I watched his face for signs of disgust but he just smiled.

"I love the Renaissance art, Mrs. Adams, and the placement of each piece, like your walls are telling a story."

"You have a very good eye, Tyler. Are you an art aficionado?"

"I am, actually. My grandma used to work for Le Bronte, this fancy art gallery in New York while she was in school. Anyway, when she used to babysit me and my little brother, she'd talk all about it and show us pictures of all the paintings. Mostly contemporary stuff and some cubits, but my favorites were always the renaissance."

First linguistics and now art. I was beginning to think that Tyler was always going to surprise me.

"Yeah ok, Margo honey, never let this one go."

"Mom!"

Tyler and my mom both laughed.

"Kidding. I spent a year studying art history in Italy and fell in love with the Renaissance movement. These were my favorite pieces. I'd love to one day have an original."

She stared at the painting of *The Creation of Adam* with a longing, like she was remembering some other time, maybe wishing she'd never met my dad in Italy and gotten pregnant, thinking of what she might be doing with her life instead. Turning back to Tyler, she pointed at the flowers in his hand. "Tyler those are lovely roses."

"Oh, thank you. Margo, I brought these for you. I hope you like red." He handed me the bouquet of roses. I didn't have the heart to tell him I prefer pink.

"Thanks. They're pretty." I said, bringing them to my nose and inhaling. Mom squeezed my elbow as she moved in to take the roses. She knew I preferred pink but I was glad she didn't say anything.

"Here, let me take those and get them into some water. They really are lovely, Tyler."

While she tended to the roses, I folded my hands in front of me and walked around the room.

"Okay so, now you've seen where I live. As you can see there isn't actually much *to* see. This is the living room, that over there is the kitchen and down the hall are the bedrooms and ONE bathroom."

Tyler rested a warm hand on the small of my back, calming my nerves. "It's nice. Quaint. I love it."

"You're just saying that."

"I'm not. This place feels homey. My house is, well you'll see. It doesn't feel lived in. It doesn't feel like a home. Speaking of," he glanced at his watch, "we'd better go. Mom said 7pm sharp."

"Hey Mom, we gotta go," I called out, grabbing my purse from the hook by the door. She came around the corner with the vase and placed it on the book shelf next to the purse hook.

"Alright, sweetheart have a good time." She gave me a tight squeeze and then moved in on Tyler. He welcomed it as if he'd never been hugged by a mother before, wrapping his arms around her.

"Wow, that's what I call a hug."

I yanked at his arms. "Okay bye Mom, love you!" I hollered as I opened the door and sped down the stairs.

Tyler's house was the size of a football field. A slight exaggeration sure, but that's what it felt like as we rolled down the long drive to his estate. I'd always thought Jillian's house was huge, but Tyler's Kardashian sized house made hers look like a yurt. I wasn't sure my jaw would ever close. We parked next to his mom's cherry red Jaguar. Of course, she drove a Jag. I mean, why wouldn't she? Tyler opened my door and held out his arm for me as we walked up the stone steps leading to his front door. Inside the foyer was like literally being inside one of the houses from that old show about the rich and the famous. The floors were stunning, swirls of gold and cream that sparkled when the light hit it at certain angles. Across from the entrance was a set of ivory chairs, and above that was a family portrait. The perfect nuclear family dressed alike in deep maroon and grey sweaters; blonde hair perfectly styled not a single fly-away. Crisp white smiles, the kind that take up the entire face. I was so enthralled with the portrait that I didn't notice Mrs. Ashford descending the stairs to the left of me.

"Miss Adams, how wonderful it is to see you again," she said in her sing-song pompous voice that made me want to hurl. I plastered on my best smile, released my grip from Tyler's arm and met Mrs. Ashford at the bottom step, my hand outstretched. She regarded it with something akin to disgust but accepted it nonetheless, sliding her long fingers into my hand but not squeezing or shaking at all. Then Alexander came down the stairs, stopping behind his mom. He leaned against the rail, arms folded across his chest, a disgruntled look on his face.

"Alexander, I believe you know your brother's girlfriend, Margo Adams." He turned up his lip, jumped down the last few stairs and brushed past me.

"Sup weird Indie girl," he said as he passed. Tyler opened his mouth to say something but a set of doors flew open and out came his dad, the buttons on his white shirt undone, a lavender colored dish towel draped over his shoulder. His smile was welcoming and sincere, a complete contrast to the bitchy one always super-glued to his wife's face.

"Ah, Margo you're here, welcome! I've heard so much about you." He wiped a hand on the towel and extended it to me. His grasp was firm and his shake strong.

"I hope you like tapas. I don't get in the kitchen much with my busy schedule, but when I can I love making tapas." There was something about the way his eyes twinkled when he smiled, so warm and welcoming that made me wonder why on earth he was even married to Mrs. Ashford.

"Yes, of course I love tapas."

"Great!" he beamed. "Dinner will be ready soon; I'm just working with Alma on the finishing touches. Tyler why don't you give her the grand tour. Xander, come help me in the kitchen." He winked and turned back to the kitchen. Alexander rolled his eyes as he followed his dad behind the double doors. Mrs. Ashford came to stand beside Tyler, gently taking him by the elbow.

"Tyler, let's show your guest around, shall we?" He nodded, leading the way past the kitchen doors and into a formal dining room. I'd have preferred for a tour with just Tyler, but something about the grip on his elbow, once gentle but now possessive, made it evident she was coming along.

"The flooring in the foyer is beautiful, Mrs. Ashford," I said.

"Ah, yes. It's Breccia Oniciata." She paused to look at me, as if she expected I'd be too dumb to know what kind of marble it was. Granted, I didn't know a thing about marble flooring, but no way in hell would I give her the satisfaction. She continued, pointing out various paintings on the walls, sure to indicate that they were all the original. The living room housed two gunmetal grey oversized couches and the biggest television I'd ever seen. It was like Barney's TV in *How I Met Your Mother*. We were still rocking a boxy 16-inch television that required a good five to ten seconds of "warming up" before the volume could be adjusted. I ran a hand along the backside of one of the couches as we passed, the material soft underneath my fingers. Mrs. Ashford noticed and said, "These couches were specially made and imported from Italy. They truly are the most comfortable thing."

"Mom, she really doesn't care where the couches come from," Tyler said. She smirked, shrugging her shoulders. We climbed a different set of stairs to the second floor where there were five bedrooms, each with their own on-suits. I couldn't even imagine what it would be like to have my own bathroom. We'd only ever had one bathroom, which is fine now with it just being Mom and me, but for as awesome as Nate was, sharing a bathroom with him was gross because teenage boys are gross, enough said.

We went back downstairs and then out through a set of French doors leading to the backyard where I was shown to the outdoor summer kitchen, the pool, the hot tub, and the stables, because if it isn't enough to have a huge ass house, they also had their own horses. Past the stables was a small apple orchard, which really wasn't small by any means but I was told by her royal highness that it was in fact, as far as apple orchards go, very small. As we were about to press on, the watch on Mrs. Ashford's wrist chimed.

"Looks like dinner is ready. I'm going to go freshen up and meet you in the formal dining. Don't be long."

"Yes Mom," Tyler said.

When I was sure she was out of ear shot I grabbed Tyler by the arm, squeezing. He looked at me confused, and then cracked a smile.

"Dude, what the hell? You never said anything about having horses, or your own apple orchard."

"Psssh this? Nah. It's just a bunch of trees that bear fruit. Hardly anything worth mentioning."

"Yeah, and the horses?"

"What horses?"

I shook my head at him, looping my arm through his as he led me back into the house.

"This place truly is amazing, Ty."

"It's okay I guess," he shrugged.

"It's more than okay. It's beautiful. The stable, the furniture, the freaking marble floors, I can't believe you live here."

"Like I said, it's huge and it's home, but it doesn't feel homey. It's a statement piece for my mom. There's not a thing in there that wasn't custom made or imported. Believe me, your house is so much better."

I'd never really been a jealous person. I'd accepted early on in life that people were always going to be better off than me, have bigger houses, better cars, fancier clothes, fatter bank accounts. I was comfortable with what I did have mainly because I had my friends who loved me and reassured me of my worth. And I was okay with that. But seeing Tyler's massive estate, and how he brushed it off, how he felt MY pathetic cottage was better than all this, well let's just say that ugly little green-eyed monster was itching to rear its head.

The formal dining room table looked like it was a page torn from a copy of *Home and Garden* magazine. Cerulean blue square porcelain salad plates were placed on top of matching dinner plates, gold cloth napkins folded in to triangles on top. Three different forks were lined up on the left side of the plate while on the right were two knives and two spoons, also varying in size. I was legit having a *Downton Abbey* dinner and it was freaking me out. I was ninety-nine percent sure that I would use the wrong fork at the wrong time and it would be all the more reason for Mrs. Ashford to disapprove of me. I could see her now gabbing about it with her little Sunday fun-day brunch friends. In between sips of her pinot she'd say, *"Oh and then the poor girl used a fish fork to eat her salad. A FISH FORK!"* What the hell even is a fish fork??? There was absolutely no way I was going to make it through this dinner without screwing up.

Tyler pulled out a seat for me and then took the one next to me. I grabbed his leg and leaned into him. "What the hell am I supposed to do with all these forks?" I whispered.

"You'll be fine. Just work your way in." What the heck did that mean?

His parents sat at either end of the table leaving Alexander to slump into a seat across from Tyler. His face still regarded me with a moderate level of distain and no matter how many times I smiled at him or asked how he was doing, it didn't get any better. Prior to entering the dining room, Tyler pulled him aside and whispered something into his ear but he responded by shoving out of his way with his shoulder.

Once seated various platters were brought out by kitchen staff and served onto our plates in courses. I'd never eaten any meal in courses. We were firm believers in grabbing a fork and hoovering over the pot. This was just bananas. Tyler probably ate like this nightly, with fancy plates, cloth napkins, and people serving him. Sometimes we didn't even have napkins at home so we used dish towels

"How are you liking everything, Margo?" Mr. Ashford asked.

I finished the bite in my mouth, washed it down with the water from my goblet, and dabbed my mouth. "Everything is wonderful, Mr. Ashford. I especially like these bread thingies," I held up one of the slices of toasted bread with some sort of tomato and cheese.

"What kind of cheese is this?"

"That is called Pan con tomate with garrotxa cheese. It's a Catalan goat cheese. I'm glad you like it. It can be an acquired taste."

"Probably better than the government cheese she's used to," Alexander snarked and then yelped as Tyler kicked him under the table. Mrs. Ashford brought her glass of wine to rest at her lips, hiding her smile. His comment stung but I did my best to not let it show. Instead, I took a bite of the garlic shrimp and said, "This shrimp is delicious. I love garlic."

"Our cook is from Spain," Mrs. Ashford said. "Well, her family is. I think she was born here. Anyway, most of what she makes for us is infused with something from her country. She teaches Mr. Ashford here and there, indulges his need for a cooking hobby."

"Please, I spend over 60 hours a week in surgery. I need a release and cooking relaxes me. Plus, you've never once complained."

"Tell me Margo, what are your hobbies? What do you like to do for fun, when you're not busy slaving away at the bookstore that is?" Mrs. Ashford asked, probably trying to find something to throw in my face, use against me in her case for why her son shouldn't date me.

"Well, I like to listen to music and go to concerts, and I like to run."

"Are you on the cross country team?"

"Yes, and the track team. We've actually just begun practices this week."

"That's great, dear. I myself don't really see any point to such sports, ones that are just running and nothing else. There's no skill involved, not like with basketball," she said nodding at Tyler, "but to each their own. What matters is you enjoy it."

"I do. Very much so."

"Margo is one of the fastest runners on the varsity team, Mom," Tyler said. "And Andy said she'll for sure go to State in track this year." I glanced at him, completely taken by surprise. I wasn't aware that he and Andy talked about me enough for my running to come up. Then again, they are best friends so it would only be natural to talk about their girlfriends, right? Besides, Andy is the team captain of the distance runners. So he'd know I guess.

"So, do you do any other activities at school, Margo? Key club? Leadership? National Honors Society?"

"Nope. Just cross country and track. I really don't have much time to join afterschool clubs. I work after school most days."

"Such a shame. Colleges like to see extra-curriculars."

"It's okay Mom, she'll get in on scholarships anyway, you know, for being poor," Alexander said between bites. Tyler kicked him again. "What? You know that's how she's going to Marshall. Mom said she's on an alumni scholarship. Those are for the poor kids."

"Alexander..." Mr. Ashford coughed but I put up a hand to stop him.

"No, it's okay. Yes, I am on an alumni scholarship. Yes, I am poor by your standards. I live in a small cottage, I drive a crummy car, and I work more hours than I should. But I'm not ashamed of who I am."

Tyler grabbed my hand under the table and squeezed. It was taking all that was within me not to cry, but Alexander wasn't ready to give up. Cocking his head to the side and baring his teeth he continued.

"Hey didn't your brother try to off himself? That's why he's in that rehab isn't he?"

"Alexander James that's enough!" Mr. Ashford yelled, rising to his feet and tossing his napkin onto the table. Alexander's eyes widened then looked to his mother for backup, but she had zero interest in doing anything other than pouring another glass of wine. Accepting he'd not receive help from her, he pouted his lips and crossed his arms.

"What's the big deal? She doesn't belong here! I don't know why you're all pretending like you're okay with Tyler dating her."

Tyler released his grip on my hand, slowly pushed his chair out and stood up, puffing out his chest before leaning across the table onto his knuckles. "Choose your next words carefully, little brother."

"Or else what? You gonna beat me up too like you did Blake?"

"If I have to."

Mrs. Ashford slapped a hand down on the table, our glasses shaking under the vibration.

"That is enough from both of you. I'll not have you attempting to fight one another at the dinner table."

"Are you just going to let him sit there and insult my girlfriend?" Tyler seethed.

"Alexander is just speaking his mind, Tyler," she said, glancing at me before bringing her glass to her lips and taking a drink. I fought the urge to whack the glass out of her hand. "He's entitled to his opinions just as you are yours. No need to be sensitive."

I felt nauseous and hot and I wanted to get the hell out of here before I could be insulted any more. I pulled my napkin from my lap, placed it on the table and stood up.

"I think I'd better go now. Mr. and Mrs. Ashford, thank you for inviting me to dinner. The food was wonderful."

Tyler pulled my chair out of the way and placed a hand on the small of my back. "I'm taking her home," he said. He ushered me out of the dining room; I could feel their eyes on us as we left. Mr. Ashford opened his mouth to say something, but snapped it shut at the sound of Mrs. Ashford clearing her throat. Tyler yanked my coat off a hook by the door and helped me into it. He grabbed his and shoved his arms in, and just before grabbing the door handle, he shook his head, mumbled for me to hang on, then marched back into the dining room. I couldn't hear what was said, mostly in part to the closed door but also because my ears were still ringing form the verbal assault and my brain was having a difficult time processing. Tyler stormed back into the foyer, face beet red and brows firmly set. He yanked open the front door and ushered me out.

The ride home was quiet, just the hum of the I-5 and the gentle whirl of the heat coming out of the vents. I pressed my face against the window, the cool of the glass comforting. Tonight sucked. There was no doubt about it. Linz would have served me a big steaming bowl of I-told-you-so if I told her. I won't, though. Tell her that is. What would be the point? I'd been insulted before. When I transferred, I didn't have a license and my mom couldn't drive me to school every so I had to take the city bus. No one at Marshall took a city bus, so yeah, nothing said "girl from felony flats" more than riding a city bus to school. I learned fairly quick to develop thick skin. But tonight, the looks that killed from Mrs. Ashford and the full-on assault from Alexander, I was afraid to admit how much it had hurt. Worse than that though, how did Alexander find out about Nate? Had Tyler totally broken my confidences and told him? We were moments from the freeway exit. I couldn't end the night without knowing.

"Did you tell him?" I asked, my voice catching. Tyler turned to look at me, his face still screwed up into a scowl.

"Tell who what?" he asked.

"Did you tell your brother about Nate?"

He tilted his head, eyes softening but hurt. "No, Margo, of course I didn't tell him."

"Then how did he find out?"

"I don't know," he said. "Probably my mom since she seems to know everyone's business. I mean, it wouldn't have been hard for her to sweet talk one of the nurses at the rehab facility into telling her what his story was. She's a real "see you next Tuesday" but people generally don't figure that out until later."

Of course. Leave it to Amanda Ashford to go around the facility asking questions just to be a bitch. If that was the case though, someone sure did risk a lot because I'm pretty sure there's a whole HIPPA issue, and I know it wouldn't have been Sari. She'd never betray us like that. I felt bad for even assuming it was Tyler that said anything. I placed my hand on his arm. He tensed but then eased, crossing his left arm over to touch my hand with his.

"I'm so sorry about tonight," he said. "I really thought they'd be different. Alexander isn't usually such a dick."

"He's clearly a mamma's boy," I said.

"Big time. And my dad, well he doesn't generally tolerate Mom and her antics but ever since she became Counsel woman Ashford and started acting like she was the shit, he's backed off, focused on work and his hobbies."

We pulled up to the curb next to my house and parked. I was so disappointed the night hadn't gone well, not because I'd been burned, but because Tyler had put so much faith in his family and tried so hard but in the end, I wasn't the only one who'd been hurt. I unbuckled my seatbelt, slid as far as I could in my seat closer to him and gently placed both hands on his cheeks, turning his head so we were face to face. The blue of his eyes still so bright and vivid even in the dimly lit car. I didn't know what the future held for us, if his mom would ever accept me. But he'd defended me and I knew it would cost him.

"I love you, Tyler Ashford," I said, feeling my body freeze up. What if he didn't love me back and I'd said the three most powerful words for nothing? I scanned his face, searching for any sign that he was going to chuck me out of the car and speed away, but instead he pulled my hands away from his face and moved in, pressing his lips to mine soft and gentle. Then he brought his lips to my ear and whispered, "I love you more," and then he returned to my lips and kissed me again, this time full and deep, shooting hot sizzling sparks all through my body.

15

— · —

The summer after I transferred, Jillian would invite me over to her house for sleepovers every other weekend. At first, I wasn't into it. In my mind sleepovers were meant for twelve-year-old girls, not sixteen-year-old's. Also, I'd never actually *been* to a sleepover before since I wasn't ever close enough with anyone growing up to do the whole sleepover thing.

So, the first few weekends were super uncomfortable and I didn't sleep at all, but Jillian and her family were so warm and cheerful, eventually I looked forward to the weekend sleepovers. Junior year when I started working and Jillian got busy with dance, we swapped sleepovers for movie nights once a month and got Donny and Linz involved as well. We'd rent a couple movies, buy Costco size bags of Doritos (no one else shared in my love of Funyuns so I relented and went with my second fave, for the good of everyone else) and Dr. Pepper, and holed up in Jillian's family room, under mounds of blankets and plush floor pillows.

The movie rule was we watched a scary movie to satisfy Linz and Jillian's love of the horror genre, and would follow it up next movie night with a cheesy rom-com for me and Donny. It was difficult for me to get through a horror film without thinking about Nate, so I usually scrolled through my phone until Linz would start to grumble, and then I'd find excuses to go into the kitchen. Of course, I could have just told them why I didn't watch horror movies anymore, and they'd have totally understood, but it was just easier to let them assume I was a scaredy-cat.

Rom-coms weren't exactly my favorite, but I was the only in the group who liked art house films, and Donny didn't like anything without a love story. It was fine, I mean, rom-coms are cute and all but they are totally ridiculous. Who says they're in love after only just meeting and spending exactly ten days together? That's not love, that's infatuation. The one with the old people was sort of believable in that the couple fought just as much as they got along. Not that I'd had much experience with healthy relationships, but I'd been told that if you're not fighting at least a little it's not real. So far, *You've Got Mail* had been the most believable because it wasn't just overnight that they fell in love. There was time for those feelings to develop. Infatuation will either dissipate or develop into love depending on how long it took for a person to reveal all sides of themselves and whether or not the other person was willing to accept all those sides. Like, how much can you actually know about a person until you've seen them at their worst, their absolute ugliest?

So when we'd spend our weekends stuffing our faces and watching these movies I'd roll my eyes as Donny would swoon. But then I met Tyler and we'd said those three words that changed everything. Changed how I felt about love, how I felt about relationships, how I now appreciated the sentiment of these movies because for the two weeks since the "the dinner from Hell", since Tyler told me he loved me and we'd spent every day together, I felt like I was living in one of those romance movies.

We hadn't had a movie night since Christmas because of all of our work schedules (and my wanting to spend all my free time with Tyler), but I could tell we needed to get together so we went with a mid-week movie night. A coin toss decided on horror.

"Alright bitches," Donny said, flicking on the Roku and opening Netflix. "I'm peeved that we have to watch a horror movie, but Linz's brother said we have to watch *Veronica* because it's probably the scariest movie he's ever seen."

"I heard that the movie was so scary people were turning it off halfway through. Like it's scarier than *The Ring* was," I said, securing my spot in the middle of the oversized maroon sofa.

Jillian smiled maniacally and rubbed her hands together. "I know! I'm so excited. I've wanted to watch this for, like, ever."

"Jilly, it's been on Netflix for months now. Why haven't you watched it already? Thought you lived and breathed horror films?" Linz asked.

"I do! But I didn't want to watch it by myself, in case it was, you know, actually so scary that I had to turn it off. Better to be scared with my bff's than alone."

"Fair enough. So let's get this started." Linz snagged the remove from Donny and pressed play.

Well, we didn't have to turn the movie off completely, but we did have to stop it not once but three times. Linz's brother wasn't lying when he said it was balls scary. The couch cushion would forever have the shape of my nails embedded into it. Even Nate would think it was scary.

When it was over, Donny clicked off the television and stretched. "Well Linz, Jillian, I hope that satisfied your need for all things scary. I declare the next five movie nights to be comedies. No more scary movies."

Just then Jillian, who'd been scrolling on her phone, squealed and squeezed my arm, a smile so big stretched across her face, she looked like the Cheshire cat from *Alice in Wonderland*. "Girl what are you smiling about?" Donny asked.

"I don't know, why don't we ask Margo?"

Three sets of eyes focused on me. I shrugged my shoulders and held up my hands.

"What are you talking about Jilly?" I asked.

"Have you not seen Tyler's Socials?"

"I'm not on Social. You know that. Why? What's wrong with it?" I snatched her phone from her and scrolled. I hated the idea of everybody's business being all over Social, so I'd only ever had an account for one year. After people kept going on and on about my riding the city bus and the things people always said about Donny, I deleted the account. I was probably the only person at Marshall's not digitally chronically online.

Donny wedged himself between me and Jillian to see the contents of the phone as I scrolled Tyler's page. I covered my own cheshire-esk smile with my hand. His entire page was plastered with photos of us. From our dates to the movies, coast trips, our random getaway to the zoo when he'd convinced me to call in sick. Under each picture he'd commented "me and my girl" or "I love this girl."

"So? Spill Margo," Jillian said taking back her phone. I swept my hair over my shoulder and began to braid it. The only other time I'd actually talked about me and Tyler had been when I'd first told them about Tyler and the mood had been quite different.

"I don't know! What do you want me to say?"

"Just how serious is this relationship?" Jillian pressed.

"I mean, how serious is any high school relationship, right?"

"Girl don't play coy," Donny said. "So, are you guys like, in love or whatever?" Linz rolled her eyes at him but then she looked back at me, eyes dripping with anticipation.

I told them about the dinner at his house and how it was a total utter nightmare, how his mom and brother had been huge dicks but then about how sweet and generous Tyler was and how I told him I loved him and he'd said it back.

"And now, I don't know. Every time we see each other it's like there are fireworks but only we can see them. And the way he looks at me, like either in class or from across the room, the way the corner of his eyes crinkle and his lips curl, it's like everyone else fades away and there's only us."

"Wow," Donny swooned. "That's so freaking romantic. It's just like a movie."

"Donny, are you crying?" Linz asked. Sure enough, tears were streaming down his face. He wiped them away and tossed back his hair.

"Shut up, bitches. It's just so beautiful."

Linz rolled her eyes harder this time. One of these days she was going to roll her eyes so hard they'd get stuck up there inside her head.

"You guys are ridiculously sappy, you know that?" Then she looked over at me and did something I never ever thought she'd ever do, let alone be capable of doing. She placed a hand on my knee, smiled up at me and said, "I still think his friends are shits and you're being stupid, but if he makes you happy, I'm glad for you."

We all stared at her, totally not believing that she'd actually said something nice and touched someone in a way that couldn't be considered assault.

"Um, thanks Linz, yeah. I am. Happy. Really, really happy."

"So like, how happy are you?" Donny asked, jerking his eyebrows up and down. It took a moment to register just what he was asking, but once it hit, I felt my cheeks flush and I chucked a pillow at him.

"None of your beeswax!"

"There's no need to be prudish about it, Margo. You're either smashing or you're not. Which is it?" Linz asked, clearly having returned to her normal asshole-ish self.

"No, guys. We haven't had sex yet. Sorry if you were hoping to live vicariously through me."

We'd had some heated make-out sessions in his car or in my car after our dates, but it had never gone any farther, not because we didn't want to. Trust me, I most def wanted to, but I got the feeling he was so worried he'd mess something up by moving too fast and I didn't want to spook him or anything by bringing it up. Besides something like that, something so intimate should come about naturally rather than forced.

"That's alright girl, when it happens it happens. And when it does, I'm sure it will be magical," Donny said whimsically.

"Or it will be really gross and awkward because sex is gross and bodies are gross," Linz said. We all couldn't help but stare. Never not once had Linz ever talked having done anything physical with another person.

"What?" she said, mouth full of Doritos. "My sister told me!" And with that we all laughed so hard it felt as if something had split open.

***

Mr. Dan hated office hours. He'd always said if he ran the school, once the final bell rang, that was it. No teacher-teacher meetings, no teacher-student meetings, definitely no teacher-parent meetings. Nothing. So when he'd stopped me in the halls earlier in the day to say he needed to see me during office hours, I panicked. What could possibly be so important that he'd break his own policy? Also, if he wanted to talk to a student, he preferred to ambush them while they were quietly sitting somewhere, not stopping them and addressing them all formal-like. I was so preoccupied with what Mr. Dan needed to say that I hardly heard a word Tyler said while we were having smoothies at lunch.

"Ok so what are your thoughts on a limo?"

"Huh?"

"A limo. What are your thoughts?"

"Like in general as a mode of transportation? A little ridiculous."

He laughed and slurped from his smoothie. "I meant for Prom night, weirdo," Tyler said, sliding his cup into the cup holder, then scooping up my free hand and bringing it up to his lips.

"Ack. How very stereotypically prom. What's wrong with taking your car?"

"Nothing, I just thought we could go as a group and a limo would be cool."

I narrowed my brow. "Who's group? My group or yours?

"Any chance our groups might call a truce for one night?"

I laughed. "Not even the smallest. I thought we'd just go the two of us.

Truthfully, I hadn't given much thought to Prom since Tyler asked back in February. I'm sure for other girls, Prom night was the highlight of their year, the night to end all nights, THE single even that defines Senior year. Whatever, it just wasn't my thing so no, I hadn't thought about it at all. He'd also asked super early. But it was April and Prom was less than a month away. I needed to attempt to be psyched about it for Tyler because I knew it was a big deal for him.

"Ok so no limo, and no big group. Any strong thoughts on The Electric Station for dinner?"

"Their steak is great."

The rest of the day flew by and the copious amount of sugar in my smoothie kept my brain peppy and alert, and not at all thinking about what Mr. Dan might need to talk about.

When final bell ended, I packed up and headed for Mr. Dan's classroom. I knocked twice before walking in, stopping suddenly at the sight of my mother sitting in one of the chairs at the table across from Mr. Dan. Her lips were in a thin straight line and her hands were clasped so tight in her lap it looked like her fingertips were about to push holes through her knuckles. Mr. Dan mirrored her appearance and the aura in the classroom seemed to be mirroring the both of them, a murky swirl of frustration and disappointment. There was only one reason my mom was in here sharing grumpy faces with Mr. Dan. They both knew, and I was totally screwed.

Mr. Dan cleared his throat and chucked a hunk of chalk at the open chair beside my mother. "Have a seat Miss. Adams."

I looked back at the door, I don't know why, maybe expecting Tyler to be there to whisk me away, or see if I could make a run for it and not totally be pegged by chalk on the way out. Reluctantly I slung my backpack onto the floor and lowered myself down into the chair. I glanced at my mom but she stared ahead at a space beyond Mr. Dan's head. Mr. Dan slammed his elbows onto the table and cradled his chin in his hands, eyes boring into mine like they were trying to see right through my skull, which made him look like some creepy/angry demonic creature.

"So hey, Margo, you're a bright kid, why don't you tell us why we're all here, in my classroom, during office hours."

I had two choices. I could do the smart thing and just tell them the truth. Mom needed to hear it anyway, she needed to know exactly why the tests were important to me. Even if she didn't like it, even if she'd have to give up whatever religious reason she was holding on to, she needed to understand my needs. Mr. Dan would totally get it and he'd forget that I'd lied, and anyway, as far as lies go, really, it wasn't that big of a lie anyway.

My other option was to do the teenage thing and say I had absolutely no idea why my mom was here for office hours and if it was about the assignment I'd promise to do better. Teenagers had been mastering the art of shoulder shrugs, long sighs, and lengthy excuses for years. Mr. Dan would never buy that thought, not from me, but my mom was staring at me with wide eyes and her nostrils were flaring, and Mr. Dan was now tapping his fingers on the desk, waiting for me to answer.

"I don't know what you want me to say."

Mom swiped a hand across her brown. "For fuck's sake Margo."

Mr. Dan held up a hand. "Let's hang on to the expletives for a sec, yeah? We may need them later. Margo, if you knew your mom wasn't going to change her mind, like, ever, you should have just said so."

I snuffed. "Yeah right. For the record I tried to tell you she didn't want the tests. You were the one who insisted."

"That's hardly the case. If you recall you came to me and said she'd changed her mind. Regardless, the position you put us all in was unfair and uncalled for."

"What about the position I have been in?"

"The position you've been put in?" Mom cried. "What possible position have you been put in?"

"Oh, I don't know how about finally having the chance to know if my brother is alive but not being able to because of your stupid religious convictions!"

"Ok first of all, your mom's religious convictions aren't stupid, and secondly, your brother *is* still alive. These tests aren't going to determine that, I mean, that's already a given."

I rolled my eyes. "You know what I mean Mr. Dan."

"Margo, I don't know how many times, in how many different sets of words, in how many languages I need to say this to you to get you to understand. I am not going to allow for these tests."

I crossed my arms over my chest and slunk down into the chair. "See, this is exactly why I lied to Mr. Dan. You only think of yourself and couldn't give a crap at all about what I think. Fine, whatever. I'm sorry that I lied to you Mr. Dan. I really was hoping I'd be able to talk to her before you called her, and I know that's still not an excuse, but I'm sorry."

Mom shifted in her seat. "What about me, huh? Don't you have something to say to me?"

"I don't have anything to say to you."

"Fine. Just so you know you're grounded, for lying."

"Fine," I huffed. "Can I go now? I have homework."

"I think we're about done here," Mr. Dan said. I didn't wait for another word before scooping up my backpack and leaving the classroom, slamming the door behind me.

I'd never been grounded. No matter how many times I had mouthed off, or blared my music, or left my dishes in the sink, my mom had never followed through with any form of punishment. Granted, in the grand scheme of things, I'd probably never done anything that would have warranted a grounding. When Mom had said I was grounded, it sounded like she choked on the unfamiliarity of the words as they came out.

Nate pretty much spent every summer grounded for some reason or another but the thing about Nate was that he excelled at getting Mom to forget she'd grounded him. The way he'd pay her compliments- *"Mom you look good today, is that a new shirt?"* the extra chores he'd do around the house- *"Mom I know it wasn't my week to do the dishes but I did them for you"*, how quickly he'd go from grounded to hanging out with his friends in a second.

Doing anything that would be construed as stepping out of line was accompanied by a strong sense of fear. What would I lose, what books or amount of TV time would be taken from me if I did something wrong? Would I miss The Decemberists play? I suppose I never saw a need for it, to be disobedient. There'd never been any wild parties I'd wanted to attend (not that I'd have been invited anyway), my friends never wanted to sneak into clubs or anything. Asking permission, calling every hour if I was going to be at a show late, it just seemed like a way better idea than the alternative. So, I'd managed to avoid a grounding my whole life. It felt weird, to be grounded. When Mom came home a few hours after I did, she sat down with me at the table and quickly laid down the rules of my - no hanging out with my friends after school, no talking to Tyler at the rehab center, and cleaning Sir Rusty's litter box daily which was dumb because I already did that anyway.

Tyler texted me five times throughout the night. It was after ten pm before I could text him back.

> ME: hey. Sorry. My mom's been hovering

> TYLER: There you are! WTF? Are you okay?

> ME: Not really. Mom found out about the lie. She grounded me. Can't hang out with anyone.

TYLER: Wow that sucks! I'm sorry, babe.

ME: Yeah. Me too. She's never been good at sticking to a grounding, I think it will blow over. Maybe. Hopefully. Can't see you at the Rehab anymore. Just school.

TYLER: It's ok. We'll be ok. Love you.

ME: Love you.

News Flash, it didn't blow over. For some reason, Mom was super ultra-focused, not just with her daily routine, but with everything to do with me. Oh, and she was also hell-bent on sticking to her word. I even tried to slip past her last weekend to meet up with my friends for a concert but that didn't work. She'd been preoccupied in the kitchen baking cookies for work (something she's never ever done before) and I tried to lift my keys from the hook but as if she had eyes and ears in the back of her head, she said, "If you're trying to sneak out of here, you really suck at it, and also it's not gonna happen."

She'd also been hovering. She wanted to know who I was texting every time I was on my phone, *what* I was texting, checked all my homework, and at the rehab center she'd only give me five minutes to walk to the visitor lounge to grab a snack and get straight back. I hated this version of my mom.

When Nate was awake, for lack of better word, she exhausted so much of her time being all over him, checking his phones, arguing with him about curfews, trying to make sure he wasn't getting into trouble, for all the good it did. I had basically been able to skate by unnoticed. Then for the past two years she'd been the checked-out kind of mom, but now she was back to being the helicopter mom and it was all focused on me and it was super frustrating. I know that it was my doing, had I left things alone I'd never have gotten grounded and she'd not be monitoring me like I were a felon.

School was the only place I had room to breathe, and the only place I was free to see my friends. I really missed spending time with Tyler. We tried to go off campus for lunch every day, but as if the Fates had it out for me as well, that quickly changed.

"My mom is making me do the Mr. Spartan pageant," he said after taking a bite from his Quarter Pounder. I dredged my fry through some ketchup and popped it into my mouth. The Mr. Spartan pageant was basically like Miss America but for high school senior boys and it was put on by Children's Miracle Center in order to raise money for the neonatal unit at local hospitals. All of the high schools in the area competed. Marshall Academy was Mr. Norseman, Crescent Grove had Lion King, Valley Central had Mr. Irish. You get the picture. Usually, it was the popular boys who were voted as contestants, and they performed a number of skits, talked about their experiences touring the neonatal unit, and charmed their way into donor's wallets. The strapping young lad who raised the most money AND exhibited the most character was declared the winner by a panel of Judges. No trophy or moon man, just bragging rights.

"Okay. You don't want to do it?" I asked.

"Not really. I mean, I'm all for supporting the babies, but I think she's just forcing me to do it because she and my dad are on the board of CMC, and it looks good to have her pride and joy as a contestant." He took a sip from his drink. Was there anything in this town his parents didn't have their hands in?

"Also, I think she's doing it because she knows it means you and I will spend less time together."

I hadn't spoken to Mrs. Ashford since the craptastic dinner. She'd walked by the bookstore a few times with some of her minions but never dared to come in. She did though flash the most epic resting bitch face at me through the window one time while I was stocking shelves with a coworker.

"Margo, why is Counsel Woman Ashford glaring at us?" my co-worker had asked.

"Ugg not us, just me. She's glaring at me." I'd then went on to explain to said co-worker how much of an uptight B with an itch she was but they were disinclined to believe me, declaring her to be awesome. Wolf in sheep's clothing was more like it.

I dredged another fry through ketchup. "What do you mean it will make us spend less time together?" I asked.

"Well, until the pageant ends, I have to spend my lunches with the rest of the contestants and the organizers, and after school at various locations getting donations, touring the NICU, doing charity events. The week leading up to the actual pageant I'm basically living at the school doing rehearsals."

This sucked. I thought we'd be able to spend all our lunches together, kind of as our dates since we weren't going to be able to see each other outside of school.

"So, you won't even be able to come see me at work?" I asked.

He shook his head. "Probably not. Mom says every free moment will be spent doing this. Coach pretty much had to beg her to let me squeeze in gym time. The only reason she agreed is because she knows it's important for scholarships and such that I keep up with playing club ball."

"Have you heard back yet? From any of the schools you applied to?" I asked.

He didn't answer right away. Instead he took a last bite of his hamburger, chewing slowly, like his jaw only masticated at one speed. When he finished, he crumpled his wrapper and dumped it onto the tray.

"I was accepted to all of them," he finally said.

"All of them? How many did you apply to?"

"Three on the east coast, three on the west coast, and a few somewhere in the middle."

"Damn. That's insane, but also pretty crazy you were accepted into all of them. Why don't you sound happy about that?"

"Because I don't know which ones accepted me because of my academic achievements or because of how much money my mom promised them." He rose up, slid the tray off the table and walked the few steps to the trash can, dumping the contents of the tray and then returning.

"You really think she offered money?"

"Oh I don't think it, Margo. I know she did. It's what they do, rich people. They promise to give huge endowments, be a benefactor if you accept their kid." He crossed his arms tightly across his chest.

"What are you going to do? Which school are you thinking of responding to or will your mom be selecting that for you?" It had been meant to come out sounding like a joke, but there was no hiding the thick layer of distain. I knew it wasn't his fault that his mom was the way she was. I suspected there was always a part of him that feared if he acted out too much, she'd cut him off completely, and then he'd have to fend for himself.

"What about you? You hear back yet?" he asked.

"I'm sure I'll hear soon. It's still early April."

"Well, I'm sure you'll get in. I still think you should consider UCLA just as much as U of O."

"You know why I couldn't, Ty." Now that there was no chance of Mom letting the tests happen, I knew for certain I couldn't go to school out of state. If he woke up, by some amazing miracle, I needed to be close.

Tyler dumped my tray. "Should we head back?" he asked. I nodded and pushed back form the table. This was probably our last lunch date and already I felt the sadness creeping in.

"How are we going to make this work if we'll barely be able to see each other? We only have one class together," I said. He took my hand in his and squeezed.

"We'll make it work, M. Trust me, we will."

16
— • —

I used to love going to psychology class, but ever since the whole teacher-parent gang up on Margo meeting, Mr. Dan had refused to look me in the eyes. Before the start of class while everyone was filing in and taking their seats, I stopped beside him at the chalk board and waited for him to talk to me, but he just acted like I wasn't there. He kept scribbling some junk about learning and memory

"I think you meant to write seven," I said. He twisted his head at me, a sour look on his face, then back at the board.

"What?" he growled.

"Miller's short term memory magic number. It' seven, not six. The capacity of short-term memory is like, seven bits of information." Ordinarily he enjoyed when I acted like a showy know-it-all, but today he looked more annoyed than I'd ever seen him.

"Oh. Yeah, thanks," he mumbled, erasing the word six with the sleeve of his sweater and scribbling in a seven. When he didn't say anything else, I walked to my desk and slid in. Donny kicked the back of my desk.

"He looked really pissed at you, girl. What happened?"

"I kinda messed up, lied about my mom wanting to allow for some tests to be done on my brother.

He stared at me, mouth agape. "Damn girl."

"Damn girl is correct. My mom grounded me for it too. I can't hang out with you guys, I can't hang out with Tyler, all I can do is go to school, go to work, and go to track practice. Oh and Mr. Dan basically hates me now, so there's also that."

Linz clacked her pen against her desk. "So you keep secrets and you lie to authority figures. Guess there's a lot we don't really know about you Mar."

It felt like she'd sliced through me with a knife, and what's worse is I didn't know if it were her words or the fact that she was absolutely correct that hurt the most. From the moment I transferred and was welcomed into their little circle, I'd done nothing but keep secrets, and now I was adding lies onto it, even if it had only been a small lie.

"That was super harsh, Linz," Jillian said.

"It's okay, Jilly. She's right."

Mr. Dan cleared his throat beckoning our attention to the front of the class. "Alright. Let's get started. So here's what's happening. Your papers on *The Grey Zone* are due in two weeks. I want empirical studies people. Nothing from Wikipedia. It doesn't count. And it needs to be in APA, not MLA. Also, I was hoping to have had an opportunity to assist in a similar test with a local subject," he paused and looked directly at me in a way that totally made my spine stiffen, "-but there's been a change in plans. So just make sure your papers are completed and ready to hand in. And I expect stellar group reports. I'll have group sign ups next week."

When class was over, I waited around until the room cleared to talk to Mr. Dan. I couldn't go the rest of the year having him be pissed at me. As he picked up the eraser to clean the board, he sighed a deep belly sigh.

"What is it now, Adams?"

"Um yeah, I just wanted to say, again, that I'm really sorry I lied and for whatever position that put you in with my mom and also with your old professor or whatever. I'm sorry."

Setting down the eraser in a plume of white chalk dust, he sat on the edge of his desk and rubbed his pinky and thumb through his eyebrows leaving a dusting of chalk.

"You have no idea how humiliated I was. To speak to your mom on the phone, to have her screaming on the other end of the line, not once, but twice. I felt like a freaking idiot, and I'm sure she must have felt the same. It really sucked, kid."

"I know, it's just, you were super sad about your breakup and I felt bad for you, thought you needed a win. I thought I'd be able to convince my mom to change her mind before you had the chance to call her but I kept chickening out."

"Wait, that's why you did it? Because you felt bad for me?"

"Well sort of. I mean, you seemed really pumped about getting the opportunity to do the tests, and I really just...I know that the chances of Nate waking up decrease the longer he remains in a coma, but if your tests were able to prove that he can understand what we say to him, then I could tell him I was sorry for what I said to him the day before he...the day before he shot himself."

I didn't know when I'd stated crying but Mr. Dan reached over to yank a couple tissues out of the box on his desk. I wiped my face and slunk down into the chair by his desk. I hadn't intended to open up and basically bare my soul to Mr. Dan. It's not that I didn't trust him, or felt uncomfortable unloading this all on him, it's just I couldn't even admit all this to my own mother, or the group of people I called my best friends, but there was just something pulling within me, like my whole system was finally saying enough is enough and before I knew it, I was telling him everything.

"My brother was super messed up. I mean he was dating a girl who basically got him hooked on drugs and he fell for her hard but she was bad news. She strung him along and they kept breaking up and getting back together, and every time it happened you could just see him getting worse and worse. I just knew if she stayed in his life it was going to ruin him. I kept telling him to break up with her for good but he said he needed her. Then after she dumped him for the last time, I told him not to try to get back together with her because she was this piece of trash and he was gonna be trash too. We got into this huge fight about it and the next day he went all psycho in the convenience store by our house, shot himself in front of the clerk, and I can't stop blaming myself."

"Margo, your brother suffered from a mental illness that had nothing to do with you."

"Yeah, but if I hadn't tried so hard to get him to break up with Khali, if I'd been more supportive of him, maybe he wouldn't have felt he had to kill himself. I should have been a better sister. That's why I need him to wake up so I can tell him how sorry I am and know that he understands what I'm saying."

"Have you told this to your mom?"

"Yeah right. She's so focused on her own making amends with Jesus that she won't even listen to what I have to say."

"I think you should give her more credit than that, kid."

"You don't know her, Mr. Dan."

"Fair point. Still, you're both trying to grieve and figure this stuff out in your own way, but it's still super important for you guys to communicate. No matter what she's dealing with inside, you should still tell her how you feel. This is a lot to carry on your shoulders.

"It's not gonna make her change her mind about the test."

"Maybe not," he said. "But kiddo, it's not about the test, it's about you and your mom and understanding that you're both blaming yourselves for things that neither of you had any control over, and once you both let go of that, I'm not saying things will be better, but maybe you'll be able to understand each other a little better."

I cried for several more minutes, using up all the tissues left in the box, and when that was empty, I used my sleeve. Thankfully Mr. Dan just sat there, and he didn't even look grossed out at all every time I ran my snotty nose across my arm, or the fact that I was sure my face looked like a freaking blow fish.

When I had cried to the point it felt like I couldn't possibly have any more tears left in me, Mr. Dan gave me the biggest bear hug ever and then after sending Coach Kathy a text telling her I wasn't going to make it to track practice, I drove up to Skinner's Butte.

***

The rest of April played out like one gigantic suck-fest. Between the tension between me and Mom at home, and school crap, it felt like the world was against me and there was absolutely no silver-lining.

Even though I'd smoothed things over with Mr. Dan, he was still treading lightly around me. No more jokes, no more stopping me at his desk before class just to talk about life. I know I'd really taken advantage of his trust and he was probably trying to keep himself guarded, and rightfully so, but it kinda hurt.

At home, Mom was somehow avoiding me like the plague *and* riding my ass, which I didn't even know was actually possible. She asked a million questions about my school-work, wanted my work schedule printed out and taped to the refrigerator, and was having weekly calls with Coach Kathy about how practice was going. She'd gone from a free-range parent to a quasi-helicopter parent. It probably would have been okay, this whole change in parental tactic, under normal circumstances I might have actually enjoyed having a super present mother, but unless it was about one of those three areas of my life, she didn't want to talk to me much. I missed the mom from my first dinner with Tyler's family, how playful she was. There was a saying, something like trust has to be earned and it was clear that whatever trust I'd earned from her I'd lost hard core. A few times I tried to tell her about the stuff Mr. Dan and I talked about, but I couldn't get over my stupid inability to communicate.

I was also still grounded, which sucked. I really did think it was going to blow over and that she'd forget. Even when I tore a page out of Nate's book and tried to do extra chores, or complimented her on her outfit or hair, it just breezed right by her and I was still grounded. Every time I'd ask for how long I'd just get the shoulder shrug. I was lucky she was even letting me continue to go to track practice since it would interfere with me going to the rehab center on Tuesdays, but Coach told her she was grooming me for State, so Mom relented begrudgingly. I just had to make sure to go visit Nate on Saturdays before work.

At school I saw even less of Tyler than I thought I would. It seemed that every day there was some other Mr. Spartan event or activity that he needed to be involved in. I tried not to take it out on him, I knew if given the choice he wouldn't do the pageant, but then I'd see him smile and laugh with people, really play up the part and I'd get upset, convince myself that in truth he *was* enjoying the pageant and would rather do that than spend lunches with me.

"You're being totally crazy," Tyler said to me one day in the student lounge. There was a 15-minute school-wide break after third period.

Kids who were higher up on the popularity food chain hung out in the student lounge. Tyler and I sat knee to knee in one of the plush but well used sofas. Blake, Alexander, and a handful of senior girls milled around the other couches, both Blake and Alexander alternating glares in our direction.

"Don't call me crazy, you know I hate that term. I'm not being crazy."

"Alright, you're not being crazy, but you *are* making assumptions that are false. Look, I've told you a kajillion times that I don't want to do the pageant but I have to, and I have to look like I'm enjoying it. But trust me," he pulled my hand up to his lips and kissed it, "I'd much rather be sneaking away with you." He flashed his boyish grin and I caved. That smile that got me every time.

"How's the pageant been going anyway? How's Blake been?"

"He's been a huge dick like usual. Making the whole damn thing about himself and straight up refusing to work with me. We were supposed to be partnered off for this weird dance segment but he pitched the biggest fit. When I tried to tell him to calm down, he sucker-punched me."

"For real? Jeesh."

"Yeah and even though I was the one who got attacked my mom still sided with him basically. She said I needed to be more of a team player."

As if he could tell we were talking about him, Blake rose from the couch and strutted over to us.

"Talking shit about me to your girlfriend, Ty?"

"Get bent, Blake," Tyler responded, releasing my hand and stepping up to him. Blake turned an unflattering shade of red, balled his fists up. Before he could make any move, Andy slid in between them.

"Let's all just take a chill pill, alright? At least wait until after the pageant to pound each other's faces." Blake relaxed his arms, smirked and backed up. Tyler kept his stance, chest still puffed out.

"Yeah alright," Blake said, returning to the couch just as the bell rang. He tapped Alexander on the arm and he got up too, following Blake out of the room like a sad puppy, but not before turning back and flipping us off.

"I take it things are still pretty messed up between you and Alexander?" Andy asked.

"Yeah he's turned into such a little jerk. Worships the ground Blake walks on," Tyler said, slouching back beside me on the couch.

"It's not gonna last. He'll get tired of Blake bossing him around, eventually."

Tyler shrugged. "Maybe, maybe not. Doesn't matter. He's still the golden boy at home so it doesn't matter how big of a jerk he is."

I rubbed Tyler's back and leaned into him a second before getting up and straightening my t-shirt. "Alright boys, I gotta head to fourth."

"Want me to walk you?" Tyler asked.

"No, I'm ok. It's all the way across campus anyway." I pecked him on the cheek, waved goodbye to Andy and left.

The only decent thing about April was that I was doing extremely well during track practice and at the meets. This year I'd decided to run 800 meter as a warm up and finish it off with the 3000-meter, which Coach Cathy was ecstatic about.

"I think this has been good for you, to do both of these events instead of just the 3000. I really think you will do great with both of these at Districts, even have a shot at State."

"State? You really think so?" I asked, sipping from my water bottle.

"Oh yeah absolutely," she said, tossing the whistle back and forth in her hands. "I wasn't messing around when I told your mom I think you could go all the way, but you're not gonna be able to flake and skip practices like you did with cross country."

"You don't have to worry about that. I can be one hundred percent committed. I made sure that I am only scheduled to work the late evening shifts during the week, and I'm grounded for the next century so I can't go hang out with friends. That means every day after school I'm all yours."

"Good because I need you to step up and do the 4 x 400 meter as well."

My jaw hit the track faster than I could catch it. I did NOT run relays. I hated the pressure, the need for coordination, the possibility of running the third leg!

"Wait what? Coach, I'm not really the relay type. I mean, I told you about my baton pass freshman year. It was mortifying."

Freshman year track I ran not only the 3000 meters but also the 800, the 400, and for kicks the 4 x 400 relay. I figured since I ran the 800 meter and 400 meter in middle school the relay would be easy-peasy. There couldn't be much to handing off a stick, I mean, it's not like there was math involved. Yeah, I sucked. Hardcore. We came in last every race because our timing (my timing) was way off, and the last race of the year I was so frustrated I basically hurled the stick at this poor girl hitting her in the back of the head and then tripped on my own feet taking down not one, but four other runners, two of them from Marshall. From then on, I'd stuck with just the 3000 meters.

"That was then. This is now," Coach said. "Look, Margo, I really wouldn't ask you but Ashley can't do it because she broke her ankle jumping a hurtle, trying to show off for some jock straps."

Well that explained it. The past few days I'd seen her hobbling around on crutches, a hot pink cast plastered to her ankle. She'd told everyone she rolled it on a trail run which was a complete joke. Like she'd ever trail run. Well, I couldn't say no to Coach. I'd already been such a jerk earlier in the year.

"Alright, I'll do it."

"Great!" she beamed. "I'll have you practice the stick with Andy. He'll be running third which means all you have to do is bring up the rear."

I sat down by the equipment shed on a blue javelin mat stretching my legs. The weather was perfect. With the partially sunny sky it was warm enough for shorts but just chilly enough for long sleeved shirts. With my thumbs pulling through the hole in the sleeve, I extended myself forward, stretching the inner thighs watching as Andy jogged around the track, stopping when he reached me and taking a seat next to me on the mat.

"What's up, Adams? How's the shoelace treating you?"

"Still there," I said, wiggling my foot, the shoelaces flopping around.

"You ready to practice hand-offs?" He passed the baton back and forth, like Coach did with her whistle.

"Guess so. Just let me change into my spikes." I kicked off my running shoes, pulled out my spikes from my gym bag. They were by far the most expensive thing I'd ever purchased. They were last year's model, but I didn't care. I'd worked every single day of junior year and skipped a Decemberists concert in Jacksonville just to have enough money saved to get these and I'd kept them in pristine condition.

Once my spikes were on, I followed Andy to the starting line where we'd be practicing hand-offs. At first, I was apprehensive with the thought of working with him. Not because I was uncomfortable being around him. It wasn't that at all. Since Tyler and I started dating, I'd hung out with Andy countless times and I saw pretty quickly that he really was a good guy who also had the unfortunate luck of being lumped in a group with Blake. My problem was I knew I sucked with the damn baton and didn't want him to bare witness to it and then tell Tyler how much of an uncoordinated dork I was. I know it sounded silly but it was true.

At the starting line, Andy squared up to me and planted his hands on my shoulders.

"First thing you gotta do is loosen up. Shake these puppies out." He shook my shoulders until I couldn't help but laugh. "Better. Much better. It's like I could feel your apprehension the whole walk over here. Look, in order for me to effectively pass you the baton and for you to accept it, you're gonna need to be loosey-goosey and for us to be simpatico. Make sense?"

I nodded. "Yeah. Got it." I didn't. I hated this already.

"So the trick is, get a good enough feel for where I am in relation to you so that you aren't looking back at me to get the baton. If we do it correctly, I'll be able to get to you as you take off and hand you the baton without any missteps. If you're spending so much time looking back to see where I am, you'll be slow and lose, and we can't have you losing."

"Wow no pressure."

He laughed. "Nah I'm just joshing. You've done this before though right? Didn't you do relay freshman year at your old school?"

Oh crap. How did he know that? "Yeah. And every race was a total shit show."

He paused for a second before his eyes widened and a grin spread across his face. "Oh, that's right. I remember that track meet. You dropped the baton and then tripped like three other runners when you fell. Didn't you also peg someone in the head with the baton?"

"Welp, thanks for the trip down memory lane. Peace out." I turned to leave, totally mortified but he laughed and grabbed my arm.

"I can see why Tyler loves you. You're hilarious, Adams."

Instantly I felt my face flush. "He told you that he loves me?"

"Well yeah. He's my bro. Of course that's something he's gonna tell me."

"What else does he say about me?" It was lame to ask, I knew it, but I couldn't help myself.

"That you're basically like the best thing that's ever happened to him and that he's super bummed that you're grounded." I knew I was grinning like a freaking idiot but I couldn't help it.

We spent the last half hour of practice working on passing the stick. Sure enough each hand-off was a total flop as I dropped it every single time AND tripped on my own feet half the time. Andy assured me that I'd get better though there were only three more weeks until Districts and I didn't see how me getting better would be remotely possible.

***

Saturday nights at the bookstore, compared to the bustling daytime hours, were fairly slow in the spring. Most of the clientele were the locals, like Marge the florist who came in once a month to pick up books for her reading club. I asked her once why she didn't just check the book out at the library since she read so voraciously and she said she'd always dreamed of one day lining her study floor to ceiling with books, which had always sort of been a dream of mine as well. Then there was Pete who came in when we changed out the literary magazines. I don't think he's ever purchased a single one. He just sits on the bench, a stack at his side and thumbs through each and every page.

My co-worker Manny was busy organizing the CD rack by the registers, swinging his head back and forth to the Vampire Weekend song that was playing in the stereo. He was in his mid-twenties and had graduated from the University of Oregon with a political science degree, had every intention of going to law school but I guess after a summer working at the Oregon Country Fair he decided it wasn't for him, grew a man-bun and hasn't taken off his Birkenstocks. Ever. Well, hopefully to shower. And sleep. Anyway, while Manny organized the CD's I shelved the books in the children's department. A small alcove in the back of the store, it was easily my favorite place to work. It was just so magical. In the right were three navy couches with crocheted blankets strewed across the back. In the middle of the couches was a Thomas the Engine train set, three pint-size chairs on each side of the track. The far left of the section was a little stage that was designed to look like the deep dark forest, where story time was held every Saturday at 10:30am. At the foot of the stage were boxes of puppets, princess dresses, and knight outfits. When we were younger, Mom would bring us here for Storytime, and I'd pout my lips and bat my eyes in an attempt to get Nate to dress up with me. If we came when it wasn't story time, we'd dress up anyway and Nate would read to me. The costumes were different now but the memories were still the same, still just as vivid.

I folded each costume, placing them neatly into the box and swept the stage. After picking up rogue train pieces and placing them back on the track, I re-shelved a few books left on the floor, and then motioned to Manny that I was going to clean up the periodicals. Pete had been in earlier in the evening and after putting away the magazines he'd been reading, he'd picked up all of the other rogue magazines, so there was literally nothing left for me to do. I grabbed the latest copy of *Under the Radar* and sat down on the bench. Half way through an article reviewing the latest album release by Connor Oberst, a set of soft warm hands slid over my eyes which naturally caused me to go into fight or flight mode. Quickly I dropped the magazine to the floor and jammed my left elbow back as far as it would go. The hands slid away and I heard a moan. Jumping to my feet fists raised, I gasped, unclenched my fists and ran to Tyler who was curled into a fetal position.

"Tyler are you an absolute idiot? Because only an idiot would sneak up on a girl like some sort of creeper and not expect an elbow to the junk." I looped my arms under his armpits and hoisted him up onto the bench. He held up his finger, indicating he still needed a moment to collect his breath and make sure his balls weren't permanently lodged up into his abdomen.

"Guess I deserved that. Manny warned me but, in my defense, I thought it would be cute, you know, guess who?"

"M'kay but at 9:00 o'clock at night in downtown Valley River, it's not very cute. How are your balls? I didn't elbow you too hard, did I?"

"I think I'll live." We both started laughing because honestly, how could we not laugh? He leaned over, gently kissed me on the lips. He tasted like peppermint.

"What are you doing over here? Thought your mom was keeping you busy for the rest of your life?" I asked.

"Oh, she thinks I'm out picking up the dry cleaning for the pageant. Technically I am. I just really wanted to see you." He kissed me again. I missed his kisses. The past few weeks we hadn't managed much more than a few quick pecks on the lips here and there between classes.

"I've missed you," I whispered, leaning into him, resting my forehead on his.

"I've missed you too. This sucks."

"I know."

Just then the doors chimed open and Mrs. Ashford stormed in, whipping her head around until she spotted us. Her face was pinched and her nostrils flared so much I thought for sure smoke was about to come out.

"Tyler Michael Ashford, you were supposed to be picking up the dry cleaning, yet according to Find My Phone, you're all the way over here.".

"You tracked me?"

"Of course I did."

"Mom, I did pick up the dry cleaning, but I figured I could have just a minute to stop by and see Margo.

"Well you figured wrong. Say your goodbyes and meet me outside."

"Mom, chill out you're being ridiculous," he said, standing up and shifting from side to side. She stepped up to him until they were nose to nose, her eyes so wild and wide I thought she was going to absolutely lose it. Instead she thrusted her hand towards the door, index finger angrily extended. He puffed up his chest but then deflated.

He kissed my cheek before pushing past his mom for the door. She turned to follow him but right before she got to the door she stopped, pivoted, and marched back over to me, arms in full swing.

"You know, I don't know what you think is going on between you and my son but you need to know that it can't possibly go any farther."

"Excuse me?" I stood up arrow straight but made sure to put space between us. Out of the corner of my eye I could see Manny peering over the registers observing this epic showdown.

"Don't play coy. You two, you're not cut from the same cloth. You're no good for him and the sooner this ends the better it will be for him."

"You mean better for you. I bet if I were rich, we wouldn't be having this conversation," I said.

She laughed. "You could have all the money in the world and you still wouldn't be good enough for my son, so don't kid yourself."

"But we love each other." I bit on my lower lip to keep from crying.

"You're seventeen. You don't know what love is. End this now. Before you ruin everything for him." She spun on her heels and left. It felt like I'd been assaulted by ten thousand fists. Manny jumped over the register and locked the door.

"Well that was intense," he said. "She always looks so nice in her ads. Who knew right?"

My head and my heart felt like they were going to forge a mutiny and vacate my body. It was like the universe was hell bent on keeping us from being together. Dramatic, maybe but what else was I supposed to think? Being together with someone wasn't supposed to be this hard and complicated, was it?

17

I had one of those dreams where you knew you were dreaming and you wanted to wake up but you couldn't no matter how many times you yelled at yourself to wake up. Most times, the setting of my dreams tended to reflect something I'd watched before going to bed. In this case I'd watched *Carrie*, (the original from the '70's), and a few episodes of a show called *Glee* on Hulu, so naturally my dream kind of meshed the two. Sounds awesome right? It wasn't. I dreamed that Tyler and I were the "it" couple. Everyone wanted to be friends with us and all couples wanted to be like us. We ate at the popular table at lunch, people gave us high fives as we walked down the halls. It was like we were Kate and William, Marshall Academy's very own royal couple. More than that, our parents were happy with us AND my mom and Mrs. Ashford were even best friend.

At Prom we were crowned King and Queen, and as Tyler placed the crown on my head, he stepped back and that's when the whole *Carrie/Glee* moment happened. Something wet, sticky, and ice cold hit my head and dripped down my neck, my shoulders, my spine. And then everyone in the audience chucked big- gulp sized cherry red slushies right at me. I turned, frantically searching the stage for Tyler, finding him off to the side sipping from a mother fucking cherry red slushy. Standing next to him on either side were his mother and his brother, both holding slushies. His dad stood next to his mom, wearing a black leather choker around his neck attached to a leash held by Mrs. Ashford's free hand. His face was void of any expression at all, which seemed fitting since he seemed to be submissive to her in the real world anyway. And then the gut punch happened. I turned out to the crowd and there, front and center were my mom and Nate, their lips curled up into identical evil grins. Then they both raised their arms and chucked slushies at me, pegging me right in the freaking face, which is when I woke up.

It was by far to date the worst dream I'd ever had, probably because it pretty much summed up my biggest fears. There'd always been some part of me that worried Tyler would come to his senses and realize he'd made a galaxy sized mistake by dating me and once that happened, he'd turn on me and treat me like garbage. And of course, I'd always, *always* worried I'd been a huge disappointment to my family. To Nate. Like, if he were awake and here with me today would he be all, "Margo, you're the biggest loser in the world. Why'd you let yourself become a loser?" And I knew that in and of itself was ridiculous because Nate and I had always been super close. Even after he left, he still called me every week. But things change. What if he expected me to be stronger? Rebellious? More like him and less like myself? It made my skin crawl. I rolled the blanket down off my legs, scooped up Sir Rusty who'd been sleeping at the foot of the bed, and brought him to my lap, bending down to bury my face in his fur.

"Ugg Sir Rusty, why does life have to be so hard? And why do dreams have to remind you of how much life sucks?" He responded with a muffled mew and then began to purr wildly. I could be the most popular girl in school, or the biggest reject, Sir Rusty would always love me. Or at least I'd hoped.

There was a soft rapping on the door followed by it slowly opening, hinges squeaking in protest. "Margo, you awake?" Mom asked, poking her head in.

"Yeah Mom, I'm awake."

She stepped in and sunk down on the end of my bed, reaching over to scratch Sir Rusty on the head. "I wanted to talk to you about something, well, about your brother and all those tests."

I groaned. "It's fine Mom, there's nothing left to say. You don't want to do it so I'm not planning to ask you again."

"Actually, that's what I wanted to talk to you about. I've been talking with Mr. Dan the past few days. He told me about how he is trying to finish a Masters in Psychology, and how much a study like this would help, and I've realized that maybe my reasons for not wanting the tests have been one sided, so I've agreed to let the tests happen."

I waited for her to say "just kidding" or "fooled you". She just stared at me.

"Aren't you going to say anything?"

"Are you for real?" I asked.

"Yeah, I mean, I still have my reservations, and I don't feel comfortable doing something to Nate without his permission, but yeah. It's all been arranged. Nate will be transported up to Portland to Myer's Research Institute on May fifteenth."

I leaned across Sir Rusty to pull Mom into a hug. He let out a growl before hoping off the bed. "Thank you, Mom. You have no idea how much this means to me."

"That's not when Districts are is it? I'm not sure they'll reschedule."

"No, Districts are the twentieth."

She nodded, patted my leg and then rose up. As she got to the door, I called out to her.

"Hey Mom, do you think…I mean, would it be alright if I came to the study with you?"

Please say yes. Please say yes. She looked at me and then down at her hands, as if they held her answer. "Yeah honey, you can come."

"Thanks Mom." She nodded and left, closing the door behind her.

At school I waited for Tyler in the parking lot before the first bell, but he didn't show up. I was dying to tell him about the tests. I texted him to see where he was and he texted back that his mom had dropped him off early, which was strange because he always drove. I figured his car must have been in the shop, but then that didn't make sense because there were like ten cars at their house, so why wouldn't he have driven one of the surplus cars?

I waited for him in the student lounge at break but he didn't come, and he didn't respond to any of my texts. I was starting to feel like one of those needy annoying girlfriends, with all the texts I'd been sending but I couldn't help it. Since I'd been grounded most of our communication had been by text or super quick facetime sessions, but I felt like I was sending more of them than usual, mostly to ask where he was. It was super lame. I didn't want to be that kind of person, but being here in the student lounge by myself, around all the popular kids made me feel like a huge freak. I'd only ever been in here with Tyler, and even then, I'd felt super uncomfortable.

I reached into my backpack for my headphones, desperate for my music, but after realizing I'd be such a huge lame-o to sit in the lounge with the popular kids just listening to my music, I zipped my bag back up and took out my phone and pretended to scroll mindlessly through my non-existent Chirp feed. I was just glad that Blake wasn't in there. I don't think I could have coped with any of his verbal lashings. But it didn't keep me from feeling uncomfortable with the way the girls would look at me out of the corner of their eyes and then whisper to one another. I could have started dating Tyler the very day I'd transferred and still, to the popular crowd it wouldn't matter. I'd never be one of them. When the bell rang, I sprang up from the couch and bolted to fourth period, holding back my tears.

I didn't want to socialize at lunch, and I didn't feel much like eating anyway, so I spent lunch period in the library at the computers working on my psych paper. I still wasn't sure where I was trying to go with my report but I figured handing in something was better than nothing. I popped in my earbuds, scrolled through my music until I found The Album Leaf and stared at the blinking cursor willing for words to come. The chair next to me pulled out, startling me. I looked up to see Jillian smiling down at me before she lowered herself into the chair.

"Looked for you everywhere. Figured I'd find you in here. What's going on?"

"Just trying to work on my psych paper."

She looked over to my screen, at the blank page and evil blinking cursor, cocked her head to the side. "Wow, you've really made some progress. I think Mr. Dan will be so happy with this."

"I know. I really think it's my best work." Joking with her was so natural, so easy. It almost made me forget how numb I felt inside.

"What's really going on?" she asked, eyes softening.

I shrugged. "Just stuff that sucks."

"Care to elaborate? Be more specific? Maybe use more vocabulary?"

"I don't know, it's this whole grounding thing, and Tyler's pageant thing. We haven't really been able to hang out, like at all. We used to be able to at least have lunch together but now he's always doing stuff for the pageant during lunch. We don't even have time to text or facetime either. And his mom has been a freaking nightmare."

"How so?" Jillian asked.

"Well, he was running some errands for her or with her, I don't know which, but anyway he came into the bookstore when I was working just to say hi and it was so sweet and so awesome. Well then, his mom comes in, like she'd been following him or something, tells him to leave and then after he does, she comes back and like lays into me. Tells me how I'm basically white trash and not good enough at all for Tyler. Oh, and this was all in front of Manny."

"Wow that's pretty messed up. What did Tyler say about it?"

"I didn't actually tell him what she said. She's already been so far up his butt and his brother is really being a little prick so I didn't want to add to it."

"Maybe you should have, you know, told him. That way at least he'd know."

"Wouldn't make a difference. I already told you how she treated me at the family dinner and he was pissed but couldn't really do anything about it. What's he going to do? Tell his mom to stop being such a raging bitch and then end up being cut off?"

She shrugged. "Guess you're right. I'm really sorry M."

"I guess I'm starting to wonder if everyone is right. If maybe we aren't meant to work out. Also, what if he thinks that too but he's too nice to say it and this is his way of cutting me loose?"

"Him being a part of the Mr. Spartan pageant is his way of cutting you lose? How does that work?"

"No, not actually being in the pageant but just the fact that it takes so much of his time and maybe it's easier for him to do something that takes up so much of his time that eventually we don't see each other anymore and then kinda forget about each other."

"That can't really be how you feel."

I was about to respond when my phone vibrated. A text from Tyler. "It's from Tyler. He said he's sorry for missing me at break today, had to make banners with the pageant team, and had to work on it again now at lunch. And here's another one of a kissy face emoji"

"Well there you go. See? He's not intentionally trying to blow you off. Maybe just cut him some slack? You love him, and he loves you, so maybe give him a little credit. Nothing that is meant to be is ever easy."

After school as I was swapping my school bag for my gym bag at my car, I saw a group exit the side entrance of the lecture hall, currently being used as HQ for Mr. Spartan pageant. All the pageant contestants, including Tyler, a handful of peppy senior girls who were "on the team" followed by two of the faculty advisors. They were laughing, the girls swishing their pony tails, arms linked with the boys. I couldn't help but feel both crazy jealous and extremely sad, which sucked because I absolutely didn't want to feel that way. There was no reason for it. A) I'd never wanted to be one of those fake pony tail swishing girls who hung over all the guys, and B) Tyler had said a million times he'd rather be with me. I waved, hoping he'd see me, but he didn't, or maybe he did but was ignoring me. Again, a freaking ridiculous thought because he'd already explained his situation. Why was I having such a hard time grasping that? The group split up, piling into two SUV's and drove off. Trying to not get too worked up, I locked up my car and headed for practice.

I was surprised to find Andy stretching on the track down by the equipment shed.

"Figured you'd be out working on pageant stuff with everyone else," I said taking a seat next to him and folding my legs into a butterfly stretch.

"Nah, I do what I need to do during school, but Coach needs me to be here for practice since Districts are in a few weeks, so I don't have to do any of the after-school stuff." He pulled one leg bent at the knee behind him and folded himself forward into the hurdler's stretch. I did the same.

"What kind of stuff do you guys have to do after school?"

"Mostly it's just extra skit rehearsals," he said. "Or working on banners or canvasing neighborhoods to raise money. I do most of that with Tyler on the weekends though."

"Tyler seems to be kept pretty busy with it. I hardly see him anymore."

"Yeah, his mom makes him do a lot of extra stuff. She says it looks good or whatever, for scholarships. Mostly I think she just assumes he has a bigger chance of winning if he does more."

"Isn't that a little biased? A little unfair?" I asked.

He popped up, pulling me up with him, and then used my shoulder for balance as he stood on one leg to stretch, pulling his opposite leg, knee bent, to touch his butt. "You mean a lot biased and unfair. She doesn't care though. Anyway, there's a whole panel of judges so it's not like she has the greater say in it just because she organizes it. I swear though, if she wasn't making him, Tyler really wouldn't be doing it. Not that he doesn't care about charity and the neonatal unit or anything, but pageants are just not his thing. He'd rather be spending time with you."

I smiled. "Really?"

"Yup. Really. Now let's go work on those hand-offs." He picked up the baton, tossed it up in the air, retrieved it, and jogged down the track. I followed him, trying to take comfort in what he'd said, but the nagging bitch of a voice inside my head kept trying to convince me that Andy was wrong, that Tyler really did like spending so much time away from me, that he did like working on the pageant and being with Blake. It sucked, being caught up inside my thoughts that just snowballed.

I called Tyler later that night, hoping I could tell him how I'd been feeling lately and hoping he wouldn't think I was being too incredibly ridiculous, but he didn't answer. I refused to send any more texts. I was seriously one text away from becoming the crazy obsessed girlfriend.

The next day he texted to say he promised to meet me in the lounge at break. Having no reason to actually doubt him, though admittedly riddled with apprehension, I waited for him in the same spot on the couch taking small sips from my mocha. Kids came in and out, kids who weren't Tyler, and every one of them seemed to raise an eyebrow and whisper at one another as they walked by. The minutes passed, and ten minutes in Tyler still hadn't shown up. I was about to hoist myself up from the couch and leave when Alexander slipped in, saw me sitting by myself on the couch, scrunched up his face and sat down next to me. Every part of my body tensed. My hands gripped my cup so tightly I'd heard it crinkle. He took a bite from the apple he'd been holding, so close to my face I felt the spray from his bite.

"Sup Margo. What are you doing in here all alone?" he asked sounding evermore like the asshole he was.

"Can't really be alone in a room full of people," I said, hoping he didn't hear my voice catch.

He laughed, but it was more like a cackle, and then took another bite of his apple. The way he chewed, mouth open, pieces of apple flinging around back and forth in his mouth, was enough to make me yack. "Ever the witty one, you are. But you know exactly what I mean. Where's Tyler? Did he get tired of you already?"

"I'm meeting him here," I said, finishing the last of my drink.

"Nah. Know what I think? I think he finally realized what a huge loser you are and is ghosting your basic ass." It was exactly the kind of thing I expected to hear from Blake. He took pleasure in reminding me and my friends how big of losers we were.

I felt the tips of my ears redden. It was taking everything within me to keep my composure.

"That's a neat theory. Here's what I wonder though, are you a puppet?"

"Huh?" He looked at me confused.

"Well, you speak as if Blake has his hand wedged up your ass. Does he move your lips? Tell you what to say? How to think? So, are you his puppet?"

He spat out the hunk of apple he'd been working on and shifted in his seat to face me. His eyes bugged out and his nostrils flared the same way his mom's had in the bookstore.

"You think you're something special but you're not. You're just some weird white trash piece of shit who doesn't belong here. You should have stayed at Valley Central with the rest of the freaks."

His words should have hurt, I mean, no matter that stupid old saying about sticks and stones and bones, it should have hurt to be called white trash, a freak. It always cut every time Blake said it, but for some reason, when he said it, the way his voice waivered like the words just didn't quite fit him, made me burst out laughing. He cocked his head to the side, clearly taken off guard by my random fit of laugher. He looked around at the other kids who shared in his bemused look.

"I'm sorry, I'm sorry. It's just that, you were trying so hard to insult me. But here's the thing. Everything you can possibly think to call me, every nasty insult, has already been said. There's no possible way for you to be original. You're just a dumb rich kid whose head is so far up someone else's butt, there's no telling where he begins and where you end. A Plus for effort though."

His face turned beet red, lips pursing. Not about to give him the chance to respond, I pushed myself up from the couch, and left the student lounge, tossing my cup into the trash as I left. When I'd reached the end of the hall, I kicked open the doors and leaned against the cold brick of the building, chest heaving as I tried to gather myself. This school sucked and all the people inside it sucked even more. I should have put up more of a fight when my mom said she was pulling me out of Valley Central. I may not have had friends there, but the people at least were decent.

When the bell rang for the end of break, the doors to the hall on the other side of me flew open and out walked Tyler with Andy and Blake on either side of him. They were laughing and chummy and it made me want to barf. Before I could rationalize with the sane part of my brain, I firmly planted my hands on my hips and stormed up to them. When Tyler saw me approach, he said something to Andy, nodding his head in my direction. Andy and Blake stopped outside the door to the east hall while Tyler waited for me, greeting me with a tentative smile.

"Hey Margo, what's wrong?"

"You must think I'm an idiot," I seethed

"I don't know what you're talking about."

"For starters, you promised you'd meet me in the student lounge at break. One of us was there. The other wasn't. I'll give you a guess as to who wasn't."

He slapped a hand to his forehead. "Oh shit. Baby I am so sorry. We got caught up on some stuff and I totally lost track of time."

I nodded in the direction of Blake and Andy. "So, I guess you and Blake have worked out your differences?"

"I told you, we have to get along for the pageant. That was just me getting along."

I should have dropped it, should have believed him but that nagging voice in my head prodded me to keep going. "You know, if you're trying to ghost me…"

"What are you talking about?" he asked. "Trying to ghost you? Margo, I told you I was going to be super busy with the pageant. And you've been grounded. I'm not trying to ghost you. The pageant is in a few weeks. I've been spending literally every second working on it when I'm not doing my homework. I haven't even been into the gym to shoot hoops in weeks."

"Oh no you poor baby. You haven't gotten to shoot hoops!" I was aware of how callous I was being but I didn't care. Quiet Rational Margo had left and was replaced with Loud Raging Bitch Margo.

"Why are you acting this way?" His voice quivered and his eyes searched my face for any sort of understanding. I crammed my hands into the pockets of my hoodie.

"Look. This is too hard," I said. "We haven't spent any time together and it's just getting too hard." I bit down on my lower lip until I could taste hot salty blood pool under my tongue.

"Wait, Margo, what are you saying? Are you saying you want to break up?"

"I don't know what I'm saying. I just…I just know that things are getting complicated and we don't have time for each other, and we're going off to college next year and who knows what happens then, so I just don't know if I can do this." There'd always been some part of me that assumed in the end he'd be the one to break my heart. Standing here staring up into his watery blue eyes, it was clear as day that I was breaking his.

The bell rang for the start of fourth period. I shifted my weight, very much so aware that there was zero chance of making it to the other side of campus before the bell rang. Tyler reached out to touch my arm but I took a step back.

"I'm sorry, Tyler." I swerved around him and pushed past the gathered sea of nosy classmates, pretending not to hear his pleading voice call after me.

18

— • —

I couldn't sleep. Three cups of piping hot chamomile tea and I was still wide awake. The events of the day replayed in my head like a sappy Hallmark movie. The words that came out of my mouth, the confusion in his eyes, his quivering lip, the snickers from all the kids who had stopped to spectate. It was all too much for my head. He'd texted ten times, called five, left three voice messages, all asking the same question: Why? And I couldn't answer him because any reason I could possibly give for me wanting to break up with him wouldn't make sense, because they were all stupid. Just me stuck so far inside my own head, wrapped up in my own insecurities that I'd looked for something to be wrong.

Sometime around 3am I dozed off. When I woke, the birds chirped on the branch outside my window; a sliver of bright sunlight peeked through my curtains hitting me right in the face. I yawned, rubbed my eyes open, and then remembering that I'd just dumped the possible love of my life, I pulled the blankets tightly over my head and willed for night to come back.

I finally dragged myself out of bed at 10am after the fifth all caps text from my mother telling me to get up and clean the kitchen before going to work. How could I clean the dishes when my entire world was crumbling? I showered until the water turned cold, dug around in my drawers for some sweatpants, and schlepped to the kitchen to wash the freaking dishes. At least it had been a monotonous chore. I felt like I was functioning on some sort of auto pilot zombie mode, standing in front of the sink, rinsing, scraping, shoving into dishwasher, repeat. When I finished it was noon. I didn't have to be at work until 4pm but I didn't want to hang around here so I swapped my sweatpants for jeans, grabbed my purse and keys and drove up to the rehab center.

I knew Tyler wouldn't be there on a Saturday since it was his best fundraising day, but still, as I pulled into the parking lot, a watermelon size knot twisted into shape in the pit of my stomach. I'd spent the entire night dodging his attempts at communication. If he were there, in the visitor's room or walking the hall on the way to see his grandmother what would I say to him? What would he say to me? Would he look at me with those sad eyes, ask what gives, or would he be super spiteful and not acknowledge me at all? I'd find out soon enough on Monday at school, but just the possibility of seeing him today was nerve wrecking.

The double-doors screeched open. I walked past the visitor's lounge, peering through the window. No Tyler. I sped to Nate's room, closing the door behind me. Leaning against the door to catch my breath, I realized how ridiculous I was being. His car wasn't in the parking lot and neither were any of his parents' cars so he was so obviously not here. I needed to chill. I set my purse and keys on the chair by the door, twisted my hair up into a messy bun, slumped into the chair next to Nate. His open eyes, glassy and pale blue with rings of yellow around the iris, stared into the void. I took hold of his hand, straightening out his curled fingers. The nails were freshly clipped. I brushed the blonde curls from his eyes and folded over to rest my head on his chest, feeling the rise and fall with each breath, listening to the soft beating of his heart. I so badly wanted him to wrap his arms around me, stroke my hair and tell me everything was alright, like he used to do when we were kids, when our parents would fight, when our dad left for good. I placed his hand on my head and held it there, praying to whatever God was listening for his fingers to miraculously wiggle and run through my hair. When I let go his hand slid down my head and landed on the bed with a muffled thump.

"I messed up big brother," I whispered. "I messed it all up with Tyler. I broke up with him, and for why? Some lame reason that I don't even know what it is. He probably hates me. And the look in his eyes. I don't know what to do. I need you. Wake up, please Nate, please, please wake up. Tell me how to make things right." I spent the next hour lying next to Nate, enveloped by the sound of his breathing, the muted beeping of his monitor, the waves of rain beating on the window, until eventually I fell asleep.

A quarter after 2:00pm Sari came in, startled to see me. "Hey girl, I didn't expect to see you here on a Saturday. You doing okay?" I didn't need to answer. She took one good look at me in the light, set her clipboard down on the table and knelt beside me.

"Girl, what's the matter? Why you crying?" She reached up and gently swiped the tears off my cheek.

"I broke up with Tyler yesterday."

"For reals? What happened? I thought you two were amazing together."

"Honestly Sari, I don't even know. I built something up inside my head, things I couldn't handle and I panicked. Stupid thing is, I think I made a mistake but I don't know how to take it back." And then I started crying again, the snotty, messy ugly-cry kind of crying. She hoisted me up from the bed and pulled me into a deep hug, wrapping her arms around me until I was buried in her chest. She smelled like rose hips and I breathed her in.

"It's okay. It's gonna be okay. We all do stupid stuff, especially when it comes to young love. I got you." She held me like that, tightly in her arms, gently swaying back and forth until I'd stopped crying.

"Thanks Sari. Ugg this is so stupid. Does it ever get any easier? You know, this whole love business?"

She laughed. "I want to tell you yes, but that'd be lying. Girl, it doesn't get any easier, it actually gets more complicated. But you'll learn and each time will suck a little less. Now, go on to the bathroom, get yourself cleaned up. You look like the Stay Puff Marshmallow man."

"I don't even know what that is, Sari."

"Don't you age me. Go on. I have to get your brother ready for his physical therapy. I really am sorry to hear about you and Tyler." She kissed my forehead and ushered me into the bathroom

After cleaning myself up, I went out to the car and sent a group text to Jillian, Donny and (gulp) Linz asking them to meet me at The Daily Bagel ASAP. I had a little over an hour until my shift at the bookstore and I needed some best friend time. When we were all seated in our usual booth in the back-left corner of the shop, I cut to the chase.

"You guys, I broke up with Tyler," I said in one raspy breath.

"You what?" Donny asked.

"What happened, Margo? Thought you guys were in love?" Linz asked throwing in air quotes with her fingers. Ordinarily I'd hit her back with some witty remark but I was running on empty, which I think she noticed because she quickly apologized. "Sorry. I mean, what happened?"

"I can't even answer that without sounding like a total idiot," I began, rubbing my forehead with my hand. "So, his mom was never a fan of us, well, of me I guess. Because I'm not rich or whatever. I think she forced him to be in the Mr. Spartan pageant because she knew it would keep him busy, too busy to hang out with me, which she didn't really even need to do since my mom grounded me from having any form of a social life whatsoever. So, we hardly saw each other and he wasn't able to text as much as we thought and so…"

"You got up inside your own head thinking he was spending so much time on pageant stuff in order to avoid you because he realized he didn't actually want to date you anymore, because you're too different," Jillian interjected, annoyingly spot on as always. "Did I get that right?"

I grumbled. "Yes, ugg I hate that you can do that."

"Wait, how *did* you know all that?" Donny asked.

Ignoring him she reached across the table for my hand. "Margo, what exactly did you say to him when you broke up? Are you sure it wasn't just a fight?"

"I'm pretty sure he knows it was a break up. I mean, I told him that it just wasn't working, that it was too hard, and then he texted and called all night on Friday, and I didn't answer."

"You ignored all his calls and texts?" Donny asked.

"Yeah pretty much. You guys, what was I supposed to say? Tyler hi I'm sorry I made a mistake, maybe I don't want to break up with you?"

"Well yeah you could start with that," Jillian said.

"Okay but it doesn't change the fact that he's still super busy and I'm still technically grounded. I'm not even supposed to be having coffee with you guys right now. We still will hardly see each other and I'd be right back in the same line of thought. And then what about next year? I don't even know where he's going to school. What if it's on the east coast? What if it's in Europe?"

"Europe?" Linz said, holding up her hand. "Wait up, Europe? Margo, don't you think you're getting ahead of yourself? I mean, you'd still have the whole entire summer.

I tucked my head under my arms on the table. "Frick, you're right. I hate it when you're right. I'm such an idiot!" I wasn't planning on starting school early, so my plan was to stick around Valley River and work at the bookstore, and Tyler hadn't mentioned going anywhere over the summer. Assuming my period of groundation would have passed, and his mom got off his ass, we could have totally spent all our time together.

"Margo, there's no sense in beating yourself up over this," Jillian said. "You made a decision and you can either accept it and move forward, or if you really feel you made a mistake you could just text him and see if he's willing to talk."

"Yeah, I mean, getting publicly dumped sucks, but he might forgive you, Mar. He's a nice guy," Donny said

I shrugged. Move on and hope he wouldn't hate me forever, or try and talk with him. Those were my two options, and both meant accepting I was the idiot who broke up with the most perfect guy for no good reason.

"Alright guys, thanks for listening. I'll call him back. Hopefully he's not too pissed to talk even though I ignored all his messages." I slid out of the booth and slung my purse over my shoulder. "I really mucked this up. I truly thought he'd be the one to eventually break up with me."

"So did we," Linz and Donny said in unison.

I rolled my eyes at them and turned to leave, but remembered I wanted to tell them about Nate's tests. "Oh wait, I forgot to tell you guys, my mom said she changed her mind about those coma tests."

"No way, really?" Jillian said. "Margo, that's amazing. What changed her mind?"

"Something Mr. Dan said."

Donny and Linz exchanged glances. "Since when have your mom and Mr. Dan been all buddy buddy?"

I shrugged my shoulders. "No clue."

Turned out I was a colossal coward. On every one of my breaks Saturday *and* Sunday, I pulled out my phone, scrolled through my contacts and hovered over Tyler's name. I wanted to talk to him, explain why I'd broken up with him, tell him I might have had a mini stroke or something because I was an idiot and never should have done it, but every time I tried to touch my finger to his name it was like what happens when you try and touch two magnets together. The thing is, if he was willing to talk to me, I worried nothing I'd say would make sense and I'd only end up making it worse. If he wanted me to drop dead and never speak to him again, I'd be super crushed. So maybe it was a good thing my finger was being a jerk.

When I got home from work Sunday night Mom was extended across the couch, a bowl of popcorn in her lap watching a Hallmark movie. I was zapped to the core, my emotional cup completely drained so I was really hoping Mom was in one of her moods, preferring to be left alone. I hung my keys on the hook, dropped my purse onto the bench and walked into the kitchen. I'd poured a glass of water and was just about to head to my room when I heard the familiar click of the TV shutting off, and the clank of the remote being set back down on the coffee table.

"Margo, can you come in here a sec?" Mom said. I gulped down my water and walked into the room, leaning against the doorframe.

"Hey ma, what's up?" I asked.

"How was work this weekend, honey? I feel like I haven't seen you all weekend." Her tone was light and airy.

I shrugged. "Work was fine. Not too busy I guess."

"Did you get out to see your brother?"

"Yeah. Saw him Saturday morning. Before going straight to work."

"Honey, is everything okay? You don't quite seem like yourself." I wanted to laugh and point out the obvious. She hadn't been herself in years. "How are things going with Tyler?"

Hearing his name felt like a ginormous nail was being driven into my heart. Didn't see the sense in not telling her.

"Um, well we actually broke up."

She patted the space next to her on the couch, motioned for me to sit down. "Sweetheart, I'm so sorry to hear this. When did you guys break up? What happened?"

"Friday, I guess? I don't know. It just got too hard, to like have a relationship. We hardly got to see each other. With me being grounded and him having to do so much for the Mr. Spartan pageant and for his mom."

"Oh, honey. You know when I grounded you, I never thought it would cause for you two to break up. I really liked Tyler."

"I know Mom. It's not your fault. I'm sure it would have happened anyway. His mom would have found some reason to keep him away from me. She really hates me."

Mom tucked my hair behind my ear, running her fingertips across my cheek. "It's not you she hates. For her it's about status and position in life. If you were you with just a little more money, she'd love you."

I scoffed. "Yeah that's not what she said. She said, and I quote, I could be the richest person in Valley River and I'd still not be good enough for her son."

"I'm sorry honey. It's probably because you are my daughter and we've never gotten along." Mom said. "You sure there's no way for the two of you to work things out?"

I shook my head. "I don't know ma. He tried calling a bunch of times Friday night but I ignored all his calls. I was planning to call him over the weekend but I just couldn't do it. It might be too late."

She pulled me into a hug. I was surprised at how warm and comforting it felt. Even when I was little, I couldn't remember a time when she'd ever hugged me like this. I curled into the crook of her arm while she ran her hand through my hair.

"It really sucks, Mom," I said.

She kissed the top of my head. "I know. But you know what? If it's meant to be things will work out. You may not be able to see that while you're in the thick of it, but really honey, have some faith. Try to talk to him. It might not be too late."

It wasn't much, maybe just a shifting of sorts, but simply confiding in Mom and letting her actually mother me, I felt a little better. Maybe if I'd spent more time telling her my problems, letting her in on the things that were bothering me, even if they were miniscule, this whole stupid situation wouldn't seem so dire. Or maybe it still would have, I don't know. All I know is it felt so nice having her actually take an interest in me, and me actually letting her in.

"I think you've been grounded long enough. I truly am sorry if it contributed in any way to you guys breaking up."

"It's alright," I said. "His mom would have tried to separate us even if I hadn't been grounded."

She picked up the bowl of popcorn and handed it to me. "Wanna eat the rest of this and watch this terribly cheesy Hallmark movie with me? The acting is bad and the plot is completely contrived but it's entertaining."

I grabbed a handful of popcorn and shoveled them into my mouth. "Sure Mama."

***

On Monday morning, I sat in my car, engine idled, in the farthest corner of the school parking lot blasting Phoebe Bridgers as loud as my poor shaky speakers could manage. It would only be moments before school security motored over on their school issued golf cart to reprimand me, but I couldn't face the gossip mongers otherwise known as Marshall Academy student body just yet. I knew without stepping foot outside my car that the rumor mill had been churning for hours. Any time anyone breaks up, especially anyone from the inner circle, there are a million different tweets and group texts and basically shout-outs on any social media platform to make it known. Nothing was private. Not at Marshall Academy. Not for faculty and certainly not for a student.

I heard the familiar squeal of golf cart tires and then from my rear-view mirror saw the cart round the corner and jolt to a stop parallel to my car. I lowered the volume down on the stereo to a dull roar and rolled down the window. Mr. Sadler, head of security crossed his arms over his chest, his lips stuck in a perma-frown.

"Sorry Officer, was I speeding?"

He rolled his charcoal eyes. And grumbled. He didn't appreciate my humor. "You aware, young lady that there's a strict noise ordinance on this campus and you're in clear violation of said ordinance?" He smoothed his Ron Swanson-esk mustache with his fingers and then crossed his arms again.

"My bad," I said, stretching my mouth into the biggest grin I could muster and hoped like hell he wouldn't write me up.

He shifted in his seat, unfolding his arms and gripping the steering wheel. "Yeah well, watch your volume and uh you should get to class."

I saluted him, rolled the window back up and killed the engine as he shifted his cart into gear and sped away. My phone vibrated somewhere in the bottomless abyss of my purse and I cursed as I frantically dug around for it. It was Jillian.

"Hey Jilly bean, what's up?"

"Where are you? Are you here?"

"I'm in the parking lot. I just locked my car. What's up?" She sighed. "I was at my locker this morning to get my calc book and I heard Christy Kehoe talking to Courtney Sash."

"It's not unheard of for two friends to gossip outside their lockers, Jilly."

"It was what they were gossiping about that got my attention, and I'm pretty sure you can guess the subject."

"So, what are people already saying about me and Tyler and our uncoupling?"

"Well, Christy said Tyler accused you of cheating on him and then you started gesticulating wildly with your hands and it was like this huge ordeal."

Wow. I'd anticipated fabrications but not that extreme. Never once had I gesticulated wildly with my hands. "Clearly Christy was looking for some attention. Did she happen to tell Courtney who I cheated on Tyler with?"

"Yeah and you're not going to believe it," she said and then paused.

"Jilly, who?"

"Blake Wolf."

I stopped fast in my tracks, pushing down the bile that crept up my throat. "Blake Wolf? There's a rumor going around that I cheated on Tyler with Blake fucking-Wolf? Who'd even start that and more important, who'd even *believe* that? He's made it publicly known that he detests me."

"I have no idea Margo, I'm just telling you what I heard. Thought you'd want to know. I mean, this school is small and sucks so you'll hear eventually but thought it would be better if you had a heads up. I gotta go. See you soon."

"Yeah see you." I hung up and dumped my phone back into my purse. Well today was going to be pure crap. I didn't want to go to my locker. The hub of the entire senior class was in that hall and if Tyler was at his locker, I was certain all eyes would be on us waiting for something to happen, and I wasn't prepared to deal with that. Not just yet. Instead, I would just schlep around unnecessary books until break. He'd most likely be working on pageant stuff then anyway.

As I walked from the parking lot to first period, I tried not to notice every single kid staring at me. My face was hot, probably super splotchy, my palms were dripping with sweat, and I'm pretty sure I heard the phrase "bitchy hoe-bag" a few times but I held my head high and kept an even pace until I reached the classroom door. As I slid into the desk beside Donny, he scooted his as close to me as possible.

"Girl you broke the rumor mill," Donny whispered. "I don't think people gossiped this hard even after Amelie Bradley and Andy Risko broke up at homecoming last year."

I didn't go to homecoming last year but anyone with ears heard in great detail about it. Amelie and Andy had been on again and off again since freshman year. Andy was totally devoted to her but she strung him along. During the homecoming football game Andy found Amelie making out with some dude from Junction City under the bleachers, totally cliché. For whatever reason he didn't break up with her then but at the dance after they were crowned king and queen, right in the middle of their official dance, he called it quits and walked out, leaving her there in the middle of the dance floor totally mortified. People talked about it for months, changing bits and pieces from one person to the next. The worst one that went around was Amelie getting knocked up by the Junction City guy and then driving up to Portland for an abortion. After that rumor Amelie dropped out and enrolled in Sheldon.

"Great. Just great. So how can I like, get people to not talk about me? There has to be something else going on that's worth talking about."

"Suck it up buttercup because it's going to happen. You know how this school works." Donny scooted his chair back into position. I slumped into my desk, wondering how hard it would be to transfer back to Valley Central, because if someone started passing around a rumor that my eggo was preggo, I was out of here.

I pretended I were invisible from first to third period, like I'd inherited Harry Potter's cloak of invisibility, but I couldn't escape the curious eyes darting in my direction from everyone in my classes. If I locked eyes with someone, they'd swiftly look away, turn their heads, either to pretend they hadn't been looking at me, or to whisper to the person next to them. Math was the worst. Mr. Fisher really didn't govern what people said because it wasn't his style, so people were cavalier with what they said to me.

The moment I sat down in my desk Liberty Jackson turned to me, left eyebrow raised, a sideways grin on her pimpled face.

"So like, is it true?" she asked. The kids surrounding us turned to spectate.

"Is like, what true?" I scoffed.

Casting a glance at her friend Molly and then turning back to me she said, "Did you totally get dumped by Tyler because you stole money from his mom?"

I stifled a laugh. "Is that what you heard? No Liberty. I didn't steal from Tyler's mom."

"But he did totally dump you, right?" Molly asked.

"Does it matter?" I hissed. Both girls snickered and turned away from me. At least they hadn't asked if I'd been knocked up.

When the bell rang, I bolted from my desk without hearing a word Mr. Fisher had said about math homework and raced to the bathroom in the small gym next to the band room. It was half way across campus and I would without a doubt be super late for next period but I didn't care. I needed some place I could lock myself in a stall and cry.

Andy was stretching his leg on the back of a hurtle when I approached him at practice. His eyes were stormy and furious and they greeted me with distain.

"Hey Andy," I said, cautiously. He shook his head at me, switched legs.

"Hey heartbreaker."

I sighed. "That's not fair Andy."

"Oh yeah? And how's that? My boy professes his love for you and you repay him by dumping him in front of the whole school."

"It wasn't the whole school, there was hardly anyone in the breeze-way."

He swung his left arm across his chest, grabbing hold of the elbow with the right hand pulling for a stretch. "I don't get it. I thought you liked Tyler."

"I do, Andy. I love Tyler."

"Typically, when you love someone, you don't dump them."

"You don't understand," I said.

"Why don't you explain it to me."

I bit my lower lip. "It was just getting too complicated, too hard. We barely saw each other and his mom hates me."

"You've got to be kidding," he laughed. "It was getting too complicated? What relationship isn't complicated? You gave up so fast for stupid reasons. It's not like he cheated on you, or ignored you, or whatever. Yeah, he's been busy with school but you've been grounded."

He paused, and when I didn't say anything, he ran his hand through his hair, a sharpness running through my gut at the memory of Tyler and this same habitual motion.

"Tyler has never had a girlfriend. He's dated or whatever, but he's never actually had a real relationship with anyone he'd call girlfriend and you know why? It's because he's never met anyone he felt comfortable enough with to let his guard down and open his heart to until he met you."

He may as well have actually punched me in the gut. I didn't know what to say so I kicked at the track with the toe of my spike and shrugged, like a moron. He shook his head.

"Look, I'm going to practice with you, because it means a lot to Coach Cathy, and because Districts are soon. But we're not friends."

I nodded and followed him down the track, slump-shouldered because at this point what else could I do?

19

"Y ou guys, Neko Case is gonna be in Portland this weekend, and I think we should for sure go." Donny slapped his hands down on the table as he slid in next to me. I twirled my french fry in ketchup until it was soggy and limp.

"Can't. Have to work," I grumbled.

"Can't you get Manny to switch with you? Come on M, you need this concert just as much as I do."

He was right. I couldn't argue. Last week had been pure torture, followed by another week of sideways glances, mean-girl glares and whispers, our break-up still very much so a hot topic. Worse than that, I'd finally mustered up the courage to talk to Tyler and it had backfired horribly.

Ms. Grace had asked me to take the attendance sheets for Spanish 4 to the front office. On my way back to class I stopped short at the sight of Tyler shuffling through books in his locker. I hadn't actually seen him alone in the halls since he started the pageant, and I'd been doing my best to avoid a possible run-in. If ever there was a perfect time to talk to him it was then. Tightening and then releasing my fists a few times I slowly walked up to him and leaned up against my locker, cleared my throat. He peered around his locker door, widened his eyes and then hid again behind the door.

"Shouldn't you be in class?" he asked, a sharp click in his tone. I shoved my balled-up fists into my jacket pockets.

"Um, yeah well I was just taking attendance sheets to Mrs. May. You know, in the office."

"I know where Mrs. May works."

"Right. Uh so hi. How are you?"

He laughed once, a deep, acidic laugh that sounded just like his mother and made me shiver. "Really? You're gonna ask me how I am?" He slammed his locker door shut causing me to jump back.

"You're right. Probably pretty stupid."

"What do you want Margo?"

"I just...wanna know if you're okay."

"Okay with what? Okay with being dumped? Okay with having this broken heart that I have no idea what to do with? Okay with the fact that I still don't even know why you broke up with me, like *really* broke up with me? I called you a bajillion times, Margo." His lip quivered. He was trying so hard not to cry. It killed me to see him like this.

"I know. I know I didn't give a good reason. And I'm sorry for ignoring you. If I said I made a mistake, would that matter?"

He cocked his head to the side, opened his mouth but then snapped it shut. He slid his arms into the straps of his backpack and shifted his weight. "It doesn't matter. It's too late." He stepped past me and walked down the hall, head hanging low. I wiped a rogue tear from my cheek and walked the other way back to class. If I'd only answered his calls or texted him back over that weekend it might have made a difference. He might have been pissed but we probably could have worked it out and chalked it up to our first big fight. But no, I had to go and be an idiot.

"Hello, earth to Margo!" Donny waved his hands in front of my face, bringing me back to the present. I shook my head and swatted at his hands. "So? Can you get someone to switch with you or not?"

I probably could. I'd worked enough extra hours over the past few months, even working some of Manny's shifts so that he could DJ several EDM shows that I had no idea he even did. I'm sure he'd cover for me, and even if all I wanted to do was hide in my bed under a mountain of blankets and snuggle a fat orange tabby cat, I really did need to get away. I wasn't that big a fan of Neko Case, not like Donny, who carried a certain affinity for her, but with everything happening with Tyler, and Nate's test just a few days away, I could use a distraction.

"Know what, I think I can. Let's' do it. Who's gonna make the hotel reservations?"

"On it!" Jillian whipped out her phone, fingers flying frantically across the screen. "And done. My dad said he'd book us a room at the same hotel again. Also, we don't need to worry about the tickets, they're also going to be taken care of."

"Wait what? You're buying all the tickets?" Linz asked, pointing back and forth between us and herself.

"My dad knows a guy who knows a guy," she said. Ordinarily I'd protest to her paying for the hotel *and* the tickets, it felt too much like charity, but at this juncture in my life I didn't have the energy to put up a fight. Instead, I hugged her and welcomed the trip.

When Jillian said her dad knew a guy who knew a guy, I didn't expect for that guy to be the actual owner of the Roseland theater. When we rolled up, the manager greeted us and explained that the owner, I guess by way of Jilly's dad, arranged a table for us in Peter's Room, which was located on the ground level of the Roseland theater, but acted as a more intimate venue setting, including a restaurant and a bar. Apparently, this was where Neko Case would actually be performing and we'd been given a front row table. Donny was basically in heaven.

"OMG you guys, the last time I saw Neko Case I was in the freaking nosebleeds!" he exclaimed, bouncing up and down in his seat like a sugared-up toddler, eyes darting rapidly from corner to corner of the dimly lit room.

I leaned over to Jillian and whispered in her ear. "I think you broke Donny." It had been forever since we'd seen Donny look this excited about anything, and even though my core didn't want to feel excited about anything for the rest of my life, I found it within me to laugh, for Donny's sake. I mean, how could I not?

It was an amazing show and a perfect distraction for my brain. Best of all, before Neko Case came on set, Connor Oberst of Bright Eyes did a secret show, and he was freaking awesome. Even Linz loved it and she's always maintained that he has a voice you either really love or really hate. Afterwards, we swung by Voodoo Donuts, grabbed a box of assorted oh-so-bad for-you-but-damn-they-taste-good donuts, returned to the hotel, changed into our pajamas and posted up on the two queen beds, Linz of course preferring the overstuffed couch where she sprawled, legs dangling over the sides.

"I love this hotel," she said through bites of her fruit loop donut. "They have the best couches out of every single hotel I've ever been in."

"It's still so strange you prefer the couch to the comfy bed," Jillian said, attempting to eat a powdered donut without getting it all over the place.

"If it means I don't have to sleep next to one of you I'll take the couch every time."

"You guys, that was such an amazing show. I love love love Neko Case," Donny said.

"We know," we all responded. He frowned and then waived a finger at each of us.

"Don't be haters."

"Seriously though," I said. "It was a great show and I can't believe Connor Oberst performed, oh and also the food was amazing. Jillian please thank your father for us."

"Oh yeah sure thing. He said it was his pleasure."

"Well it's not over," Linz said. "We still have this whole box of sugar-packed gluten to finish up and we're having breakfast at Tin Shed tomorrow before heading home. The dude at the desk says it's incredibly difficult to get in cause it's always balls crowded but hey, challenge accepted."

In the morning, we woke up before sunrise, which was a miracle in and of itself because no one else besides me is a morning person, and arrived at Tin Shed just before a line was beginning to form. Once inside we ate until our bellies were full. I loved going out to eat breakfast probably more than any other meal, and as far as breakfast joints go, Tin Shed was one of the best. I tried to stay chipper, even when the waitress brought out a steaming pile of cheesy hash browns and sausage, which was my all-time favorite breakfast food, but it was hard to ignore what was waiting for me when the weekend was over.

We got home late in the evening, thanks to Donny wanting to stop at every tulip and iris garden festivals along the way. We parted ways at Jillian's house and I drove the long way down Highway 99. When I arrived at home, the cottage was dimly lit and Mom had fallen asleep on the couch again, the Bible folded across her chest. It seemed fitting that she'd be reaching out to the powers that be, in the few days before Nate's study, probably hoping for there to be hidden somewhere the answers to her questions so that the study didn't need to happen.

***

Thursday after school I rushed through a quick practice with the relay team minus Andy, put three miles around the track to score some major brownie points with Coach Cathy, and cut out early to meet Mom at the rehab center. Nate's test was in two days and we wanted to spend a little time with him before then.

I tossed my gym bag into the back of the car and sped to the center; fairly certain I'd ran more than a few red lights. In the parking lot, I still found myself searching for Tyler's car, and again scanning for him in the visitor's lounge, but he'd long since stopped coming in during the week. Sari told me that he'd been coming early Sunday mornings, and even though he greeted her with a friendly smile, there wasn't the usual twinkle in his eye. *Way to go, Margo. Way to take away a sweet boy's twinkly eye.*

I walked through the double doors, habitually turning my head to look in the visitor's lounge and stopped in my tracks. "Margo, honey there you are," my mother called to me from a table in the back. Across from her at the table was Mr. Dan comfortably dressed in jeans and a fitted Marshall Academy sweatshirt. He smiled and waved as I entered the room. Instead of sitting in the seat my mother had pulled out for me, I leaned up against the coke machine trying to push down the raging bubbles of anxiety that were trying to escape. Why was he here, at the center, with my mom? I'd turned in all of my assignments, I hadn't smarted off in class, and as far as I knew everything was still on track with the tests.

"Hey Mr. Dan, what are you doing here?" I asked, voice wavering.

"I wanted to meet with you and your mom to go over how the study will be conducted, what can be expected of the doctors', and your roles if any, in the study. Your mom said you guys would be coming here today and it was as good as any a place to meet. She also offered me a chance to meet Nate."

"Is that necessary? To like, meet him before he's brought to the hospital?" I asked.

"No, it's not necessary but I'd like to meet him, maybe I'd get a better feel for how the test questions might be directed, you know, beyond the normal neutral questions that were asked in the previous study."

If he could sense I was totally freaked out with him being here he didn't let on. I wasn't even sure *why* I was freaked that he was here, really. I think that I preferred to keep my school life and my personal life very, very separate, and while that got me in trouble with my best friends, and even though I liked Mr. Dan well enough, it just felt strange and uncomfortable for him to be here. What would we even say when he walked into the room and saw Nate laying there like a vegetable?

"Honey, you're okay with Dan meeting your brother, aren't you?" *Dan?* Shouldn't she be calling him Mr. Miller, his actual last name? It was weird, the way she said his name, how it rolled off her tongue with ease, like she'd been saying it casually for years. I shook the thoughts out of my head and nodded. "Yeah. Why wouldn't I be okay? Mr. Dan, you should meet Nate. I'm gonna head in there now while you two finish up. See you in there."

"Don't you want to hear what Dan has to say about the study?" Mom asked.

"No, I think I'm good with whatever he tells you. I mean, they are the experts, right? So I'll just meet you guys in there." I spun and left the lounge for Nate's room. After shutting the door behind me and catching my breath I slid into the chair beside Nate's bed and leaned in.

"Alright big brother, so check it. My psych teacher Mr. Dan wants to come in and check you out. He's a cool guy. I think you'd like him. Sometimes he's super dorky, and the front of his pants are always covered in chalk, but he's still pretty chill." I waited for a response that wouldn't come. In the past he'd roll his eyes whenever I'd say something he felt was childish or just stupid. I watched his eyes to see if they were going to roll, imagining they would, but they remained vacant, affixed to the same spot on the ceiling.

I hoped more than anything that this study would prove he was still in there, in any capacity. I knew it wouldn't change anything. Having electrodes hooked up to his skull, his brainwaves recorded as questions were asked wouldn't just miraculously cause him to wake up, or even reveal how to get his brain to snap out of it. But it was something. I hated being hopeful. It made me feel vulnerable, or maybe a little ridiculous. My mother was hopeful and I always gave her a hard time for it. Now I realized I wasn't that far off from her. But was being hopeful such a bad thing? I guess it wasn't so long as in the end, you didn't wind up crushed.

There was a soft knock at the door and when it opened Mom and Mr. Dan slipped in. I stood up and moved away from the chair, folding my hands in front of me, fingers lacing and unlacing. Mom moved in front of me, turned to where Mr. Dan still stood at the door and offered her hand.

"Dan, this is my son Nate. Nate honey, this is Margo's teacher Dan Miller. He's going to be spending some time with you in a few days and wanted to come meet you." She motioned for him to come closer. He hesitated but after I nodded, he shuffled in and stood beside my mom. She rested her and in the middle of his back.

Mr. Dan cleared his throat. "Hi Nate. I'm Dan, Dan Miller. Kids like to call me Mr. Dan. Right now I realize how totally uncool I sound." He nervous-laughed and I sympathetically smiled. He was trying, which was more than I could say for anyone else.

"Your mom tells me you like to listen to music. Me too. I'm really into this heavy metal band called Mental Disorder. I know, it's a terribly insensitive name, but the lead guitarist can really shred."

I slung my arm across my face to hide my wide-mouthed grin in the crook of my elbow. I'd never pegged Mr. Dan for being a metal-head. Admittedly we'd never discussed his particular taste in music, but I always figured him for more a soft rock, easy listening kind of guy. He glanced up at me, smiled out of the corner of his mouth and continued to talk to my brother. My mom looked like she was just taken away with him and the way he so comfortably and effortlessly talked to Nate, like the fact that Nate was basically a stick with eyes didn't creep him out. Or the fact that the lingering smell of hospital and old people permeated the nostrils didn't send him running. Granted, he was a psychology teacher and before that he worked in a lab; being around test subjects wasn't some new thing for him. But there was still just something about how much of an interest he took that proved he was so much better than any of the other teachers at Marshall's, and that he actually cared.

When he was finished getting to know Nate, he thanked my mom, told me to finish my paper and left. Mom still wore the same playful smile as the one she'd had plastered to her face when I found them in the lounge. Was my mom totally crushing on Mr. Dan? It would be weird if they started seeing each other, I mean, he was my teacher and I was almost pretty sure she hadn't been on a date since my dad left. Still, it was nice to see her look like she was happy.

We said goodnight to Nate, checked out with Sari and headed for the parking lot. "I'll swing by Little Ceasars and pick up a pizza. We can eat it picnic style in the living room and watch Lifetime movies. What do you say?" I wanted to say that I had loads of reading to do for lit and a psych project to complete, and a crap ton of math homework from Thanos but a bigger part of me knew that I should take advantage of her good mood because these "pizza picnic moments" were few and far between.

"Sure Mom. That sounds great. I'll see you at home."

The morning before the study I was a ball of nerves. It felt like a giant gnarled hand with long boney fingers was gripping my insides, releasing my organs, and then gripping them again. I ran to the bathroom, the sudden feeling that I was going to hurl taking over me, but as I squatted there, head hanging over the toilet bowl that was in need of a cleaning, all I could do was dry heave.

It was just slightly after 5:30am and I had a good half hour before I'd need to get ready for school so I slid into some sweat pants, zipped up a hoodie, laced my shoes and went for a run. The early morning air was crisp and sweet, the only sounds were that of the babbling brook next to our cottage and birds singing. I started out at a nice even pace but by the time I'd crossed the foot bridge to the trail next to the highway I was in a full-on sprint, running as if my life depended on it. I couldn't slow down and I didn't want to. It was as if all my frustrations, all the emotions that had been clogging up my head about Tyler, these past two years of Nate being in a coma, my mom, were being released with every stride and I didn't want to stop. I wanted it all gone so like Forest Gump I just kept running. I ran until I'd reached the mouth of the pond, then turned right and ran until I reached the historical society.

I folded myself over, hands on my knees, breath heavy and quick. My cheeks were damp; I wasn't aware that I'd been crying. I found a soft patch of grass by the steps that wasn't too wet with dew and laid down, the light rays of the sun warm on my face. They say that things get better when you're older, that the teenage years always feel like they are the worst, that you're going to die. I hoped they were right because I absolutely hated the way I was feeling right now. It was like someone was sitting on my chest with their full weight, crushing me and just as I felt I were about to die, they'd get off of me long enough for me to catch my breath before they hopped right back on.

More than anything I hated the way I'd made Tyler feel and there wasn't a damn thing I could do about it. I wanted to talk to him, to tell him about how nervous I was for Nate's tests, ask him how things with the pageant were going, talk about his summer plans, and mine. Two weeks. It had been two weeks since he stopped talking to me and I missed him so much. After my lungs had recovered, I stretched my legs, stood up and then ran home, a steady even pace this time.

Mom was in the kitchen when I got home, leaning over the counter on her elbows reading the paper, a steaming mug of french roast resting between her hands. She looked up over the rim of her glasses as I rounded the corner making a bee line for the pot of coffee. I was drenched in sweat and probably smelled like a sewer but nothing could stand in the way of me and a good cup of fresh hot coffee. I sipped it slowly, all too aware of her pale blue eyes focused on me, a half grin on her face.

"Morning kiddo. How was your run?" she asked.

"It was good. I only saw two tweakers this time, down by the historical society."

"I really don't like you running down there sweetie. It's just not very safe."

"Mom, there are tweakers, like, on every corner in this town. And also, I run fast so like try and touch me."

She chuckled, taking a drink of her coffee and turning back to her paper. "Mr. Spartan pageant is tonight. You thinking about going?"

"Hard pass."

"Why's that? Oh, is it because Tyler is in the pageant?" I picked at the chipped corner of the counter. Was that the reason? Partly. Ok mostly, I guess. She turned back to me, waiting for a response. I shrugged.

"Is it still awkward between you two?"

"A little. I guess a lot actually. I tried to talk to him a week or so ago and he basically told me it was too late. So I guess I'd feel weird being there. Like I don't want him to see me in the audience and fudge up or whatever if he was still mad at me."

"What if you sat in the very back?" she offered.

"Nah. I'd feel like he would still see me, feel my presence or something. I know it sounds stupid."

She shook her head, put her mug down and stepped toward me, pulling me into a hug. I was really enjoying her recent increase in hugs. "Not stupid, honey. It's okay for you not to be there."

"Are you gonna go?" I asked, face buried in her chest.

"And be in the same room as his she-beast of a mother? Not very likely." We both laughed. It felt good. Right. Almost dare I say normal. She tucked my hair behind my ears, kissed my forehead. "Okay. I have to get ready for work and you need to shower before school. You smell like a foot." I stuck my tongue out at her and walked to the shower. She was like a whole different person. Like how a mother was supposed to be and I was afraid I'd become too used to it. No matter how pleasant she acted, I knew deep down it wouldn't last for long.

All anyone could talk about at school was the upcoming pageant at 5:00pm tonight. Tyler was projected to win, of course, which would probably piss Blake off if he did, even if they were currently on speaking terms. Surprising yet also not so surprising was the fact that there was a good chunk of student body who were putting their support behind Griffin. I could see why. Despite being twinned with a demon seed, Griffin was a total sweetheart.

What pleased me more than anything about the student body obsession with the pageant was that I was no longer the hot topic of conversation. Frankly I couldn't believe I had been talked about for so long. If all the girls at school wanted to do was talk about which one of the McHotties was going to win and how their skits would go, well, more power to them. Now I could go back to being the nobody weird indie girl no one gave a crap about.

Jillian on the other hand was obsessed with the pageant. As we walked down the hall after lit class, her lips flapped on and on, hands flying in sync with every word. Donny and I were good at rolling our eyes and letting her get it out of her system, but Linz just wasn't having any of it.

"Oh. My. Gosh can you puhlease stop talking about the stupid pageant!" Linz yelled, stopping in the middle of the hall. It was third period break and we were heading to the benches out in the quad. Jillian brushed her off, looping her arm through mine.

"There's nothing wrong with being excited about something Linz," Donny said.

"Yeah maybe if that something was a topic or an event that didn't kill brain cells. It's a freaking boys' pageant. It's not some scientific study that's going to change the world, or a presidential election."

"Be a hater all you want Linz, you're not going to make me any less excited to go," Jillian said.

We found an empty bench by the fountain and spread out. Jillian stood behind me and started to french-braid my hair. She loved to braid hair and always wished for a sister to practice on but since she didn't have one and my hair was super long, I'd been her guinea pig. I didn't mind. I found it relaxing, the way her elegant fingers gently combed through my hair aided in my need to mentally work through all the things that were bothering me. Donny watched, a pleasant smile stretched across his face.

"I absolutely love your hair Margo. It's so thick and rich," Donny said, reaching across Linz to run his fingers through a loose section of hair.

"Thanks, Donny. I kinda like it."

"Ever think about cutting it?" Linz asked, looking up from her graphic novel. Her jet-black hair was short, razor cut and angled to the chin, a deep blue streak down the left side. She's had the same hair style since we met, the color of the streak the only thing to change. In second grade my mom took me to Great Clips for a trim and I wound up with a choppy pixie cut. My mom flipped out and Nate couldn't stop laughing for hours. It had taken me forever to grow my hair out from that horrific cut and ever since I've had the long hair.

"Nah, I think I'm good with this length," I said. I could sense the smile that spread on Jillian's face. She alone was the only one to have ever seen my second-grade horrible pixie cut photo. "Besides, I'd never be able to pull off your style."

Linz chuckled. "No one can pull off my style."

A throat cleared behind us. We turned to see Father Dave, the campus Priest accompanied by Mrs. Fergie, the junior/senior guidance counselor. Instinctually my stomach seized. Nothing good ever came from an encounter by both the Priest and the guidance counselor together.

"Good afternoon, ladies," Father Dave said. He caught Donny's gaze and correcting himself said, "and gentleman. Nice to see you all taking advantage of this beautiful spring day." It was weird, listening to these words spill forth from his mouth. I recognized it must be on account of Mrs. Fergie because ordinarily Father Dave rolled with more of a sailor mouth and was never so formal. It's what the student body liked about him, how down to earth and real he was.

"Yeah, Father Dave, it is a fabulous day," Donny replied.

"Margo, I wondered if we could have a word. In the Dean's office," Father Dave said. I stood up, running my hands through the braid shaking it loose. "Is everything okay? Is there something wrong with my scholarship?"

"Why don't you just come with us and we'll discuss this in the Dean's office," Mrs. Fergie said. I scooped up my backpack and headed towards the office with Father Dave and Mrs. Fergie, turning back only once to look at my friends who all shared the same look of concern. Mrs. Fergie kept a hand lightly at my elbow as we walked from the quad to the office and around the corner to the Dean's office. Mrs. Driscoll, the Dean of Students sat behind her oak desk in a plush leather chair. She motioned for me to take a seat in front of her desk, Mrs. Fergie sliding into the seat next to me while Father Dave posted up beside Mrs. Driscoll. It was unsettling, the whole thing and my mind was reeling with all the reasons I'd been called into the office. There was one month left of school so I couldn't imagine there being something wrong with my scholarship, and I hadn't defaced school property, bullied a student, or bad-mouthed a teacher (though Mr. Fisher was asking for it like all the time). Maybe it was about one of my college applications.

Mrs. Driscoll folded her hands on the desk in front of her, cocking her head to the side.

"Margo honey, I know you're probably wondering why you have been called in here."

"Pretty much, yeah," I said.

"Well, there's no easy way to say these kinds of things so...honey we got a call this morning from your mother. She called to inform us that your brother Nate passed away. As far as the doctors can tell he didn't have a seizure or anything, he simply stopped breathing."

I don't know what she said after that. All I heard was Charlie Brown's mom talking, the wonk wonk wonk wonk wonk. I focused on the same three words over and over. Nate passed away. Nate passed away. Nate...what? It wasn't possible. For two years he had just been a vegetable. No strokes, no movement, nothing. How could he have just passed away? The study was scheduled for tomorrow. How was it possible that he could die the very day before this super important study? Mrs. Fergie's cold plump hand gripped my arm lightly and I yanked it away.

"Margo, did you hear what Mrs. Driscoll said?" she asked, trying not to look hurt by my sudden move. I stared at her, at the jagged crack in the left corner of her purple frames. "Margo, Margo are you okay?"

I met her gaze and then slid my eyes over to Father Dave and Mrs. Driscoll. Three sets of eyes stared at me clearly waiting for some sort of response, an outburst of tears, wailing maybe. Something that registered as sadness or disbelief. Any normal person would have responded that way.

"Could I please have some water?" I croaked. In a split-second Father Dave was in front of me with a small paper cup filled to the top with room temperature water, almost as if he'd anticipated the request. I downed it in one gulp, crushing the cup on the desk.

Mrs. Driscoll cleared her throat. "Margo, I know that's a lot to take in, and I'm sure you have many questions for your mom. If you'd like we can arrange for someone to drive you to the rehab facility where your mom said she'll be spending the day. It's not advisable that you drive yourself. You'll of course be excused from classes today." She pulled her creased crimson red lips into a thin smile and once again paused to wait for a response. I slipped my cell phone out of my pocket and tapped the screen. No text or call from my mom. Why hadn't she called me directly the moment she found out? Why'd she leave it for the school to tell me?

"I think I'll go back to class. There's a uh, test or whatever in my math class."

"Margo, we're excusing you from the rest of your classes today and from any upcoming tests. We understand how dire this situation is and we understand it will be difficult for you to study when you're grieving." I shook my head. I knew I should take them up on the offer, let someone drive me to the facility but I couldn't go there, not yet. I needed time to process. How could I grieve something I hadn't yet even processed? If I went to the facility where Mom was doing well, who knows what, it would be sad and depressing and oh my gosh would his dead body still be in the bed? No, I wasn't ready to face that. I needed to be here.

"I appreciate the offer, and I will consider it, but I think I need to go to class today. Please? I just can't go there. I can't be there. Not right now."

Mrs. Driscoll nodded. "Alright. But if you start to feel it's just too much, please come to the office and we'll get you out of here, okay?"

I nodded and pushed off the chair. Mrs. Fergie led me out of the room followed by Father Dave. At the end of the hall before it opened up into the main office, Father Dave gently took my arm, spinning me to face him.

"Kiddo, I see what you're trying to do. Putting on a brave face. It's okay to not be brave. It's gonna suck like hell. Death sucks like hell. You come find me if you can't be tough anymore, okay?" He squeezed my arm. I lightly brushed his fingers with mine, nodded and left for class.

The quad was empty. Fourth period had started just over five minutes ago. I'd been tardy to fourth period more times the past few weeks than I was proud of and I just didn't want to deal with the annoying look on Mr. Fisher's face yet again so instead I cut left around the fountain and slipped into the library. Ordinarily we needed a pass to be in the library during class time but I'd volunteered enough shelving books I hoped the librarian would look the other way.

At the sound of the door clicking open, she looked up from her perch at the circulation desk, lowered her glasses down the bridge of her nose and smiled. "Margo dear is there something I can help you with?"

I swept my hair over my shoulder, slapped on a fake as hell smile, approached the desk.

"Hey Ms. Card. Um, I was wondering if I could hang in here and work on my psych paper? It's due next week and I'm only like half finished." It wasn't far from the truth; I just hope she'd buy it.

"Aren't you supposed to be in math class right now? Did Mr. Fisher excuse you?" she asked.

"No not exactly. It's just, I had to meet with Mrs. Driscoll in her office and the meeting ran late and Mr. Fisher hates when people are late and I just really can't stand being embarrassed by him. Any other day and I could suck it up and take it but just not today. So please, Ms. Card would it please be okay if I worked on my psych paper in here?" It came out as one big gulping sob. She wasn't sure how to handle me, it was so easy to tell by the way her eyebrows twitched.

"Sure honey. If he asks, I'll say you were helping in the library and didn't hear the bell."

"Thank you Ms. Card. Really, thank you." I headed for the group of desks in the back of the library, slid into one of the study booths and dumped my bag on the floor next to me. I yanked my headphones out of my bag and set my music on shuffle, then texted my mom.

> Mom. You need to call me. Please. ASAP.

I knew she most likely wouldn't respond but I felt better sending it anyway. I thought about sending a text to Jillian, to let her know what had happened, but I just ended up staring at my phone, waiting for a response. Mom should have called me right away. No, wait. She should have gotten in her car and hauled ass here to tell me in person so I wouldn't have had to hear it from the stupid Dean and then have to sit here waiting to hear from her. If there had ever been a time that anyone needed a mother it was now. Nate had died. Nate had died. Nate. Had. Died. I yanked the hood of my sweater up over my head, pulling tightly at the strings before resting my head face down on the table. I didn't even know how my brain was supposed to process those words. Nate. Dead. It didn't compute. For my entire life he'd been the most important person, even in vegetable form, and then there was Tyler. Well, I'd screwed things up with Tyler so he was gone, and now Nate was literally gone from this world so what was I left with? I really wanted to run and find Tyler, feel his strong arms wrap around me, have his lips kiss the top of my head. Surely he'd not turn his back on me in a time like this, even though I'd done the same to him.

When the bell rang indicating the end of fourth period, and since my mom still hadn't responded, I grabbed my bag and headed to AP Government. Mrs. Grace decided it was time for a pop quiz, which I totally bombed because I didn't answer a single question.

Halfway through sixth period, my phone vibrated. Flipping it over I saw it was my mom finally calling so I snagged a bathroom pass from the door and slipped outside.

"Mom?" I squeaked.

She sighed. "Hi honey."

"Mom what happened?"

"They don't know. They say it looks like he just went to sleep and didn't wake up."

"How is that even possible? Did he get sick? Did one of the nurses not clean his tubes properly?"

"No honey nothing like that. They said he just didn't wake up."

"There's gotta be something else, Mom. He just doesn't *not* wake up. Someone must have done something wrong."

"Margo, honey, nobody did anything to him. It was just his time to go."

"So what now?" I whispered.

"I'm working with the center on that, honey. I will take care of everything okay? You don't have to stay at school. They said you could leave. Do you want me to come get you?"

She sounded calm. There wasn't even a crack in her voice, the kind you expect to find in people passing on bad news while also trying to hold it together, but she just sounded too calm. It so wasn't like her.

"No. I'm going to stay. I have track practice.

"Honey I really think I should come get you, I need to talk to you about something."

"Well I have my car here, can't it wait?"

"No honey, it can't."

Ten minutes later, Mom whipped into the school parking lot, screeching to a halt alongside the curb where I'd been waiting. When she'd first pulled in, I thought I could make out the silhouette of someone sitting next to her in the passenger seat. When she stopped, and I was able to get a better look, for half a second, I thought it was the ghost of Nate. The lanky build, rust-brown mop of hair, almond-shaped eyes, and a crooked nose. Then the thing smiled and I knew it wasn't Nate's ghost because Nate rarely smiled.

The Nate-look-alike opened his door and stepped out. Mom got out of the car and came to stand beside him, sliding her sunglasses to rest on the top of her head.

"Hey honey, um, so you remember your father."

20

— • —

"I'm sorry, I think I just had a mini stroke. Did you say that this dude leaning against your car is my father? As in the man who walked out when I was five-years-old never to be heard from again?"

Mom sighed. "Yup. That'd be him. Listen, there are things we need to talk about so get in, we'll grab a bite to eat and I will explain."

My absentee dad lowered his aviators down the bridge of his nose and took a step towards me, then pulled me in to the world's most awkward half-hug.

"Wow. Margo. I can't believe it. You've shot up like a weed. When did you grow up so fast?"

I wiggled out of his hug. "Well gee, Paul. Last time I saw you I was a child, what do you think happened?"

"Margo," Mom warned.

"It's alright, Christa. Should have seen that coming. Guess I kinda deserved it."

"Ya think?" I said.

"How about we catch up over some food? You guys hungry? My treat."

"That sounds like a great idea. Margo?" Mom says.

"Yeah, sure, whatever," I said and then climbed into the back seat.

We drove to Denny's (gross) where Paul proceeded to fill me in on his whereabouts the past twelve years (traveling the world) and how he eventually settled in Denver, Colorado and owns a music store, and how he's so sorry he missed me growing up, and never reached out, and blah, blah, blah. I nodded along because I just didn't have it in me to put up a fight even though a fire was raging inside of me and I desperately wanted to let loose on him. Also, even though Mom looked like she was keeping it together, I knew at some point she'd break. I mean, she basically stopped functioning when Nate attempted suicide, how she was maintaining a cool now that he was actually dead was beyond me. There would be a breaking point, I just knew it.

When we finished our meal, Paul excused himself to take care of the bill, so I used the few minutes Mom and I had alone to bring on the inquisition.

"Mom, what the hell? We don't hear from this guy in over a decade and he just randomly shows up?"

"I know how it looks, but there are things you don't understand."

"Try me, Mom."

"Honey, how else do you think I'm affording South Junction?"

I shrugged. "I don't know, I thought it was paid by the State or something."

She let out a clipped laugh. "Yeah. Right. I wish. Look, when Nate tried to kill himself, I called Paul. He was devastated, and don't look at me like that, he really was. He asked if there were anything he could do and I just told him to take care of all the finances."

"Hang on a sec, he's been paying for Nate's hospital bill these past two years but he's never even once sent in a child support check? Wait, no, scratch that. If you knew how to contact him this whole time how come you told Nate every single time he asked, that you didn't know where Paul was and didn't have a phone number for him?"

"I *didn't* know where he was, I wasn't lying about that. I've had his cell number, the one he gave me when he left and I was just lucky that he'd never changed it, and I never told your brother because I didn't want him...I didn't want him getting hurt."

"Yeah, well how'd that work out for ya?"

"That's not fair, Margo."

Before anything else could be said, Paul returned, placing a tip under a half empty glass of water.

"So, I called The Hilton and they have a room available."

"Oh no, Paul, don't be ridiculous," Mom said. "You can stay with us."

"What's that now?" I said but Mom shushed me.

"You don't have to do that, Chris, I don't mind the hotel."

"No it's fine. Besides, you have your dog with you. Don't stay in a hotel."

"Margo, would that be alright with you?" Paul asked. What was I going to say? *No, Paul it's not alright with me for you to stay in our small house, you can stay in a dumpster for all I cared.*

After Mom dropped me back off at my car, I drove aimlessly around town. I wasn't ready to go home, not when Paul was going to be there. I couldn't believe that my mom had known how to contact Paul this whole time. All the times Nate asked about where he was and she'd flat out told him she didn't know. Every time he looked so rejected. Let down. If she'd just given him the number and let him make the decision to contact Paul, even if Paul ignored his calls, or said he didn't want to talk, or even if it had been the wrong number, at least Nate would have been able to have that. Maybe then he wouldn't have even...no. I wasn't going to allow myself to go down that rabbit hole of what-ifs, because there was no point. Mom could have given Nate Paul's number and I could have been more supportive during his breakups with Khali. But none of that mattered now because Nate was dead.

I found myself driving through the hills and down the long estate drive leading to Tyler's house. I hadn't meant to, but I guess I let my heart lead the way. I just needed to see him. Even if all he did was glare at me, I needed to be where he was.

I parked and walked up to his door and rang the bell. Once. Twice. On the third ring, the door opened. Alexander smirked down at me.

"What the hell are you doing here, trailer trash?"

"I don't live in a trailer."

"Doesn't matter. What do you want?"

"Is Tyler home?"

He was about to answer when the door was pulled open farther by Mrs. Ashford. Her nose wrinkled as she took me in. Self-consciously I swiped at my eyes and straightened my shirt.

"Ms. Adams. To what do we owe the pleasure?"

"I'm looking for Tyler? I really need to see him."

She pulled her lips up into a wicked grin. "Surely you know Tyler doesn't want to see you."

"I know, but if you could just tell him that it's an emergency? It's about my brother."

"Ah yes, Nate. I heard the news about his passing. Such sadness. About time if you ask me. I'm sorry for your loss, but Tyler isn't home."

I squeezed my eyes shut. "Okay well, will you please tell him I stopped by?"

"I'd like to tell you that I will, honey, but we both know that I won't. Goodbye." She closed the door without another word. I drove the whole way home in tears.

Sir Rusty sat on my head hissing. Shoving him off and swiping my nest of hair away from my face, I turned my head to find a smushy-faced Pug named Beavis sitting in the rocking chair next to my bed snort-breathing at me. Sir Rusty popped back up from behind me where I'd shoved him and hissed again.

"Stop it Sir Rusty. He's just a dog. Paul's stupid smelly farting dog," I grumbled, kicking off the blanket and chucking a pillow at Beavis, who snorted, roll-jumped out of the chair and charged out of my room.

"Yeah you'd better run."

When I got home from my drive to Tyler's I was too crushed to further discuss this whole ordeal so I'd gone straight to bed, hoping Paul would be gone when I woke up. No such luck. He'd slept on the couch, and somehow his smelly dog had found his way into my room.

I fumbled around my nightstand for my phone to check the time. Three missed calls from Jillian and several group texts I'd ignored. After leaving them in the quad yesterday to go talk to the Dean, I'd avoided them during lunch, and skipped psych to leave with my mom. It was lame for me to ignore them, I knew it. I'd made a promise not to keep anymore secrets, yet here I was preferring to crawl inside myself rather than lean on my friends. I was lame.

There was another text from Coach Cathy informing me that my mom had contacted her to tell her the news and that she'd excuse me from practice the rest of the week. I hated receiving special treatment. It was bad enough that I was going to be excused from taking my finals, but now I was being excused from practice even though Districts were next week.

My gym bag was by the door so I changed into some running pants and set out for a run while Mom and Paul were still asleep. If I wasn't going to be able to hide in my room for the rest of my life, I'd at least get a few miles between me and this cottage.

"Alright Sir Rusty, I'm out. Try not to kill Beavis," I said, scratching him behind the ears. Beavis was curled up in a snorting mound next to Paul on the couch, and I stuck my tongue out at them as I left. I didn't care if it was childish, fuck Paul and his stupid dog.

At the bottom of the steps, I stretched out my legs, waking up my calves, and swung my arms across my chest a few times. Then I set off on the trail behind the cottage along the river, slow and steady at first and then a dead sprint. I knew today was going to suck hard core. Today I was supposed to go with Mom (and stupid Paul) to the funeral home to talk about "our options," and there was a slew of other things I'd rather do besides that. Stick bamboo shoots under my nails. Sit on a mound of fire ants. Guzzle hand sanitizer. The thing is, if I got in that car and drove to that stupid funeral home, and talked to some stupid mortician, it would mean Nate was actually really dead and I didn't want to accept it.

I could feel the bile rise in my throat, churning hot and slow, my lungs a raging inferno. A searing pain tore through my calves but I pushed it all down and kept going past the historical society, through the shady neighborhoods and up to McFarland Butte until I'd reached the gates to the old McFarland Cemetery. I hopped the rusted fence and tore off through the overgrown brush, dodging jagged gravestones until I'd reached a knotted old oak tree next to the patriarch McFarland headstone where I sank to the earth with a deep swallowing sob. It was the heaving, snot all over the face ugly crying which made me super glad there was no one, at least living, around to witness. I knew I should just call Jillian and the gang, tell them what happened because maybe at least with them around to support me I wouldn't feel like this huge black pit of despair was ten seconds from sucking me in. But just like I'd kept Nate's existence a secret, I was probably going to keep his death a secret too and suffer alone. Because I was a moron.

Once my sobbing stopped and I was sure there couldn't possibly be any more snot in my nose, I stretched out on the grass, my entire back side soaked with dew. I stared up at the sky, pale blue with hues of sunrise pink. White-yellow beams of early morning sunlight shot out from a patch of clouds and I wondered if Nate were up there. I wasn't sure what I believed about God and the afterlife, not anymore, but if there was one, a God up there in the heavens, would he have let Nate in last night? Mom always said Nate's comatose state was really him in purgatory working through his issues before God would let him in. Maybe it just took two years to get his shit straight. Or maybe there was no heaven, no God, and Nate just decided not to give a fuck any more.

My phone vibrated, a text from Mom telling me she'd gone ahead early to the funeral home and asked if I could bring Paul, then sent a follow-up text in all freaking caps asking me not to argue. Whatever. Yeah, sure I'd bring Paul with me, but she had just better not expect me to bond with him. All I really wanted to do was punch him in his stupid child-abandoning face.

When I got home, Paul was sitting in the rocking chair, a steaming mug of coffee in one hand while petting dumb Beavis with the other. We locked eyes for a moment before I looked away and headed to the kitchen for a glass of water.

"Hey, kiddo. Your mom had to meet the funeral guy early so I said I'd wait and ride with you."

I gulped down another glass of water. "Yup. Got the text."

"Thought maybe it would be good for us to spend some time together, get to know one another."

I snickered, then walked into the living room, leaning against the door frame. "Why even bother?"

"What's that now?"

"I mean, you're just gonna vamoose back to Colorado once this whole thing is over, and I'm 99 percent sure I won't hear from you again, so like, why bother with the getting to know one another."

"You're really not gonna make this easy for me, are ya?"

"Nope."

"Alright," he sighed. "Well, just let me know when you're ready."

We drove to the funeral home in silence. My hands gripped the steering wheel, ten and two, white-knuckled, my shoulders straight and tense. Paul kept his gaze out in front of him, but every few minutes I'd see him out of my side eye look over at me and begin to say something before clamming back up.

"How about some music?" he finally said, clicking through stations on my stereo. "What kind of music do you like to listen to?"

I flipped the knob on the stereo until it turned off. "Actually, I'm not really that into music, Paul."

"Really? Didn't figure there was a teenager who didn't like music."

"Yeah, well there's a lot you don't know."

The silence was deafening, but I'd developed my love for music from Nate, who'd developed his from Paul, and I wasn't about to give him the satisfaction. I didn't want him thinking we had anything whatsoever in common. So, even though there was an ache radiating from my shoulders down to my butt and music had always been my go-to-stress reducer, we drove in silence. Thankfully the funeral home was only a ten-minute drive.

I pulled into the lot, parked next to Mom's Volvo, and was out the door before Paul had even unbuckled his seatbelt. Mom was at the counter deep in conversation with a middle-aged balding man in a two sizes too big suit. He clutched a portfolio tightly to his chest. I was surprised to see Mr. Dan standing on the other side of Mom. He nodded when he saw me, offering a welcoming smile. Mom looked up as I approached and slung an arm around me, kissing my cheek.

"Good morning, honey," she whispered.

"Hey Mom," I replied. I was about to ask what Mr. Dan was doing here when Paul walked in.

"Don't you want to lock your car, kiddo?"

"There's nothing worth stealing in there, and don't call me kiddo."

He put his hands up. "Alright. You win." Then he extended a hand towards Mr. Dan and introduced himself.

"Hey, how's it going? I'm Paul Adams."

Mr. Dan shook Paul's hand. "Hey there, uh Mr. Adams. I'm Dan Miller, Margo's Psychology teacher.

Before any other unpleasantries could be exchanged, the balding man coughed into his fist and then motioned for the four of us to follow him into a room to the left of the front desk. Inside the room the walls were beige with framed photos of various bouquets of flowers, which I felt a little too befitting of a funeral home. What had I been expecting though? Walls lined with photos of the deceased or coffins? We gathered around a circular table, and balding man who introduced himself as Mr. Fields, placed his portfolio on the table and then folded his hands in front of him. I shuddered at the thought of those hands touching and embalming my dead brother.

"Are you the one that, you know, takes the insides out of the bodies and makes them look, well, not so dead?" I asked.

"Margo!" Mom gasped. Mr. Dan tried to cover a smile with his hand.

"You'll have to excuse my daughter," Mom said, pinching my arm. "She lacks social graces."

Mr. Fields cleared his throat. "It's quite alright. It's actually not the first time I've been asked that question. No, young lady, I do not prepare the deceased. I am more a facilitator for the family." He wiped is brow before moving on. "Ms. Adams, first let me start off by offering my condolences. I'm sure your son was a wonderful human being."

"Thank you," Mom said.

"Now, there are several options," he said, opening his portfolio and flipping slowly through the pages. "Here are a number of coffins priced highest to lowest. And here, if you chose cremation, are a selection of urns, from basic to the more elaborate."

He slid the portfolio across the table so Mom could flip through it. She bit her thumb nail anxiously as she did so. Mr. Dan noticed and gently took her hand in his pulling it down into his lap. She stretched a quick smile at him and turned back to the portfolio. So it looks like my assumptions had been correct. Mom and Mr. Dan were more than just friends.

When she was finished, she slid the portfolio back across the table to Mr. Fields and sighed. "There are just too many options. I mean, I haven't even spoken with the priest at the church yet to figure out when to have the service and-,"

I threw up my hand to stop her. "What do you mean service? There's not actually going to be a service is there?"

"Of course there's going to be a service, Margo," Paul replied. I shook my head at him and continued.

"Mom, you can't be seriously thinking of having a service."

She chewed her bottom lip. "Well I mean, I guess I sort of figured that would be the thing you do."

"Yeah but what's the priest going to say? Here lies Nate Adams whose failed attempt at suicide landed him two years in purgatory? Mom, come on. You know that's not gonna fly.

"You don't know that Margo," Paul said.

"Yeah I do. And with all due respect, Paul, you don't know the first thing about us. You haven't been here. For starters, Nate hated organized religion. He'd be pissed to know you had a religious service. Secondly, who's going to come to his service? None of his so-called friends even came to see him, nor did they call to ask about him. Not even *you* came to see him, Paul. All you did was send some stupid checks. So, excuse me, but you don't get a vote here. We should just cremate him, which is what he'd want, and spread his ashes."

"Margo, honey, I just don't know how I feel about a cremation. I don't know how I feel about any of this. I'm just trying to," she stopped, digging the palms of her hands into her eye sockets. "I don't know what I'm trying to do." And here it comes. The breaking point.

I tried to keep the tears pooling in my eyes from pouring. Mr. Fields sunk into himself, hugging the portfolio, uncomfortable by the family drama unfolding. Paul crossed his arms and glared at me, probably wishing he'd never even come back. Mr. Dan slid back from the table and put his arm on my shoulder, turning me towards the door.

"Hey, let's go get some fresh air, okay?" I let him lead me out of the room into the lobby. When the door closed, I took in a few deep breaths and wiped my eyes with the sleeve of my sweater.

"You okay?" he asked. I nodded, shaking out my arms.

"It's just so stupid. Nate wouldn't want to be shoved into some wooden box and covered in dirt. He hated being in one place for too long and he definitely hated the church. No way would he want a funeral service."

"I'm sure you're right. No one knew your brother more than you did. But kid, attacking your mom isn't the right thing to do."

"I wasn't attacking her! Or at least I hadn't meant to. It's just she's not thinking clearly and stupid Paul doesn't even know anything about Nate! Why he thinks he can be gone for this long and then waltz back in with opinions is, well, stupid!"

"Of course your mom's not thinking clearly. Her son died and she has to make all the hard decisions. Put yourself in her shoes. This is going to be one of the hardest things she'll ever do in her life, having to bury a child. Cut her some slack. And as for Paul, I guess just remember he'll leave when this is over, so find a way to deal with him. Don't you run to deal with these things? Go on one super long run."

"I already tried running today, Mr. Dan. Blah. This all just sucks.

He chuckled, rubbing the back of his neck. "It does. It sucks a lot. Just try to be supportive of your mom. You two are going to need each other now more than ever."

I sighed. "You're right. Thanks. Ok so now that that's over with, what's the deal with you and my mom? Are you guys, like, a thing?"

He blushed. I'd never seen that shade of red on a man before, like ever. "After she laid into me about the study all those months ago, and once she wasn't pissed any more, we kept talking and sort of connected. I guess you could say we're dating?"

"You guess? You don't sound very certain about that."

"It's complicated adult stuff Margo, no one said oh hey do you want to be boyfriend/girlfriend? We spend time with each other and we like it. So, whatever that is." He was squirming. It was obvious he wasn't comfortable talking about his feelings and relationships with a student.

My phone rang. I pulled it out of my purse to see it was Jillian. "I think I'm gonna take this. Can you tell my mom I'm gonna be outside?"

"You got it," he smiled his boyish grin and squeezed my shoulders before heading back into the room.

"Hey Jillian, listen I'm so sorry I haven't returned any of your calls or texts. Something happened…"

"I know. I'm so *so* sorry to hear about Nate."

"Wait, how'd you know?"

"Father Dave. He pulled us aside after religion on Friday. Told us what happened and said you might need us."

"Father Dave, eh? That guy. Well, he was right. I do need you guys. Turns out I'm not handling this very well and I could use you guys."

"That's' what we thought. Why don't you come outside," Jillian said.

"Huh?" I moved towards the door and pushed it open. There they were in the parking lot, leaning against Jillian's SUV. I hung up, dumped my phone into my purse and ran out to them. They circled around me, wrapping me in a tight group hug.

I texted Mom to let her know I was leaving with my friends. It wasn't like I'd be much help at the funeral home with all the Nate stuff anyway, and I didn't want to be around Paul anymore. She seemed ok with me bailing, probably because Mr. Dan was there with her. Maybe he'd be able to convince her to A) cremate Nate like I knew he'd want, and B) Tell Paul to go sleep on someone else's couch.

After we were seated in a quaint far corner booth at Lion and Owl, our orders taken, I addressed the gang. "You guys, I really do appreciate you all coming to the flats today, and again, I'm sorry I didn't just come find you yesterday after school and tell you about Nate. I think I was still in denial, and then on auto-pilot the rest of the day. I seriously don't even remember what happened once I got home. I know I promised not to be secretive anymore." I didn't tell them about where I'd gone before heading home. Too embarrassing.

"Really M, it's okay," Jillian said, reaching across the table for my hand. "I mean, at first for like a fleeting second, we were pissed that you didn't answer our calls or texts but we get it. Your brother died. I'm sure your brain was just a mess and we figured you'd reach out when you were ready."

"But then we got impatient and tracked you down anyway," Donny said.

"But how did you know I'd be at the funeral home this morning anyway? Pretty sure Father Dave didn't know that."

"We drove to your house and your nosey neighbor, the one with the walker, she told us you and some dude were fighting about meeting your mom at the funeral home," Linz said, popping a tater tot into her mouth. "Anyway, we asked which funeral home, she told us we were idiots because there was only one funeral home in the flats and Google maps led us to you."

I seriously had the best of friends. "Wow I mean, I've never been stalked before."

Linz threw a tater tot at me and laughed. It was still such a strange thing to see, Linz laughing. Or even smiling. It was kinda like seeing Wednesday Addams in *Addams Family Values* smile in front of the campers. A frighteningly beautiful sight to behold.

"So who was the dude you were arguing with?" Linz asked.

"That'd be Paul, my absentee father."

"Shut up. The one who walked out when you were five?" Donny asked.

"I thought your mom didn't know where he was?" Jillian asked. "How'd he know about Nate?"

"Welp, turns out my mom *did* in fact know how to contact him, she just didn't want us to know that. Thought she was protecting us by not telling. Anyway, he's apparently been paying the bills at South Junction and when Nate died, they contacted both my mom and Paul."

"So what's his story? Why'd he stay gone so long?"

I shrugged. "Who the fuck knows man. He had some lame-ass story but I tuned everything he said out. I have like zero desire to have a relationship with him."

Donny picked at his scrambled eggs with is fork. "Um, so have you told Tyler?"

I shook my head, staring down into my coffee. "We haven't talked in weeks so it would just have been weird for me to call. Don't you think?"

He shrugged his shoulders. "I mean, he's hurt and all, but he's not a monster. He would have taken your call if he knew about Nate."

"Did you guys go to the pageant? How'd he do? Did he win?

"No, actually Griffin won," Jillian said, wide smile on her face.

"Seriously? Wow everyone thought for sure Tyler would win."

"Yeah no, Tyler actually sucked balls. Totally bombed it. Like, hard core," Linz said. "His mom was pissed. And then Blake got all butt-hurt that Griffin won. It was bananas."

"Wait, what do you mean Tyler bombed it?" I asked.

"Dunno," she said. "He just couldn't get anything right, stumbled all over the place. Missed his queues a bunch. It was weird. He's always so put together."

In everything Tyler had ever done, be it a basketball game, a school play, a freaking school assignment, he'd always been a shining star. Even if he tried, he couldn't screw anything up. He could run around campus waiving his middle finger at everyone and all they'd see were an enthusiastic thumbs up. Something serious must have gone down for him to royally suck. I was sure his mom went ape shit on him. I just hoped she'd had enough decorum to not do it in front of everyone.

After brunch we drove out to Fern Ridge for a few hours to walk around the lake, and then I met up with Mom and Paul at the rehab facility to pack up Nate's room. Paul shot sideways glances at me the entire time, maybe hoping to get a chance to talk to me, maybe hoping I'd apologize for my behavior since he's been here, but it so wasn't going to happen. I could tell he was uncomfortable being in the room, packing up the belongings of a boy he didn't know, a boy he abandoned, so Mom suggested he head back to our place. He didn't think twice.

When all that was left to do was sign some documents, I left, but I didn't want to go home so I drove up to Skinner's Butte. I needed to be somewhere I could sit and think. Having my friends around me had been the perfect distraction to the tornado of emotions whirling through my system, but now I needed to be in a place where I could clear my head. I popped in my earbuds, turned on The Decemberists and sat on my usual bench. I waited for that moment of clarity that always came with listening to my music, but all I felt was sadness. Tyler and I had sat here on this bench so often it had become "our" bench. We'd even gone full cliché, scratching our initials into the warped wood of the seat with a knife. I traced them gently with my index finger, letting my mind wander back to that day in January. It was one of those bone chilling but blue sky for miles kind of days. We'd bundled up and hiked to the top, stopping to snuggle close on the bench and share a thermos of coffee. It had easily become one of my favorite dates with Tyler.

I was so wrapped up in my thoughts that I didn't hear a car pull up, or the gravel crunching under footsteps. When a hand gripped me lightly on the shoulder I jolted, sliding the length of the bench, arms swinging blindly behind me. Whipping my head around I saw Tyler crouched behind the seat of the bench.

"Hey, karate kid it's me!" he called out. I tore my earbuds out of my ear and sprang up.

"Tyler, what in the actual fuck! I told you not to sneak up on people! Holy shit!"

"Is it safe to come over?" he asked, peeking over the bench.

"Yeah, come on," I rubbed at the side of my butt where I'd slid on the bench. "I think I got a splinter in my ass." He uncurled himself and walked around the bench to stand in front of me. I crammed my hands into my pockets and balled them up. We were silent for several moments. He kept his eyes on mine, though I darted away several times. When he finally spoke, his voice was soft and sweet, sending my stomach into summersaults.

"Thought I might find you up here," he said.

"You were looking for me?"

"I tried to call you but it just went straight to voicemail."

I pulled my phone out of my pocket and noticed my phone had been set to *Do Not Disturb*.

"I went to the rehab to ask Sari if she had your mom's number, but then I saw her there, your mom, and she told me you needed to get some air. Figured this was where you'd go."

I nodded and sat back down on the bench. Tyler sat next to me and continued.

"Andy told me about your brother."

"Andy? How did he know?" I asked.

"He said your coach called him. Said you'd be missing some practices, explained why. He told me last night before the pageant. Mar, I am so sorry about Nate. I know today was supposed to be the study."

"Is that why you bombed at the pageant? Because Andy told you about my brother?

"Someone said I bombed?"

"I think 'sucked balls' was the term used," I said.

He laughed, rubbing his forehead. "Yeah, I guess I did kinda suck balls. I just couldn't think straight. All I could think about was you and what you must have been feeling, and how much I just wanted to be with you."

My heart seized sending spasms through every part of my body. He scooted closer, closing the gap between us and pulled my hands out of my pockets, cradling them in his.

"I wanted to come find you right away last night but my stupid mom refused to let me leave. After the pageant we fought because she kept saying I sabotaged it and that Griffin didn't deserve to win. He did by the way. He was amazing. Anyway, then my mom told me you'd come by looking for me and she turned you away and we just had it out. I told her to stop trying to control me and even my dad backed me up."

"I'm so sorry that I was such an idiot. I never should have let you walk away, and when you tried to talk to me, I should have let you. I don't care what my mom thinks, what my friends think, and I don't even care about what happens after graduation. All I care about is that I love you, Margo. So much and I just want to be here for you."

At some point I'd stopped fighting the tears. I felt them run like hot rivers down my cheeks. I didn't want to let go of Tyler's hands so I rubbed my cheeks on my shoulders. Tyler released my left hand and brought his up to my face resting it on my cheek. With his thumb he rubbed at the tears my shoulder had missed.

"Tell me what you need Margo. How can I help you?" Without hesitation I leaned into him, crushing my mouth onto his. He wrapped his arms around me, pulling me in tighter and when we kissed it felt like the world was exploding around me. I saw nebulas, a big freaking supernova, somewhere a marching band started to play. When we came up for air, he pushed my hair back behind my ears and stared down into my eyes like he was staring into my very core. The icy blue of his eyes shone like Swarovski crystals.

"I just need you," I whispered and then pulled him back into me until we were laying on the bench, his full weight on top of me, my legs wrapped around him. We stayed like that, two bodies melted into one, until the breeze picked up, and then we moved into his car where things unfolded from there. It wasn't how I'd always imagined my first time. Actually, I'd never given much thought to how it would go other than it wasn't going to be with some rando or someone I didn't care deeply about. I wasn't under some grand illusion that it would be on a bed of roses and doves would fly (though that would have been amazing), but I never thought it would have been in the back seat of a BMW the day after my brother died. Yet here, fumbling around in the backseat, grasping at each other with desperate hunger, it felt right, as if it were meant to be, as totally ridiculous as that sounds.

When we were finished, I laid nestled against Tyler's chest, his arms wrapped around me, fingers running through my hair.

"What are you feeling right now? Is that a weird thing to ask?" I whispered.

He chuckled, jostling my head as he did so. "It's not weird. It would be weird if I were asking you, cause it's a girly thing to ask."

"A girly thing? That's sexist," I said.

"Maybe a little. I'm feeling happy. Complete. Being with you makes me feel complete, and I know how totally cheesy that sounds but..." He paused, sucking in a deep breath of air. I maneuvered myself so that I could prop up on my elbow and look at him.

"What?" I asked.

He blew out a puff of air. "I probably should have told you earlier, though I'm sure it was totally obvious. I've never been with anyone else. Like this. You...this is my first time."

I covered my gigantic grin with my hand. Andy mentioned Tyler had never seriously dated anyone, but I'd made the assumption long ago that he wasn't a virgin. Not that it mattered.

"Oh God, you're laughing because it was totally obvious, aren't you?" he said. I rested my palm on his bare chest. "No not at all. It wasn't obvious at all. And I wouldn't even have anything to compare it to because this was so clearly my first time too."

"Really?" he asked. I nodded, lightly kissing him on the lips. He wrapped his arms around me and squeezed. "How are you feeling? I mean, was it okay? Our first time? God, I feel ridiculous asking that."

It was cute, when his insecurities showed. "Everything was perfect," I said. "I mean, the timing for it isn't what I'd have imagined. My heart feels like it's filled with too many conflicting emotions and could burst at any moment, but I'm glad that right now, in this very second, we're together. I'm so sorry I broke up with you, Ty. I was stupid and got scared and didn't believe in us enough to be patient."

"It's okay," he said kissing my head. "I was too hurt to understand at the time, but I do understand."

"Thanks for being here for me."

"I'm always here for you, Margo. I love you."

"I love you too. I really wish Nate could have met you."

"Me too. I'm pretty awesome."

"You're pretty self-assured," I said. My phone pinged. Grumbling, I unfolded myself from Tyler, sat up and reached into my bag. A text from Mom asking if I'd be home soon. I responded, dropped my phone into my purse and groaned.

"It's my mom. I should probably go. I don't want to, because that means I have to interact with Paul, but...oh crap I totally forgot to tell you about Paul."

"Who's Paul?"

"Well, he's my dad."

I was about to tell him more when my phone pinged again and then started to ring. "Shoot, I really have to go."

Tyler sat up, pulled his shirt over his head. "Your family needs you. As much as I want to hear the deets on this long-lost father of yours, your mom needs you. I'm just a text away though. Don't forget."

I kissed him softly, exited his car and got into mine. After turning on the ignition my phone pinged. I picked it up, about ready to send an all-caps response to my mother about her impatience, but laughed when I saw it wasn't her.

TYLER: Miss you already.

MARGO: Dork.

TYLER: <3

21

—·—

I t had been one week since Nate died, and while every day still sucked, by the end of the week we'd figured out how to be okay. Mom decided to go ahead with the cremation. Turns out after two years of a coma and absolutely zero visitors, an actual service would have been pointless, which is exactly what I had said in the first place.

"What about the whole afterlife thing? Aren't you worried that Nate won't be able to return to his body when Jesus comes back?" I asked Mom as we drove home from the funeral home with the urn containing Nate's ashes. It was modest, cerulean ceramic, his name etched around the base. She flicked me a sideways glance and smirked.

"I really don't care," she said.

"Well that hardly sounds like something a born-again Catholic would say."

"Jesus knows where my heart is and I think I can leave it at that. Besides, you were right. Nate wouldn't have wanted a service or to be buried. He was too wild to be contained, even in death." I reached across the seat and grabbed hold of Mom's hand, gently squeezing her fingers.

We printed a small obit in *The Valley Guard*, nothing too long or too specific, and a few days later drove to Depoe Bay to scatter his ashes. Paul of course opted not to come, said something about how he hadn't earned the right or whatever, and took an Uber to the airport. He promised he'd do better at staying in touch but I told him I wasn't going to hold my breath.

The coast was busy, clogged with tourists come for the whale watching, but we managed to find a secluded part of the shoreline. Huddled together against the slashing wind, we took turns reaching into the urn to grab a handful, holding tight before opening our fists, and together releasing Nate into the wind.

"When you guys were little, your father and I used to drive us up here for daytrips. I used to love the ocean so much. Drove out to Florence whenever we could," Mom said, fighting with the hair that whipped into her face. "Anyway, we'd drive up to watch the whales, you were just a toddler, strapped tightly to my chest and Nate would lean up against the rail and point out into the ocean whenever he'd spot one, yelling "Mama! Mama! I see one!" Then he'd get this far away look in his eyes before stating someday he was going to ride a whale."

She poured the remainder of the urn into her hand, held her clenched fist to her chest, eyes closed, before opening her palm to allow the wind to blow away the ashes. "Ride with the whales, honey, ride with the whales." She clasped the lid on the urn and then pulled me into a long deep hug. I collapsed into her and sobbed.

"Honey, it's okay. We're going to be okay."

"It's my fault," I wailed into her chest. She pulled me back and held my face.

"What do you mean it's your fault? What's your fault, honey?"

"Nate shooting himself. It's my fault. I knew he was hung up on Khali and I kept telling him she was bad for him and when she dumped him, I basically gave him the cold shoulder. I didn't pay attention. If I'd been more supportive, if I'd… I should have seen the signs."

"Margo, listen to me. Everything that was going on with Nate, and what he did, it wasn't your fault. You hear me? There was nothing you could have done. Sometimes people get depressed and...and things happen in their lives and instead of reaching out for help they try to find a way out on their own."

"I should have been a better sister. Maybe then I'd have been able to help him."

"If anyone should have helped him it should have been me, his mother."

We spent the next several minutes huddled on the bench crying until we'd decided we'd spilled enough of our tears into the ocean. No matter how much I blamed myself for what happened, Mom was blaming herself even more and I didn't know what was going to happen from here on out, but I sure hoped that wherever Nate's soul went that he'd forgiven us both.

I'd been excused from school the past week, and Mom had taken bereavement leave. We spent our time streaming old 90's movies and working our way through McCovey's Pizzeria menu, but while I'd loved the mom-and-daughter time, I had to return to school, and Mom had to return to work. The Dean called once again trying to convince me to skip out on finals but I was adamant on taking them.

"Margo, you really don't have to take your finals. The Dean wants for you to be able to grieve and not also have to worry about studying. Why don't you take her up on that offer?"

I stabbed at a bunch of noodles, cramming them into my mouth. "Because Mom, it would be like getting a hand-out and I'm just not cool with that. Life isn't just going to give me a free pass when bad stuff happens. I'm still going to have to face it head on. If I can study and pass my exams, which I know I can, even though my heart is hurting I know I'll be able to face anything out there in the real world."

"Fair enough Margo. Fair enough. When are finals?" she asked.

"Next week. After Districts."

She sucked in a breath through her teeth. "Cutting it close. Gonna be some late nights."

I shrugged. "I'll be alright. Besides, Jillian is wicked smart and said she'd help me. And so did Tyler."

She dropped her fork and started at me mouth slack. "Tyler?"

"Um yeah. Didn't I tell you we got back together?"

"No, when did this happen?" she asked.

"Last week? Saturday, I think?" I thought I'd told her but apparently, I hadn't, so I filled her in on our epic reunion, minus a few steamy details.

"Honey I am so happy to hear that. I really do love the two of you together. Does this mean you'll be going to Prom? There's still time to get a dress."

I shook my head. "Nah. Tyler's gonna take me to dinner, but we're skipping the dance and I'm more than okay with that. Since we're talking about dudes, what's the deal with you and Mr. Dan? Seems like there's more than a friendship there."

She narrowed her eyes at me but then softened. "You're right, we're more than friends. But you already knew that because he already told you. Don't give me that look. He told me you asked about us at the funeral home. He's been helping me work on my issues. I didn't like the person I had become when Nate was in his coma. I'd lost myself and spending time with Dan has helped me figure some things out. I like who I am when I'm around him. He makes me feel special. Oh and I've even started to see a therapist."

"Good Mom. I'm really happy for you. I'm glad you've found someone who makes you happy. And also that you're taking care of yourself. No more sad, mopey nights hiding under covers."

She nodded. "No more hiding under covers. Hey, I'm also thinking about taking classes at Valley Community College this summer."

"For real?"

She'd never say it, but I knew one of her biggest regrets was that she never got a chance to finish her art design degree.

"For real. Dan's been encouraging meme to finish my degree. Figured now's a good time. Maybe I'll start my own interior design business. Enough about me though, I have something for you." She got up from the table and slipped around the corner into her bedroom, returning a moment later carrying a blue bag with gold handles. She placed it upon the table in front of me. I gave her a sideways glance and then reached into the bag, gasping as I pulled out a charcoal grey hoodie with UCLA lettering across the chest.

"I ordered a large. It might be a little big, but I think it will be comfy that way," she said, returning to her seat.

"I...how did you find out?" I asked.

"Honey I'm your mother. It's my job to know which colleges you were accepted into."

She slid two envelopes across the table at me. One was an acceptance letter to U of O, and the other was an acceptance letter to UCLA.

"Mom, I didn't think they were going to accept me at UCLA. I just applied because Tyler thought I should go for it but, you're not mad, are you?"

"Why on earth would I be mad?"

"Because I didn't tell you I'd applied out of state. But I wasn't planning on going, I didn't want to go too far away in case, well, in case Nate woke up. And I guess I didn't want you to be alone." She slid out of her chair, kneeling beside me and taking my hands.

"I don't ever want you to feel you have to stop your life to make sure I'm living mine. Okay? I am going to be fine. More than fine. I see how hard you worked these past few years and I know it wasn't easy transferring half way through your high school years, but your hard work paid off. If you want to go to UCLA, if that's really where your heart is telling you to go, honey I couldn't be happier, and I know Nate would want this for you."

I threw my arms around her neck. "Thanks, Mom"

On Prom night, we went to dinner and a movie as planned. I convinced him to see an independent film at Bijou Art cinemas. He was clearly out of his element but years of putting on a show for his mother and being dragged to various charity events made him a pro at faking comfortable.

Afterwards we grabbed a table at Yogurt Extreme. I dug into my pile-high bowl of vanilla frozen yogurt topped with gummy bears and Oreos while Tyler worked on his vanilla with literally every single topping.

"That is by far the sickest thing I've ever seen. Pretty sure that I can no longer date you," I said, scooping a bite into my mouth. He laughed before stuffing an unflattering bite of who knows what into his.

"What are you talking about? It tastes awesome," he mushed. Who was I kidding? Even with his mouth stuffed full of frozen yogurt toppings he was still super adorable.

"You're lucky you're hot," I joked. He wiped his mouth with a napkin and stuck his spoon straight up into his yogurt.

"This feels good. Being on a date with you. I missed this," he said.

I smiled. "I missed this too. I was such an idiot for doubting you."

"Mar, you don't have to keep apologizing. It's okay. You're forgiven."

"Yeah I know, but I just feel like I have to."

He reached across the table and grasped my hand. "Well don't. It's in the past. I love you; nothing will change that."

With my free hand I poked around at my yogurt, a familiar feeling of anxiety bubbling up in my chest. "What about when the summer is over and we leave for college?" I asked. "I should have told you earlier but I found out I got into UCLA as well as U of O and after talking with my mom I'm gonna go to UCLA in the fall."

When I looked up at him, he was grinning. "What? Why are you grinning like that?"

"Because I'm going to UCLA."

I dropped my spoon and slammed my hand against my mouth to stifle a scream trying to escape. He laughed. "I got in on a basketball scholarship. My mom was pissed at first, not about the scholarship, but because she didn't even know that I applied. It wasn't really on her 'List of approved Universities'."

My insides were going crazy, juggling anxiety and euphoria at the same time. Did he actually just say he was going to UCLA? He cocked his head to the side and squeezed my fingers. "Will you say something?"

"Just to make sure I heard you correctly, you said you're going to UCLA in the fall?"

"Yeah weirdo! We'll be there together." It was the very thing I'd wanted to hear since we'd started dating, that we'd be together after graduation. So of course, it was only natural for my brain to try and self-sabotage, concoct stupid issues that weren't even actually issues- like what happens when we get to school and he meets other girls in his class? Or what happens when he's super busy with basketball practice and I'm busy studying like a maniac? Will we have time to see each other? Before I could say any of this, he slid out of his seat and into the one next to me, taking both my hands in his and squeezing tightly.

"Hey, don't do that. I know where your brain is going, you're already thinking of all the things that could stand in our way next year, but don't do that, okay? Let's just be in the moment now together?"

I closed my eyes, breathed deep until the loud crazy-talk in my brain had settled to a dull roar and the mad man juggling emotions in the pit of my stomach ceased. I reopened my eyes and smiled.

"You okay?" he asked.

I nodded, squeezed his fingers. "I am. I'm more than okay."

***

The last three weeks of the school year flew by without a hitch, which I was beyond grateful for given how much of a shit show the whole year leading up to graduation had been. Districts were a week after Tyler's big news, and I wasn't sure if I were still riding that wave or what because I made it to the podium in all of my events, including the 4 by 4 which I was so sure I'd fuck up since the last few practices I'd dropped the baton at every hand off. Not only did I *not* drop the baton, but I even handed it off a full 20 seconds faster than the other competitors which gave Carly Lyle the win, thus giving our relay team the win.

When graduation day finally arrived, I was a ball of nerves. It felt like fifty thousand hands were fist-bumping inside my stomach. There was so much to think about, so much that was going to happen after I walked off the stage, diploma in hand. I knew what I wanted to do with my future. I wanted to study neuro-psychology, figure out what the fuck happens in the grey zone. Maybe be part of the team that studies coma patients, give someone the answers I was never able to get. I also wanted to spend as much time as possible with Tyler, away from the stupid social circles that for so long had defined us. Mostly I was scared about what leaving would feel like.

We were the perfect sea of blue and gold, filing in from opposite corners of the gym and filling the rows of seats set out in the middle of the floor. I sat next to Tyler, a tight grip on his hand. He smiled and winked. "This is it," he whispered into my ear before lightly brushing his lips across my temple.

After all the diplomas were handed out and the speeches were made, we met in the quad for pictures and refreshments. It was a whir of group hugs, camera flashes, and smiles stretched across faces until we felt like we'd never want to smile again.

"I'm so proud of you, honey," Mom said after she'd taken so many pictures her phone had run out of space. "I know it was a rough few years but you did it, and I am just so proud of you." Tears streamed down her face, catching in her dimples as she smiled. I pulled her in to a hug, burying my face in her hair. I was really going to miss her hugs so much next year.

"Thanks, Mom," I said. My eyes locked on Mr. Dan, standing a few steps behind my mom. I never in a million years would have imagined Mr. Dan and my mom together, but I was totally happy they'd found each other, and knowing she wouldn't be alone made me feel more comfortable about leaving in the fall.

When all the photos were taken and the goodbyes were said to teachers and classmates, the gang met for one last gab sesh at The Daily Bagel. We ditched our cap and gowns in the trunks of our cars and filed in to our usual booth. Vinny gave us our usual drinks on the house, in honor of graduating, for which we thanked him profusely.

"You guys, I can't believe that we aren't high schoolers anymore," Donny said, his voice catching. Jillian reached her arm out and placed it upon Donny's.

Linz scoffed. "I don't know why you look like you're about to cry, Donny. High school was a living hell for you. You should be glad AF that you don't have to go back."

He narrowed his eyes at her, taking a long sip from his iced mocha. "I *am* glad AF I don't have to go back," he said. "But I'm also just a little emotional, okay? It *also* means it's the end of us." He set his cup down and swirled his pointer at each one of us.

"Wait why does it have to mean the end of us?" I asked.

"Well because," he pouted. "Sure, we have the summer and all, but come fall you're heading to UCLA, Jilly's off to Stanford and Linz's going to Corvallis. It's just gonna be me stuck here at U of O, all by myself."

"That doesn't mean we aren't going to see each other at breaks and I'm sure we'll facetime. I can't imagine not facetiming you guys," I said.

"She's right," Jillian said. "Just because we're going in different directions in the fall doesn't mean it's like the very end of us. We're best friends and that won't change."

"Speak for yourself," Linz interjected, dumping a gallon of sugar into her black coffee, clanking the metal spoon on the edge of her cup after stirring. "Soon as I get to OSU, I'm never speaking to any of you again. I'm getting new friends." We stared at her, jaws on the floor for half a second before she winked and busted up laughing. "OMG you should so totally see your faces. I'm kidding! Like I could find any other group of weirdos who can stand my bitchy attitude."

We finished our drinks, ate some bagels and spent the rest of the afternoon relishing in each other's company. They were the best group of friends anyone could ever ask for; I only wish I hadn't spent so long shutting them out. Nate once told me that friends were fickle, they'd come and go as quick as the tide rolls in. But I think he was wrong. I think if he'd allowed himself a group of friends as great as mine, he might not have felt his life was worth ending. I needed my friends, and no matter where life would take me, no matter what happened between me and Tyler, as long as I remembered to always be up front and honest with these three amazingly awesome people, I was going to be okay.

Acknowledgements

Obviously, thank you to my family. Sandy, Jason, Brian-you're a million years older than me (yup I went there) and as far as siblings go, you guys rule. Kim, my brother's better half- you're a superstar. Thank you for all your encouraging words over the years.

The Keith clan. Thanks for putting up with my special brand of crazy for all these years.

Ian and our half-pint hooligans. You're all a bunch of nerds but I wouldn't have it any other way. I love you.

A million thanks to Sarah Ellis Higgins who read the first few versions of this story years ago and helped me with development every step of the way. You had so much faith in me and loved my characters almost as much as I do. I would not have been able to complete this without your input and support.

Rach-Face, I love you to the moon and back. You root for me when I'm not rooting for myself. Remember when we cut holes in Walmart bags and wore them over our heads when it was raining? Yeah, that was awesome.

And to my little brother. I wish you were here.

About the Author

Angela L Keith is the author of *A Swirl of Colors and Jagged Edges*. She lives with her family and rather large corgi in Salem, Oregon. When she's not writing and schlepping kids to various activities, she loves to read, practice yoga, and sing silly songs totally off-key. She also prefers salty chips to chocolate cake because she is a weirdo.